DREAM WALKER

BY LARRY PROSOR

Dream Walker

Published by Bookbaby

Produced by Larry Prosor and Tuamotu

Dream Walker - Copyright 2018 by Larry Prosor. All rights reserved.

ISBN: 978-1-54392-985-0

Edited by - Susan Schader and John William Walker Zeiser

2% of the royalties from *Dream Walker* will be donated to select environmental watchdog organizations.

Cover photo: William Bradberry - Shutterstock

Larry Prosor

Dedicated to Cindy, Whitney and Will.

CHAPTER 1

A fin rises to the surface before me, offering a scary hint of the size of the owner below now blocking my path. Positioned deep in the tube and trimmed for maximum speed, my escape options narrow as the hollow wave shuts. The powerful swell clings relentlessly, sucking me up the face, then pitching me forward into a free fall. I'm offered a final glimpse of the lip of the heaving wave as it closes in. The first whiplash hits, the dense liquid tonnage plunging me deep, throwing me into a full body stress test with rag doll shaking fury. A self-imposed elbow strike to my face follows as Mean Mother Ocean tosses me toward a shoreline littered with solid rocks. Blind in the turbulent chaos of the frothy whitewater storm, struggling to surface against mighty powers, I have one thought: Breathe!

Released by the whitewater grip, I grab the lifeline strapped to my ankle and pull up the stretched-taut cord to the surfboard at the surface. Gasping in lungfuls of air, I turn toward the horizon to see if there's another wave bearing down.

A lull calms the impact zone, offering temporary relief. Blood dripping from my nose splashes onto the board, joining driblets of saltwater draining into the sea. Pinching my nostrils, I anxiously scan my surroundings, looking for the owner of the dorsal. The fin turns,

Over my shoulder, I look for a gap in the set waves. Matching the speed of the swells, I stroke hard to stay in front of the impact zone while riding a diminishing wave to a skidding stop on the sandy beach. Relieved at another successful landing, I drag the kayak beyond the reach of the surging waves, unload the surf gear, and shoulder the boat over the wind-sculpted dunes to the rack of Old Red's camper shell parked next to the chain-link fence.

On approach in the near distance, a growing dust cloud comes my way; beneath it, a black SUV with frantic yellow lights. The imposing high fence gives me a chain-link filtered view of the rapidly approaching vehicle as I struggle to remove my stubborn layer of wetsuit rubber skin. "NO TRESPASSING!" signs prominently displayed on the pad-locked gate yell at me in English and Spanish.

I find the box of roofing nails in the truck bed and fling a stealthy handful over the gate where they dive into the dust.

Pulling up tight to the barrier fence, the security guard tests his brakes and then door hinges. The private militiaman, his bulk squeezed into an official-looking black uniform, marches up to me behind the gate. Besides all his muscle, he's well equipped with handgun, ammo, cuffs and pepper spray. His costume is boldly accented with a golden ENGR logo on his shirt and across the front of his seriously angled cap. A corporate mercenary on a mission.

Reaching the gate, he adjusts his alpha male stance. "No trespassing!" His warning is loud, his eyes hidden behind mirrored aviators.

"I'm on this side of the fence," I reply, my bare ass to him as I casually pull up my surf trunks. "Besides, I've got deep roots here. My ancestors once called this place home."

"Welcome to the present. ENRG holds the title to Rocky Point."

"Only a paper title. We were here long before E-N-R-G." A whiff of sea breeze filled with his thick sweat drifts my way.

"Couldn't help but notice your corporate branding. What's it like being employed by a global goliath like ENRG?"

"Picnic compared to another tour in the Middle East. What do you do, besides surf?"

"Heritage figure. Sharp costume you've got. That weapon real?"

He draws his real looking gun.

I dive behind Old Red, ducking for cover. When I peer out at him, a strange silence descends in a temporary truce. He holsters his portable killing device and settles into his vehicle, then offers a stiff middle-finger salute out the open window as he guns the engine.

I turn away and shield my eyes from projectiles flying off his spinning tires.

Turning my back to the gate, I take a pull off my water bottle to rinse down ancestor dust.

CHAPTER 2

Checking the tie-downs on the kayak, I glance up to the blazing sun and confirm the time on my watch. Leaping into Old Red's cab and onto the duct-taped seat, I reach for the key, and mutter my familiar wish. With a rumble, the old girl struggles to turn—then nothing beyond the dying clicks of the starter. Prying open the creaky door, I lean into it. As she starts rolling, building speed, I jump in, clutch, second-gear, clutch and ignition!

Through the windshield, jackrabbits sprint for their lives to get out of my way. Through the rearview mirror, dust swirls behind Old Red, up into the hot sky, obliterating my view of the Pacific in a brown earth cloud. My sweaty fingers crank up the tunes to poetic tribal tales as a covey of California quail takes flight, gracefully gliding in unison to the indigenous beat.

The coastal dirt road twists far behind as Old Red rolls down the widening asphalt path. Over Red's faded hood, it appears like a twenty-four hour sunrise—a blindingly bright marquee consuming a hefty flow of electrons. It flashes relentlessly in a regular loop, silently screaming, ALL YOU CAN EAT BUFFET, BINGO, SLOTS ARE US, 24-HOUR KINO! Two steel pools bookend the seriously bright signage, thrusting toward the stratosphere. Two monstrous flags compete for wind—the Stars and Stripes and the state's, featuring its long-extinct state animal, the California Grizzly Bear.

The parking lot surrounding my Noqoto tribe's massive casino is a rippling hot asphalt sea. Like tiny islands of green life sprinkled on the lifeless blacktop, a few token trees struggle to survive on small squares of brown earth. From the parking lot perspective, the casino attempts an "Indian" look. In reality a series of expansive, multi-storied, industrial-sized structures of concrete, steel and glass. The interiors are stuffed with options to gamble-your-money-in-hopes-of-wining entertainment, eating, drinking, shopping, accommodation and discount tobacco. To attempt to transform the cold, straight lines of the commercial buildings into Native American authentic, the exterior panels are painted with depictions of towering tribal totem and cave paintings of ancient ancestors.

The personally elusive "Employee of the Month" parking space is marked with a nice looking sign in the shade. The full parking lot on this busy summer day sends me to the familiar distant edges of the pavement.

Sprinting across the scorching asphalt, the pull of the clock keeps me hustling toward the employee entrance. Hugging a sliver of afternoon shade, I swipe my well-worn badge in the card reader and wave at the dome-covered camera while offering a nervous smile. The door clicks open and the air-conditioned hallway hits me with a cold wave.

Except for the exotic mixed-bouquet of lingering scents of other employees, I'm presently the only person in the empty locker room. Hastily blowing my first attempt with the spinning locker combo, I risk a quick glance at the prominent digital clock glowing in red, taunting me for my tardiness. Frantically prying open the door of my locker reveals a crumpled pile at the bottom—The Costume, 100% polyester, dry clean only. Hastily I slip it over my head and ditch the surf shorts for the lined loincloth. Must not forget to remove wristwatch to disguise evidence of modern man.

With a twist of the faucet, I splash water on my face. Still dripping, cram fingers in ears and stick my head under the turbo-powered dryer. With hearing in reverb, carefully trace blood-red makeup in memorized designs onto my best-mean-look-warrior-face. Don't even bother combing the windblown, salt-crusted hair. I gather up the wad and settle the feathered headdress on my head with little respect for tradition. I freeze and take a look in the full-length mirror at The Indian Heritage Figure.

Down the sterile hallway, the employee time clock awaits, ready to document late arrivals. I check the time glowing my direction and dutifully insert the employee badge into the scanner-snitch. The clock beeps to confirm the presence of the historic character from another place in time, having arrived late in the present, which is now in the past.

I open the employee door as an actor opens a stage curtain to an audience, only to be frozen in place by an assault on all my senses. Our casino offers up copious amounts of noise directed at eardrums in attempts to lure those drawn to games of chance. The bright visuals all around are a deer-in-the-headlights wild rainbow of vibrant colors splashed on the ceilings, down the walls and spilling across the card-dice-themed carpet under my moccasins. I shield my eyes as every color on the planet leaps at me. The blinding lights bounce laser-like from polished mirror displays. In front of me are casino canyons lined with legions of gamblers perched on red vinyl chairs, desperately yanking slot machines. "I won!" an excited lady screams and leaps to her feet in front of me. She thrusts out her arms with greedy pleasure to catch the clinking coins pouring into her plastic mini-bucket featuring our tribal logo of a white hawk.

Strolling through the casino like I know what I'm doing, the Indian Heritage Figure silently observes that the blackjack tables are close to full capacity. Wannabe winners impatiently wait their turns, oblivious to everything but the cards, chips and dealers' hands. As the roulette wheel spins in blurs of hopes and dreams, the eyes of the anxious lock on the wheel, willing it to stop in their favor. At a craps table, a player fondles the dice and rolls it with a kiss and a prayer that fate is on his side. Women in tight black skirts with pushed-up cleavage on display lurk around, crying out "Keno" in alluring voices. Aged bingo room hangouts loiter at tables, their cumulative ages historically impressive. A thick gambling plague spreads incessantly throughout the casino, linked to Money.

Suddenly, like a gift, a poker chip falls to the floor unnoticed from the direction of the crowded craps table. It rolls toward my feet and circles to a stop. Two zeros leap out. I shift my foot, drop my rubber weapon, bend down and slip the chip into my moccasin. Prop weapon back in hand, I rise to see no one looking my way, beyond the normal stares.

I glance over at the Change Girls to see who might be working. Two friendly, familiar ladies occupy the booth, their eyes tightly focused on the change, cash and chips. Matching the word emblazoned on their outfits, a bright red neon "Change" sign flashes above them.

I stroll over, a noble warrior in my fake Indian outfit, headdress filled with rows of turkey feathers, rubber tomahawk poised in my hand ready for mock battle.

"Excuse me, I'm trying to find my way in time."

"How predictable, Peter, you're historically late."

"I was distracted by coastal research."

"Surfing?" The change girls question me in unison.

"Good guess, Waves were pumping." I respond with a post-surfing smile.

"Not much of a guess. And the Boss will erase your blissful grin." The head of change reminds me of what I don't want to be reminded of.

"There's a price to pay for surfing today." I reflect on change all around. "Oh, Giver of Change, is change constant?"

"Twenty-four-seven. You could change and wear a watch?"

"I do have one, but wearing it would not be keeping in character." I silently zip my lips with my fingers and turn my back on Change.

Glancing above the heads of seated patrons at the California Cantina, Steve spots me and waves me over with his holy spoon. He's hustling hard behind the counter by the looks of all the steaming plates lined up waiting to be served beneath the glowing heat lamps. As I walk among the tables, customers' conversations stop abruptly in the presence of the Heritage Indian passing by. Following familiar terrain, I poke my head through the commercial kitchen doors. The air of fried food sticks thick.

"Hey Chief, how is it in the outside world?" Steve says, as he glances longingly toward the entry doors.

"Chef, you should be grateful for air conditioning."

"Loving the deep fryer," he trails off. "So why's Indian fry bread so popular anyway?" he asks, while sliding one of the well-lubed skidders under the heat lamp.

"Those seeking stents?"

"You got that right." He looks me over like a freak. "Anyone ask where they can get a costume like yours? Maybe around end of October?"

"Mime job."

"The Wooden Indian speaks."

"Native American Heritage mime," I intone, erasing the smile from my face. "Got to get going, so I can do nothing," I ventriloquize out the corner of my mouth.

"You're are The Man when it comes to employees who do so little."

"Speaking of free time, who's playing in the showroom this weekend? Anyone worth seeing?"

"Guess."

"Not again."

"Survival band, only one original member left standing."

"Prop him up, who knows where we'll be when we're that old?"

"Not slinging fry bread."

"Not wearing this costume. Later, Steve. To my post!"

"Watch out for woodpeckers."

"Ha! Ha!"

I exit the kitchen and shuffle along in my beaded moccasins toward the red "Exit" sign above oversize, impressively polished revolving doors.

A bright, noisy casino is a sensory overload on all fronts. Walking through it dressed as a full-blown Hollywood Western Indian considerably heightens the over-stimulation effect. I've observed that very few things will stop a gambler from pulling the handle on a slot machine, but clad in my costume, complete with war paint, realistic looking rubber tomahawk and rubber knife, I often freeze them mid-pull.

I work my way through the calculated gambling maze of the casino floor and position myself in front of the cavernous entryway. Focusing on not batting an eye, controlling breathing to minimal sign of human life. There can be no hint of movement as The Frozen Heritage Indian. Stand still long enough, and it's entertaining to see people's reactions to Frozen Indian, unsure if I'm real or a statue.

But sometimes I just have to mess with people. Subtle movements leave them wondering, but they usually freak when I spring to life!

People often like to shoot selfies standing next to Frozen Indian. A two-fingered peace sign above someone's head and a cross-eyed look makes for the simple pleasures of bombing a photo. Retirees come by the busload for the death-defying blood pressure boost of gambling away their hard-earned retirements. They slowly pour through the door in front of me, come to a crawl, and inspect me closely with fading eyesight. A sudden movement on my part could send a nice old person to the ER, so I stay frozen. Some customers seem to never notice me standing right next to them. Coming out of the casino they're lost in thought, their money likely left behind in the wake of the odds. They pass through the doors into the harsh reality of a lighter wallet with nothing to show for it. But sometimes, happy winners with huge grins pass in front of me as they struggle to hold in their cashed up excitement of beating those odds. I allow my highly trained professional poker face to break into a smile for their good fortune.

My still-life working day appears to be beginning badly as two sketchy characters stagger up. With a fresh carton of cigarettes under arm, the one with the man-baby pushes his face into mine as his stomach checks the distance. He reeks like a human ashtray, and holds in his crusty fingers a discount butt smoking with toxic fumes billowing into my sad, frozen face.

"Hey, Donnie, it's one of those wooden cigar store Indians, like in the old black and white Westerns," he says, flicking ash.

"Sure looks real," his buddy replies.

"Let's see how real," he says, reaching toward me with the lit end of the cig.

He eyes me as the heat comes closer. I hold still, call his bluff, until I smell my hair burning. "You asshole," I mutter.

He attempts to inflate his chest with his ample abdomen. "What did you say?"

I turn my head slowly his way. "You heard me! Asshole!" I shout, raising my rubber tomahawk high, and firing a piercing war cry into his fear-filled face.

Just then, a lumbering weighty customer passes through the exit, sees the tomahawk raised and frantically holds his arms up in panic.

I glance back toward the man who burned me, ready to scalp him.

"Whoaa! Take it easy," the arsonist trembles.

"Hit the road!" I threaten, slashing the air with my rubber weapon. As he and his buddy flee, I fling the fake tomahawk at them for good measure.

Glancing back over their shoulders, on the lookout for a deadly rubber hatchet, they hustle fast to their cars as the gummy tomahawk bounces to a skid harmlessly behind them. Note to self: Work on range.

I walk over and gather up my phony weapon lying on the asphalt battlefield. Returning to the exit, unbelievably, the big guy still has his hands in the air when I approach him.

"Wild West show for our valued customers. Pretend tomahawk. I'm pretend too, sir."

He lowers his arms. "Scared the shit out of me! Thought you were a terrorist! You will be hearing from a lawyer on my behalf!" he threatens, as he points to the security camera with a smug look of easy bogus lawsuit money.

I try to calm down and regain my pose to wait for the next customer to come through the entry. Minutes later, another customer approaches with a little dog sporting a sharp haircut and a tiny vest labeled, "Comfort Animal." I can't help but notice the owner, which the dog walks, rather than *vice versa*, looks vainly desperate in her attempts to artificially salvage her former youth. The little dog decides that my leg is the place to have a pee. As it lifts a leg, I defend myself and shove it with my foot, sending it into a dog roll. Fortunately for me, the lady with the expressionless stare doesn't see what caused her little precious to roll over and yelp.

Briefly, I think there won't be any repercussions, but I should know better with the all-seeing security cameras. A familiar face costumed in his large casino security uniform steps up and tells me the words I don't want to hear.

"I got a call on the radio, and I quote, 'The Heritage Indian is out of control again.' The Boss is pissed at you, wants to have a word right now."

"I'm sure there's more than a word," I mutter.

"Couldn't help but notice you're late, again. Why don't you show respect to fellow workers who, somehow, manage to show up on time?"

The old guilty conscience creeps in. "Had Rocky Point to myself, except for the dolphin. I lost track of time. Truck wouldn't start..."

"Excuses are like fill-in-the-blank, Peter..."

"My priorities get in the way of work," I acknowledge.

"I'm sure your priorities will be the main topic of conversation between the two of you."

I'm pretty sure no one has ever pushed the revolving doors so hard. I run to keep up with the first revolution. A blast of air whooshes through and shifts my headdress in front of my eyes. Darting through the narrowing gap, the door clips me from behind as I'm flung into the casino.

Shuffling through the gambling floor, it seems every one of my tribe and fellow employees gives me that look that says they know I'm in trouble again. I have nothing against those who work here. It's just that money doesn't motivate me much, even when I'm surrounded by all the cash at the casino.

As I snake my way to the elevator, I cringe at the thought of facing the boss. The elevator door slides open and I'm on my way up to get let down.

The horizontal mine shaft of a hallway leading to the management offices looks especially forbidding. The door I don't want to enter awaits me. My long journey toward job destiny lies beyond heavy security in front of me. I fumble for my employee ID and look up to the all-seeing dome glass eye. The door clicks open. Hanging my headdress low, I enter the command center of my tribal casino to face the real chief.

Her back is to me, side-by-side with an armed security guard staring at a full wall of NSA-grade monitors that show every angle of the casino. Silently, I stand behind her in Frozen Indian mode, her deceptively small silhouette replaying and viewing the cigarette and dog kicking incidents.

Slowly, she turns to me and throws a look I've seen too many times. "Peter, what the hell are you doing? You can't threaten customers with a tomahawk and kick their dogs!"

"It's a fake tomahawk. That guy was trying to burn me! What would you do if a dog was pissing on you?"

"Maybe it was trying to put out the mystery cigarette. I don't see anyone burning you!"

"The fat jerk blocked the camera! Look at my burnt hair!"

"That jerk is a customer! The bottom line is: You cannot abuse our patrons!"

"Abuse patrons? Hello? Wooden Indians are not fire retardant, and they are not immune to bogus lawsuits either."

"I hate to lecture you, again, but your actions today let down our tribe."

"Mom, let's face it, Frozen Indian is a lame job, I'm the last wooden man standing. No one else in the tribe wants to demean themselves like this."

"You should be proud of your Noqoto ancestry. Just imagine yourself as an actor playing the role of an Indian of the past, who doesn't move. And besides, customers love it, as long as you don't try to scalp them."

Time seems to slow and "playing the role of an Indian of the past" echoes in my head. I gaze, glassy-eyed, across the wall of screens showing the casino.

"I am proud of our past heritage, not sure about the present. Sorry, Mom, I can't take it anymore. I quit."

"When you get to your phone you'll see the text. I already fired you. Your actions today are inexcusable! I swear, I'm going to replace you with a robot!"

I should have just walked away. "A robot? So what. Grandfather refused to work here."

"Both you surf bums seem oblivious to the hard times our tribe had before the casino!"

"I'm worried about you, Mom. You hardly see the light of day anymore. What about your circadian cycle? Is driving a flash Euro car and living in a McMansion what you really want from life?"

"Well, Mister Living-In-The-Past, grass huts, hunting and gathering don't cut it with me! Times are hard out there in the real world. I thank God every day I have this job so I can be independent and make my own way. And don't you forget, we're in the same tribe. And, thanks to this tribal casino, we contribute to each other and to the surrounding community."

"Not everyone loves casinos. My conscience sure struggles with peddling vices."

"We don't hold a gun to customers' heads, like we've had held to ours."

"You're right, it's their choice, like it's your choice, like it's my choice."

"The casino gives self-determination for our tribe," she says with conviction.

We both stare at each other in silence.

"Of course it's your choice, Peter. I know you're not happy here," she concedes.

"Thanks for the acknowledgement. You should take a walk up the road to see the old surf bum. How long has it been?"

"Awhile."

"He's not getting any younger."

"Bring him the usual for me."

"Those are gut bombs," I point out.

"While you're there, tell him to keep that cell phone charged. What if he has an emergency?"

"Come on, Mom, it'd do you good to get outside and walk up and see Grandfather. If you had a window in here, you'd see it's a beautiful day."

"I've got lots of windows," she points out as she scans the security camera screens. "Now that you're out of a job, you're the one with the free time."

A large smile grows on my face. "Maybe later. I've got field work at Mission Santos for Dr. Evans, to finish up my thesis."

"Oh, you mean the higher education you've been dragging out? The one the casino's paying for?"

"Ah... yes, that one."

"Peter, Peter, you've always been such a dreamer. There comes a time when we all have to face reality."

"Reality? You're speaking to a fake Heritage Indian."

"You should be thinking about your future."

"Sometimes I think I'd rather be living in the past." I stare down at my mock leather moccasins and turn to go.

"I'll need your employee pass, Peter," she says regretfully. "The tribe can't afford to have you working here. You're a lawsuit waiting to happen."

"Remember, I'm innocent."

I look down and find the employee ID badge hanging from my neck. I don't want it anymore, but in a plastic covered way, it connects me to my mom and the tribe. My dated employee photo stares back at me as I hand it over. "Chief, here's my badge."

I turn to leave but realize I've forgotten what's most important. "I love you, Mom."

"I love you too, Peter," she answers as she gives me a warm hug. "No matter what questionable choices you make," she adds with that familiar look of concern. "Don't you have something else to tell me?"

"Oh yeah! Almost forgot." I bend down and dig out the one hundred dollar poker chip. "I found this on the casino floor."

"We saw you," she states firmly as she takes it from me. She turns her back and looks around to the camera monitors of the casino.

Making my way back to the locker room is almost like floating. Weightless, set free, the burden of my compromise of conscience to chase dollars lifted from my shoulders.

Throwing the fake Indian costume in the dirty clothes hamper is liberating when it drops in with a swish. Exiting the front revolving door of the casino in my surf trunks, I pass by the security cameras, turn, and wave goodbye. Cool whispers of man-made air conditioning fade behind me as heat rises in ripples from the parking lot. The doors close, and I'm blasted with hot air scented with oily asphalt.

But deep down, hiding beneath my smile, there's the unmistakable sorrow of an unemployed outcast recently banned from his tribe.

CHAPTER 3

Leaving the wide concrete expanse of coastal Highway 101 behind, I turn off onto a narrow side road. A steady flow of vehicles filters towards the sign for "Mission Los Santos." Going down this narrow road is like stepping back in time, taking a journey into early California colonial history.

An informational entry sign on fringe of the mission grounds provides visitors a bit of history. "Once destroyed by an earthquake in 1787, Mission Los Santos now stands as an accurate reconstruction of an early California Spanish Mission, allowing modern visitors a glimpse into mission life. The restored mission buildings look as they would have hundreds of years ago, as a far distant outpost of European culture. The hillsides surrounding the mission are covered with native trees and plants. Crops of the era grow on the flats of the surrounding valley. Even the sheep in the paddocks are the same breed that grazed here hundreds of years ago."

Recalling personal recollections, inside the buildings, the historic charade continues, from the rough-hewn wooden truss ceilings to the cracked adobe walls meeting the worn clay tile floors. The living quarters are outfitted with European furniture from the era, and the workrooms and outside displays are filled with the implements of manual labor once used daily by enslaved Native Indians.

The parking lot in the distance is full again, and cars and motor homes line the road cramming for space. Beyond the cars, you can see walls of old adobe and roofs of faded clay tile through the oak trees. During its heyday, the mission complex was big enough to house over a thousand people. To the side of the courtyard, standing like a beacon of faith, stands the chapel. Haunted with Indian history, its Catholic cross, plastered with bird shit, tilts at the church's gable end, where mud swallow nests are plastered beneath the eaves. And next to the chapel, the now silent bell tower, no longer peeling out calls to wake, eat, worship, work, and mourn.

I pull off the side of the road, park, and shut off the engine, but make sure I can roll start Old Red again. Silence, save for the motor home generators droning away, sending the aroma of burned petrol into the air. In the courtyard and around the mission buildings, tourists stroll. Remove them, their cars and motorhomes, and it could be hundreds of years ago, when the Spanish empire builders sailed across vast oceans to stake claims in Alta California in the name of the King of Spain. For decades, Spanish colonists were led by a small man with a big vision, Father Junipero Serra, the founder of the El Camino Real chain of California Missions. Serra, driven by the Roman Catholic faith, and other invaders attached to the Spanish, selectively ignored who had the deepest roots in California.

Like many others before me, judging by the deeply worn path, I step up to another informative tourist sign covered with fresh gang graffiti on the edge of the parking area. A white passenger van slows, its lone occupant staring out at me. He pulls over and parks in front of Old Red. The door slowly opens. Out steps a man who appears to be from the historic past, with car keys. He's fully dressed as a Franciscan friar from centuries ago, from baldhead, to hooded robe, to cracked leather sandals.

"Peter?"

A long moment and then it comes to me. "Hello, Father Arguello," I say, memories clogging my head.

"Haven't seen you in church for ages, barely recognized you. How've you been? Still curious as to your religious beliefs?" he asks.

"I'm having a hard time believing you're wearing that get-up."

"It's an authentic historical costume. Please tell me you aren't abandoning our faith."

"Lost faith in a lot of things."

"Faith tests many of us. How's your Mom?"

"Working too much at the casino."

"I won't see her there given gambling is a sin. I do miss her attending my services."

Arguello sports a historically unique bowl-cut hairstyle topped with shaved bald dome. Draped over him is a brown, rough, woolen robe with a prominent hoody, a throwback to the Spanish Mission era. "Very retro outfit," I comment.

"My turn to act the part for the visitors and school children who study California history, I'm dressed historically accurate."

"I see. What about the original Native Americans?"

"Are you offering to play the part?"

"Bad actor, just lost mime job."

"Sorry to hear that."

"I'm not."

"Sure is a hot one today," he says, changing the subject as drops of sweat roll off his head. Such a long drought, even the spring-fed pond at the mission is dry."

"How many well-holes can you keep punching in the aquifer? Throw global warming in the mix, and no surprise it's dried up," I point out.

"There's a soda machine in the gift shop if you want," he says gesturing toward the Information Center disguised as livestock out buildings.

"Historically accurate?"

"Likely within the use by date." Arguello looks down at the shovel in my hands. "Are you working for Dr. Evans again?"

"Working on my thesis, 'Forgotten Californian Tribes.'"

"Find anything?"

"Just got here."

"The old septic system is failing, and we really need the extra parking."

"This place is too popular with tourists, like a California Mission cult gathering. If I do find the old Indian burial ground, you'll need to adjust your plans. Maybe bus people in?"

"Odds are... Well, I don't have to tell you, archaeologists have been looking for many years. I'm sorry to say the Indian graves have been lost in time..."

"At least the priests and soldiers got headstones."

"That was a long time ago..." He notes as he checks the time on his non-historic wristwatch. "I'm short on time, I've got to run and get ready for evening mass. You should come, Peter. My sermons are always evolving to address the challenges mankind is confronted with."

"Well, since you're here, can I confess, Father?"

"Yes, my son, you can tell me anything in confidence."

"I've embraced another worship."

"I don't like the sound of this..."

"Church of Mother Ocean."

"That's a new one, but this is California… Non-denominational?"

"As far as I know, anyone can be baptized in her waters."

He carries on with renewed recruitment efforts. "So, for old time's sake, what about coming to Sunday service this weekend? You should come, I have many empty pews. Thank God for the immigrants seeking solace in the church. If it weren't for them, I'd be praying for another job." He looks at me with born-again eyes. "What do you say? Come to my service?"

"I'll pass, thanks anyway."

With a shrug, he fails to convert. "I've got to say, you're looking well, certainly in great physical shape. Amazing to see how people change when time goes by," he says, looking me up and down. "I do look forward to seeing you again, handsome young man."

He reaches to shake my hand. I opt for a remote wave.

"Bless you, son."

"Better keep the donkey reined Padre. CHP's got radar south on El Camino."

"Thanks Peter, I'll rein in the van."

Glancing down the road toward the mission, a trickle of visitors find their way to their cars. Motor homes take up lots of acreage, their generators struggling to keep the dog cool inside. Yellow school buses spread out like a disjointed snake as teachers try to herd and gather free-ranging kids. Out-of-state license plates and bug-splattered windshields mark vehicles that have traveled far for some early California history.

I turn and watch Father Arguello's fish-shaped "Honk for Jesus" bumper sticker shrinking away, followed by a honk of his horn and a friendly reverse wave. I look at my own faded bumper sticker: "Indians Discovered Columbus."

Only been out of my truck a few minutes and I'm hot already. I feel the unrelenting sun glaring down on earth that hasn't seen rain for too many months. Gusts of wind blow hot and dry, sucking the moisture out of me with each breath I inhale. I lean against the shovel to consider my options on which direction to head.

In the distance, a swirling twister of a dust devil grabs at the dry earth, leaves, and grass, taking a shape of its own. Growing up to meet the sky, it twists into the empty field in front of me, and pauses, as if waiting. Waves of heat rise around the spinning mini-tornado, mirage like. I stare in fascination at what seems to come alive before me.

I blink. He's still there. It's like a real dream. Within the spinning dust cloud is a faint image of a Native Indian, a warrior armed with spear, bow and arrows. He's dressed in traditional clothing, loincloth hanging from his waist, the effigy of a black killer whale strung around his neck. I'm drawn toward the chiseled face and into the depth of dark eyes hauntingly looking deep into mine. Hit with a gusty wall of debris, I close my eyes. Open them again in the momentary calm within the twister. He's still with me, but now lies slumped on the ground in blood spreading like a slow river. I drop to my knees. As the spinning wind returns, I duck and cover. The twister beats me with fury, then releases me from its grasp. The air calms. I open my eyes to watch the dust twister disappear. The warrior too is gone.

Heat stroke? I take a long pull off my water bottle. Moving to the spot where I saw the warrior, I look down at the dry, cracked earth. Chipping gently into the hard soil with my shovel, clumps of dirt loosen. I clear the dirt with a small trowel and pull the soil aside with my hands as the hole in the earth expands. A skeletal eye socket vacantly stares up at me. Carefully clearing away the earth, I splash water from my bottle onto the skeletal face. The water pools in the eye sockets and settles in a mirror reflection of my eyes looking back at me. Tenderly, I clear away more soil, drop to my knees and give a Native American prayer.

I look up and see tourists mingling nearby. I capture the scene secretly on my phone from different angles before gently re-burying the soul I had disturbed.

Looking down at the freshly turned earth, I'm haunted by the vision of my ancestor.

CHAPTER 4

Working my way up the mountain along the narrow gravel road, I branch off on a faint deer trail and head toward the well-hidden rock outcropping Grandfather had shown me many years ago. The large, twisted oak tree is still standing, a few green branches struggling to survive amongst the dry, cracked wood. Ducking through the dense, red-barked Manzanita brush is more of a challenge as I'm no longer a small boy. Unforgiving branches grab me and dig into my skin, clawing red tattoos of blood. The familiar monolith rock slab leans against a tall limestone cliff band of velvety green and gray lichen-draped rocks. I feel like a child again, filled with anticipation as I squeeze into the narrow crack of the entry. My eyes adjust to the low light of the chamber that widens to reveal a stone canvas with Native American pictographs. Time-faded figures of abstracts, deer, snakes, bear, whales and dolphins. Who were these artists?

I exit the darkness, squinting into the bright light of the present day and carry on toward my Grandfather's, the ache in my leg muscles a reminder of many past climbs.

Our reservation land is mostly white-man-token-leftovers of steep hillsides, and little of it is easy to build on. When the casino expansion was approved, a few of the older homes had to go as they occupied some of the only flat land. My grandfather reluctantly accepted that his home would become a parking lot, but he insisted on his terms for removal and compensation for his loss. The Tribal Council eventually agreed that he could build a small isolated home near the top of the ridge, well away from the future casino, and far away from the tribe. People wondered how he planned on getting materials needed to build his new home up to the remote site.

He enlisted me to help dismantle his old home piece by piece, pulling out all the rusty nails and stacking the lumber in neat piles. He had originally built it with his own hands and each board held a sacred memory of time shared with my grandmother when she was alive. To Grandfather, an old school carpenter, wasting material was a crime. "Good old growth lumber," he'd remind me as I wrestled another feisty nail.

We carefully removed the windows and doors next. He saved as much as he could of the old structure with plans to reuse it on the new. Only he knew how he planned on getting it all up the steep, seldom used, narrow dirt road winding to the top of the ridge. He wouldn't tell me. "You'll see," he would repeat with a knowing smile.

His pile of building material grew to include bags of cement, insulation, metal roofing, plumbing parts, electrical wire, and a generator. There was enough money from his recycling efforts left for micro wind power, solar panels, inverter, a bank of batteries, and solar hot water panel. One of his last additions was a water tank to store rainwater captured from the roof.

One day the mode of transporting all the materials arrived. The heavy rapping of the helicopter as it came swooping in over the valley was impossible to ignore. After some airborne lifting, the materials were on site. Waving to me as he passed by, Grandfather drove away to his new house site, his truck filled with camping gear, tools and supplies to see him through the long stretch before he had a roof over his head again. "Come up and visit. I'll put you to work!" he called out with grin.

I obliged, often walking up the steep road with a heavy backpack filled with food my mom put together. Sometimes I'd stay on. He welcomed the extra set of hands and a young, strong back. I helped him with the heavy work, digging the footings, mixing concrete, pouring the footings, setting the piles, laying out the joists, raising the walls, setting the roof rafters, and getting the metal roof on before the winter rain came.

We would often stay up well into the night to watch a quiet moonrise or stare up at a bright starry night unfolding above. I would ask him questions and he would give me his experienced answers. I began to see what he saw in the beauty of isolation surrounded by Mother Nature. My body became lean and muscular from all the hard work. The student was ready and he patiently showed me the way.

As I come over the rise now, his meager home stands tall above the clearing ahead. He was wise to put his cottage where he did; the old road leads to a good, steady spring hidden in a notch in the ridgeline. Elevated, but mostly sheltered from prevailing winds by a stand of thick oaks and madrone, the house is bathed in the morning sun; afternoon heat is knocked back by the shade of the trees. Large windows open to the sun, providing warmth in winter; an overhanging eave provides shade and relief from the summer heat.

In the hot breeze, I approach the familiar clearing. The tidy house stands perched on the ridge, framed by laden fruit trees and abundant vegetable gardens. The cedar shiplap siding has remained unpainted and has weathered to gray. Black solar panels line the roof, silently doing their job. High on an anchored steel pole, the wind generator spins in a blur, whispering with each gust of wind. The building looks worn but still solid. I walk up and touch the warm wall to feel the home of my grandfather, built with our own hands.

Coming around the corner to the front of the house, I see him. He sits quietly, cross-legged on the porch, eyes peacefully closed, frayed shirt and faded shorts ignoring fashion, thin white hair blowing in the wind. Twirling in the breeze at his side is a cluster of tail feathers perched on the end of carved oak totem to the whispering wind. As I have done many times in the past, I relax and let the spirit of this place and his presence soak in.

When the moment seems right, I say, "Grandfather."

He doesn't hear, so I yell, "Grandfather!"

He slowly opens his eyes and turns toward me, a big smile growing on his weathered brown face. He pulls out ear buds by the cord and shuts down his portable sound.

"Peter! Welcome!"

Anxiously stepping onto the porch, I reach over and offer my hand. He takes it with appreciation and I help him to his feet. We embrace, sharing the warmth of love. Smiles grow on both our faces as we stand and take each other in.

"You've grown into a man." Then he looks at his own wrinkled arms. "I'm sure bio-degrading," he says with the familiar twinkle of life in his eyes.

"You're degrading well. It's been awhile since I've been up here."

"It's been too long."

"Sorry, I've been busy with work, and school, and surfing."

Reaching into my backpack, I take out the golden foil-coated bag and hand it to him. "A present from Mom. Surprise! Indian fry bread!"

"Thanks. It'd be nice if she came up here with you."

"She said to tell you to keep your phone charged."

"Tell her I said she spends too much time in the casino."

"She won't listen to me. Charge up your phone and tell her."

"Okay, I'll charge the damn thing."

Rifling through my pack, I latch onto a paperback. "I brought you a book I just finished."

He takes the thick book into his hands. "Thank you, Peter. Sure is nice to get a new book to wrap my hands around."

"Thought you might be interested. It's an historical account of past societies collapsing."

"Like our tribe's past?"

"Don't want to spoil the ending. Speaking of which, I just got fired from our tribe's casino."

"Again? Good for you!"

"Wish Mom would quit. She hardly sees the light of day."

Hesitantly, he responds. "Her mind is clouded by the money-driven material world."

"She says it's her reward for going without money for so long."

"It's true, many hard times for her when you were an infant, your father never being there for you, leaving her as a single mother. She struggled."

"Guess he couldn't handle a half-breed infant named Peter."

"He couldn't handle a lot of life's commitments. Grandmother and I helped where we could. But now, all that material stuff your mom is collecting won't be much good when the Great Spirit calls." He sheepishly glances down at his pocket. "Although, I really enjoy this little sound system she bought me. My vinyl collection is sure obsolete."

"Hang onto those albums, vinyl is making a comeback."

"Good, then you can have my records and turntable when I'm gone."

With a sweep of his arm he gestures for me to join him on the well-used bench in the shade of the veranda, furniture of his making using the natural random curves of woody branches found in his travels.

The wind calls my attention, "Santa Ana is up."

"Nice offshore wind, waves look really clean."

A red-tailed hawk soars along the ridgeline riding effortlessly on unseen updrafts, pausing to look us over without flapping a wing. With a subtle adjustment of its tail feathers, it continues on its way. I follow its unseen trail until it's lost in the view over the ocean. Hypnotizing lines of waves roll toward us from the liquid horizon. In the distance, jagged Rocky Point juts into the roiling blue, meeting the swells finding shore.

"Clean swell, Southern Hemi. I just had a great surf at Rocky Point. You'd have been onto it in your prime."

"The tide?

"Incoming."

"Must have been reeling on the inside. Any tube rides?"

"One tube I'll never forget. A dolphin dropped in on me when I was deep in the barrel! I thought it was a shark! Next thing I know, the wave's closing out, I'm bailing off the board, going over the falls, getting thrashed and pinned to the bottom for an eternity."

"Your guardian spirit was with you. The dolphin wanted time to play."

"I'm jealous, dolphins have lots of free time."

"Time is fleeting. One day you'll look in the mirror and see an old surf dude, like me."

"Speaking of old dudes, I found bones of a really old Indian dude at Mission Santos," I say, as I pull out my phone to show him the images of the skull. "They want to build a septic system and put in a new parking lot where I found the remains."

As he looks intently at the images, his eyes widen.

"They already have the survey stakes in. I'm going back to look for more. It might be the old Indian burial ground," I add.

"Peter, you dare to disturb an Old One? Who gives you the right? Surely not the dead."

"But, I'm an archeologist, or almost one... It's part of my thesis."

"Archeologist or grave robber? Both disturb the dead."

A vivid image of the man in the spinning dust flashes in my mind and sends my heart racing. "Before I found the skeleton, I saw some sort of vision of the dead at Mission Santos. A tribal man of our past appeared in a spinning dust devil in front of me, fully dressed in Native wear from hundreds, or maybe thousands of years ago. A warrior in full battle gear. He seemed very alive, and then he was covered in blood. I dug down in the earth beneath the vision and found his skull."

My grandfather pauses, searching for words. "A vision, like what you saw in the sweat lodge ceremony when you were a boy?"

"Yes."

"Peter, I apologize about the grave robber comment," he says.

With well-worn hands, he slowly removes a time-polished greenstone canoe hanging from a leather cord around his lean neck. It's the same necklace he has worn since I can remember. I was always enchanted by what he called it — The Dream Helper.

"Time to pass this on to you. My grandfather gave this to me when I was becoming one with my ancestral past, like you are today. He said this *tomol* would help carry me to Dream Walks."

Gently he places the pendant around my neck and steps back with eyes fixed on mine. "The mysteries of the past embrace you. Peter, you are a Dream Walker!"

I hold the well-polished greenstone canoe in my hand, remembering when I was a boy and holding it for the first time. A bright glimmer of sunlight bounces and shimmers emerald in my eyes.

A rush of emotion ripples through me. He reaches out and grasps my hand. I glance down and see his hand looking like a wrinkled map of his life journey. Warm salty blood flows through our veins, joining us together as family of the same tribe as we sit in silent respect.

"The dust of our ancestors lies deep. Help our people rest in the soil of our Earth Mother," he says.

"I'm trying to help sort out our ancestor's past."

"I know you are, Peter. Your heart is in the right place."

"Grandfather, when I was at Mission Santos, I ran into Father Arguello. He tried to pull me back into his church, but I gave his religion pitch a pass."

My grandfather looks up into the sky as a lone cloud floats overhead, casting a fleeting shadow across us. His eyes shift down and lock into mine.

"You're wise to stay away from Arguello."

I can sense anger upwelling within Grandfather, but he sighs and lets it flow. "Arguello preys on those drawn to a church with a steeple and cross. My temple is the open sky. When I look deep into the dark night filled with infinite stars and galaxies, I travel back in time and see I'm just a speck of dust on the grand scale of the universe. My body is composed of the same elements as stardust. When I look up at Father Sky, I feel within my soul there is a Great Spirit. God if you wish. The Great Spirit is within me, within you, within everyone and everything. This is my religion, for lack of a better word."

"So many religions and beliefs… Hard to make sense of it all."

"Some are religious sheep, they graze with heads down and follow leaders blindly. Ignorance is bliss for those who flock to religious tales written by mortal men who ages ago spun their stories to suit their own outlooks. Noble beliefs, and otherwise…"

We both look to the far horizon. Grandfather turns to me slowly, then looks back to Rocky Point. "Peter, I'm afraid humans will be paying the ultimate price for our thirst for oil to feed our consumer desires." He looks out to the ocean in front of us and the oil rigs scattered on the smoggy horizon. He turns back to me, eyes narrowed with concern.

"We are raping and pillaging Planet Earth, our only home. I'm very concerned for future generations."

"Scary times. I feel like I'm helpless in the big global picture."

"You are not helpless. Your underlying fears worry many. The acceleration of human population growth and environmental change is increasing at a rate never before seen in human history. It's normal to feel overwhelmed by thoughts of an impending train wreck as you watch life rushing by in a blur. But remember, the power to change lies within you. Get off the hurtling train and go for a walk."

"Easy for you to say, you're insulated from a lot of the outside world up here."

"It's my choice to live lightly on the land."

Looking out to the edge of the ocean from our high vantage point, I visualize a spinning sphere gently balanced within the vast cosmos of time and space, a staggeringly large area expanding from where I sit. My mind soars into the zero gravity darkness of the universe.

"Join me?" He announces as he holds up the foil fry bread packet like a sacred vessel.

"No thanks, too greasy."

"I'm a skinny old dude, I need the fat."

I smile and nod. "Hand me the sound system, let me check out your music and see what you have. If I take this home, I can download you some indigenous music from around the planet off the Internet. There's a lot going on out there beyond your hermit hill. You'd be amazed at what you can find on the Web these days. Maybe you should think about getting a dish and a wireless server up here. You could surf the World Wide Web, download podcasts, banter on blogs, sort fake news, download music, play games, watch a movie, read an e-book, and get force-fed adverts so you can see what you're not missing."

Grandfather gives me a long, hard look. I shrink back at my suggestions of him plugging into the Internet that is certainly not World

Wide to him. "I'd rather surf ocean waves. All this information coming through this 'web,' do you think I'm missing out on something that wasn't in existence when I built this home? Do you think that because I don't have Internet or TV I'm somehow stuck in an electronic entertainment gap? Do you think because I'm not spending precious time I have here on Earth social networking and trolling through cyberspace I'm missing out on something?"

"It's not just an age thing. There are a lot of older people your age on the Internet," I sheepishly point out.

"It's not an age-related question. It's a question of how I choose to spend time. Personally, I don't see the point in pursuing a perceived need to stay connected to what I see as a lot of electronic distraction racing along towards information overload. People are so busy doing things on the outside, they forget the inside. Surrounded by nature, in silence and meditation are the answers to my most important questions, not plugging into the World Wide Web."

My phone beeps with a text. "Mom wants to know if you're alive.'

"Please confirm I'm breathing."

"You should at least learn how to text," I suggest.

"You should learn to unplug from electronic drugs," he counters.

"Come on, old timer, technology can be good, as long as you're selective and don't become an addict. You could check the weather forecast, we could email each other, and we can even talk face to face with phones and computers."

He chuckles at my proposal. "I check the weather at first light. I go outside on the deck, take a pee, look around and see if clouds have come over. Depending on the wind, I adjust aim."

"What about real-time calls? We could stay in touch more often."

"You and I talking now, face-to-face, sharing our presence side-by-side, in person, this is the real connection computers and machines can't make." He places his finger gently on my chest. "Listen to the intuition in your heart and soul, Peter. It tells you what a cold machine never will."

"I'd rather be here with you," I acknowledge with respect. "But I still think a lot of technology is helping this world, except maybe losing a job to a robot."

He glances over at the wind generator. "Modern life is filled with ever increasing changes and choices, isn't it?"

"It's overwhelming sometimes."

"Go into silence for your answers."

"I need a silence app."

"Peter, let's take a walk, check out the trees you helped me plant."

He proudly leads me around his abundant vegetable garden and fruit trees. The trees I helped put in the ground now tower over me. Lemons, oranges, avocados, plums, apricots, figs, almonds and olives in varying degrees of growth, the early bloomers scattered on the ground and filling the air with fermenting perfume. In the garden bed, summer squash plants ready to take over anything getting in their way, and roots of carrots and beets hiding below. Beans twist up onto rough wood frames, clinging to anything not moving, long pods dangle and swing with each gust of wind. Ripe red tomatoes hang heavily, carefully tied to thick poles to support their weight. Bunches of cabbage, lettuce, and spinach nibbled at the edges by prowling creatures of the night. Near the planters, small animal traps, simple boxes of wood made from scrap lumber to catch those who visit, some seeking dinner, others becoming dinner themselves. Grandfather's wood carvings stand around the garden like scarecrow totems waiting to be discovered, creations from his imaginative mind.

Leaving the food garden behind, I open the well-used hinges of the entry door and entering my grandparents' home with its familiar simple style. The kitchen remains small and functional, as it was when my grandmother was alive. The same worn dining table I once sat at while I helped her bottle tomatoes fresh picked from her garden remains in a corner. The comforting smell of her presence seems to fill the room. She was, and still is, the spiritual center for our family and much of the tribe. A beacon of feminine strength drawing others to her wisdom rooted in love, compassion, forgiveness, and joy. Her spirit still radiates in this room where I stand.

The living room holds the history of life lived. The same heavy cast iron wood burning stove, looking well used. On the mantle, photos of my mom when she was a girl, images of me as a baby in her arms, photos of me growing up lined up side-by-side as I morphed through changing hairstyles into a young man. And in a place of honor, a fading portrait of Grandfather when he was about my age, with his arm around Grandmother, undeniable love radiating from them in a moment captured in a fraction of a second.

Hanging from the roof rafters above, his surfboards, made by his hands. Longboards. The wood one shines unblemished, a masterful wooden art sculpture of fine lines converging with intricate inlays of light and dark wood finished to a high gloss. The other is well-used foam and glass, beaten, dinged and faded to yellow by many years of water-time chasing waves.

Across the room, the far wall is lined with shelves of books, a library testifying to a lifetime of reading. On the small table by a worn, comfortable chair is an open book. I set the book down. Looking over my shoulder, I see my grandfather standing in the doorway, the frame encompassing him like the photos on the mantle.

"*Walden Pond*, Long while since I've held it."

"As time passes, what will the future seventh generation inherit from my generation? What do you think they will see when they are as old as me?" he asks.

"What they won't see is the bigger question. Hope humans get another seven generations," I reply, the hope in my voice half-hearted.

The doorframe shrinks behind him as he walks up to face me, his hands at arm's length on my shoulders, looking me square in the eyes. "Peter, no matter what the future brings, I want you to remember, don't turn to fear. To give into fear is to give away your precious freedom. We find ourselves in a time of changing tides sweeping the old ways of humans out to sea. The tide is so swift that many will be caught up and panic. Some will desperately try and hold on. Keep your eyes open. Go with the current and see who is with you and rejoice together for the positive changes to come when the new tide returns."

"I sure hope a new tide returns."

I reach around my neck and hold the Dream Helper in my fingers, the canoe of smooth greenstone pointing me toward the current. *What life journeys will I experience and what tide changes will be revealed in our travels together?* I ask myself.

"Look at you standing there in your prime," Grandfather says with pride. "The last chapter of my human life story will be coming to an end before long. I can feel it in my soul, and I'm at peace with passing to the Other Side. Peter, when I'm gone, I want you to have this home we built together. It's already in my Will. You are to have it and all its contents, including my woodworking tools, books and vinyl records."

I'm overcome with the thought of his home empty without him. I stand openmouthed until words wander off my lips. "Thank you, Grandfather. I'll try to look after your home as you would, but I hope you're around for a long time. It won't be the same here without you here."

"I'll be with you whenever you pull up a memory," he assures me.

"A lot of good memories."

"I'm leaving you all the tools in my shed."

"I'm no master carpenter, but I'd sure love to make surfboards like you."

"Takes time and experience, but you have a good foundation."

"You're the artist."

"Art is from the soul."

"That casino zapped the soul out of me."

"Let it go, it's in your past. Peter, I have something very important to ask you. When I have gone to the Other Side, will you scatter my ashes from our sacred gateway at Rocky Point, just as my grandfather's ashes were spread? I want my star dust to float into Father Sky and settle into Mother Ocean."

I hesitate to answer. "I'll wait until it's offshore with a solid swell."

He puts his hand gently on my chest. "Thank you in advance for granting my final wish. Remember, don't be sad for my passing when I've ridden my last wave on Earth, for I'll be with you here in your heart."

Outside on the porch, he wraps his arm around my shoulder, grounding me in comfort and a feeling a text message could never provide. The fading sunset sends a bright reflection off the sea, saturating everything in a warm, orange glow. In the distance, a smoggy haze stubbornly clings to the ocean.

"Peter, keep surfing for me."

"We both have saltwater in our blood."

"Watching you as a child play in the waves is one of my greatest memories. I live through you when I see the love and the passion you have for Mother Ocean."

"Thanks for showing me the way," I say as I look out at the obscured mass of the Pacific.

"How's Old Red? Still running?" he inquires.

"Keeps running. Like you."

"Changing the oil?"

"Yes, sir, recycle the oil too," I assure him with a nod of my head.

"Glad to hear you're keeping the old girl alive."

"She does need a new battery."

"Me too, getting harder to start on cold mornings."

"You're doing well for an older model," I answer with a smile.

"Lot of miles on my old ticker."

The sun dips below the ocean with a wink as we stand together saying goodbye.

"Peter, thank you for coming up to see me. Get going down the mountain before dark. Watch for rattlesnakes on the road. Good luck. Stay healthy and keep surfing on Sundays in Mother Ocean. I look forward to our next visit."

"It's always good to be with you, Grandfather." I reach out and hold his hand. "In person," I add.

"I love you, Peter."

"Love you, Grandfather."

I slowly walk down the familiar dirt road with Grandfather in my mind. He calls to me, and I turn back to see him standing in the distance, the road connecting us together spiritually. The wind pauses and it becomes clear what he's saying. "Dream Walker!" he calls out to me with a respectful bow my direction.

I nod in recognition of what he has acknowledged in me, and I'm reminded how long it had been since I'd seen him.

"Charge your phone!" I yell at him in the fading light of day.

I hold the greenstone tomol in my hand as I walk down the crest of the ridge, glancing occasionally for rattlesnakes coiled on the path, soaking up the lingering warmth of day.

Planets and stars appear overhead as Father Sky goes into night shift. Shadows of darkness grow with each step I take away from my grandfather and his home.

CHAPTER 5

With a slight press of Old Red's brakes, I enter a tunnel in the coastal mountain range, rolling into the dark hole of concrete on Highway 101. Pre-motor travelers on foot and horseback in California would have squeezed into the same narrow pass, man and beast looking for the easiest way through these mountains, before the ease of modern earth-boring shortcuts.

Images of the past quickly depart as I emerge from near darkness of the tunnel into the glaring light of the present. I pass a crowded rest stop filled to capacity with cars, trucks, motorcycles and RVs looking for relief at the communal water hole.

Old Red is long on road wear and lives up to its name. Heavily loaded semi-trucks roar up on my bumper and careen by. Approaching downtown Santa Barbara, the traffic starts backing up all around and speed ceases to matter.

After many laps around the Santa Barbara Museum of Natural History, I find a free parking spot that can handle Old Red's bulk in a tidy residential neighborhood blocks away. Stepping out of my truck, lawn mowers, leaf blowers and weed eaters fill the air, which is also rife with the aroma of unburned fossil fuel thanks to those contraptions.

Orderly box hedges hem me in as I follow the lines of the paved path leading to the Museum.

Logging into with the security code, I'm slightly amazed it hasn't been changed. Entering the back offices and archives wing, I peer through his door, papers and books piled thick on the desk, but he's not there. My heart sinks rapidly as I want almost nothing more than to share my find in person. I call out in my native Noqoto language. "Hello?"

"Hello!" A voice answers in Noqoto.

Down a long passageway, I head for the climate controlled vault and find its door partially open. I pull the heavy door open, revealing walls of steel cabinets with a few open drawers, the contents of each, categorized and labeled. I pause and look into a drawer filled with bone fish hooks, sinkers, stone bowls, arrowheads, chipped obsidian knives, bone awls, spear points, pipes, musical flutes, and carved figurines of bear and dolphins.

Dr. Evans is bent over in focused attention, partially buried in another open drawer. "Hello, Peter," comes his muffled salutation.

"How did you know?"

His head rises from the depth of the drawer. "I only know two people who still speak your language. And your grandfather certainly never bothers to come here."

"This place creeps him out."

"Joe has a right to be creeped about ghosts of the past. Speaking of ghosts, when's your final paper going to materialize?"

"Soon, I just added an important chapter."

Evans grabs his cane and slowly rises up from the drawer while grimacing in obvious pain. Forcing a smile, he shakes my hand. "I was about to call you."

"How's the hip?"

"Damn sore."

He reaches over and picks up a lone femur bone from the drawer. "This poor man didn't have much of a choice when his joints wore out. Fortunate me, I live in this era of time."

'Poor man' sends me reaching into my pocket for my phone. "Look at the poor man that found me at Mission Santos!"

Evans carefully studies the image of the skull. His eyes widen behind his bifocals. "Mission Santos? Found you?"

"Right where they want to put the parking lot. I hope it's the Indian burial site we've been looking for!"

I scroll to the next image, which reveals the relation of the skeleton to the survey flags and nearby mission buildings.

He studies the image carefully and gives me a serious look. "Might want to buy yourself a lotto ticket."

"It was an educated guess. I'd like to keep looking for more graveyard clues at Mission Santos, if it's okay with you."

"You download these photo files onto the computer, and I'll move forward with a stop work order on the site and alert the authorities. However, we've got a more pressing project I need you to help me with. I'm afraid it's Rocky Point."

"The surf spot? I… I mean the sacred spot?"

"CEOs and shareholders always seek profits. There's a huge plan in the works by ENRG corporate development to construct an expansive petrochemical facility there to transfer and store oil and gas from offshore rigs," he informs me with a deep look of concern.

"They can't do that!"

"Apparently they think they can. I've seen the concept plans. You're really not going to like this, Peter. They also want to build a large breakwater off Rocky Point to create a sheltered harbor for protecting pipelines and for staging boats to the rigs."

"They'll kill off another surf spot! They'll make Rocky Point into a monument to oil!"

"The plan is for a sprawling facility that will cover most of Rocky Point, including the nearby surroundings, right up to the lagoon. The ENRG expansion project is backed by the Federal Government, accompanied by the beating of Pentagon war drums. Once again, the political-corporate-military-propaganda-machine is spreading fear about oil insecurity and instability overseas. The bloody military hawks are rising again!"

Evans shuffles up to face me, his body language winding up.

"Damned military madness! History repeats again! Those who gain from war never see their blood spilled in battle," he rants, while wiping spittle from his chin.

"For sure, war sucks," I add, lacking personal experience in war.

"Right now, you and I have our own battles to fight. The California Coastal Commission contacted me yesterday. The Museum has been given thirty days to do an initial archaeological survey of Rocky Point and surrounds. Paperwork is coming my way, but no solid funding. If we can come up with something historically significant, we can put the brakes on this short-term, oil-dependency folly."

Blood rushes through my head as I try to take in all the information being thrown at me. What started as a victory with my discovery of the skull at the Mission Santos is now turning into another battle, a rush to save Rocky Point. "It's a huge area. And there's not much time."

Dr. Evans looks at me like he's studying something of historical interest. "For now, it's all you've got. Thirty days."

"Me?"

"As a direct descendant of the Noqoto people who once called this area home for thousands of years, you're ancestrally connected to Rocky Point. You know the area better than anyone I know. You cut my class to surf there, which in this case plays to our advantage."

I stare down at the labeled bones in the steel drawer. "Where are the Euro bones?"

"Peter, these bones were collected long ago by people who thought these Native American remains belonged here."

"Remains? Like what's left curbside?"

"Lighten up, we're on the same side. Peter, I need you on this project. I'm a gimp right now. I can't go out there in the field and crawl around looking for historical needles in haystacks. If I blow out this new hip, I'm back to the constant pain. I want you to be my legs and do the initial survey with my guidance. I'll follow up with a crew of volunteers after you've done the first stage field work, depending on what you discover."

"What about class? What about my thesis?"

Evans lets loose a laugh. "This will be a better lesson than anything I can teach you in class. Peter, you have a gift. Just keep doing what comes naturally. Apply the skills I've taught you, and with your luck, or whatever you've got, you'll come up with something at Rocky Point like you found at Mission Santos. What others search for seems to find you. However, you should know upfront, I can't pay you much. The Museum's budget is gutted now and I can barely pay myself, let alone an assistant."

We both look down at the drawer filled with past living souls. "They deserve a proper resting place," I whisper as if not wanting to wake dead ancestors.

"Perhaps they can be given a proper burial someday. What do you say? Are you in on Rocky Point?"

"Pay me when you can."

"Good, I was hoping you'd come round. I'll put together an authorization letter."

"You wouldn't want to end up in this cold steel drawer, would you?" I have to ask.

"With all the time I spend in here, I'll probably be the first Euro in this drawer."

CHAPTER 6

As Dr. Evans works on the reference letter, I seemingly Dream Walk back in time, through the public displays of artifacts in the Native Californian history exhibit hall, a big darkened room filled with the coastal Indian history. I stop and study the largest object occupying the floor, an accurate replica of a tomol, similar in shape to the small greenstone pendant hanging from my neck. These sturdy seaworthy boats were capable of holding many people and their goods. Built like a small wooden ship with planks hand drilled and stitched together with woven cord, the joins were sealed with naturally-forming asphalt. Stained red, shaped with a deep V hull flared at the bow, and designed to handle open ocean swells, they were used by the mainland and island Indian communities for fishing and trade.

My eyes adjust to the dim light. There's another museum patron looking at beautifully crafted basketry across the room. She returns my quick glance with another.

I move on to a diorama behind glass of a serene looking Native American seaside village from hundreds, or thousands of years ago. There's a cluster of domed huts, a large central lodge, shade areas to escape the sun, boats pulled up on shore, fish hanging to dry, kids playing, men back from hunting with a slain deer in tow, and a group of women gathered in a social circle. To my eyes it looks like a past paradise, an idyllic scene of tribal village life in another time, before the name, "California" was added by Europeans. Glancing to my right is the Early California Mission Era diorama, complete with the working Native Indian occupants under the watch of armed Spanish soldiers riding the perimeter. An artist's depiction of a productive operation involving crops, cattle, sheep, adobe bricks and building activity. A hooded Franciscan friar kneels in front of the courtyard cross. Behind the priest, Indian women wash clothing in a man-made pond.

I notice a woman of the present looking at me from across the village display. I glance away from history all around me to focus on her.

Behind her glasses, her dark, intelligent eyes read me, as I read her. Sun-bleached hair is braided into a single twisted rope and pulled back, showing her face and slight smile.

"The Native Californians, what wonderful people," she remarks.

"You look wonderful too."

"I meant the past Indians..."

"Well, I am Native Californian. What about you?"

"My family history in California runs deep, but they say I'm a blend of cultures. Mexican, Native American, Italian and a dash of Chinese."

"My mixed-Indian blood cup is about half-empty. Have some conflicted history myself."

"Don't we all have skeletons in our DNA closets? The pre-European tribes on this coast seem to be a noble culture, just look around this room and close your eyes to imagine."

"Open your eyes. Very few survived the first wave of Spanish colonists and their missions," I add.

"Their art, the basketry that did survive, what a beautiful legacy."

We both look again at the village scene, soaking in its stories.

"They never would have imagined the horrors of nuclear waste, toxic chemicals, smoggy skies, water pollution, de-forestation, dying seas, and overpopulation of humans driving unprecedented extinction rates of plants and animals," she adds with a frown.

"Poor people, they had no Internet..." I say, trying to lighten the room.

"I do try to stay optimistic, even with all the depressing news these days. But sometimes, like now, the past doesn't feel far away at all," she says with a sigh.

"Day dreaming?"

"Who knows? Maybe this is a dream now?" she suggests.

"If I am dreaming, don't wake me. You come here often?"

"What original lines. Are you an actor? You do look familiar..."

"Actually, I was sort of... I didn't have any lines to speak."

"Actor with no lines, mmm... silent movies or mime?"

"Wooden Indian."

She laughs. "Should I not laugh? I'm so sorry, I don't mean to be cruel. It's not every day I get to meet a real wooden cigar store Indian."

"Former wooden Indian, I was a Native American Heritage Figure at my tribe's casino. I'm being replaced by a robot that doesn't talk back. Back to my question, do you come here often?"

"When I need to get grounded. And you?"

"According to some, I come here too often. Living in the past, they say."

"It's good you're interested in history and other cultures."

"I'm working on finishing my thesis with an emphasis on forgotten California tribes."

"Now that Wooden Indian thing is starting to make sense, sort of."

"What about you? Why are you hanging out here, dwelling in the past?" I ask.

She glances around the room, looking at the displays surrounding us. "I like to come here to imagine what it was like before tens of millions of people flooded into California."

"California here we came, and keep coming."

"Some places are still relatively pristine in California, rare sanctuaries for nature."

"Yes, some places are really worth protecting," I reply, thinking about Rocky Point.

We both look at the glass-covered display. I look at the reflection of her face. She looks over at my reflection looking at her. I stumble for something to say, and then she says it for me.

"I'm Linda, Linda Diaz."

"My name's Peter, Peter Martinez."

We both stare at each other like open books with blank pages to fill. My heart tells me there's something between us beyond random crossing of paths.

"Linda, this may seem bold, but I'm wondering, would you like to get together sometime out there in the modern world?"

"Like, a date?"

"Coffee? No time like the present?"

She digs out her smart phone and strikes the pose of the wireless communication tribe.

"Oh, shit! I'm late! I'm so sorry! I have an important meeting! Give me your number! I have to run!"

With my number in her phone, she turns and hustles toward the exit like a hurried shadow. I turn back to the glassed-in display of the Native community, and see her faint reflection fade away across the Indian village like a fleeing ghost stealing my anxious heart.

CHAPTER 7

Old Red and I inch along at rush hour, trying to get out of Santa Barbara and back onto Highway 101, my daydreams of the past left behind at the Museum. Shifting the old manual stick between starts and stops is taking a toll on my cramped clutch leg. On State Street, Santa Barbara's main thoroughfare that leads straight to the ocean, the retail stores are stacked tightly together on either side of me, looking like one big outdoor mall. Tall palm trees stretch for the sun along the concrete pathways leading to the sea. Stucco, rod iron, fake wooden headers and red tile roofs are all around. Signs above the entries of retail stores tell of designer labels tastefully displayed to lure the disposable income crowd. Boutique shops with graphic window displays flash their feathers to compete for attention and consumers.

The light changes to green and I roll on through restaurant row. Outside tables and chairs spill onto the sidewalks on this fine weather day, hosting a sprinkling of diners giving shopping a rest. I roll the window of the truck all the way down and suck in inviting aromas. All around me on this stretch of road, a world of taste traveling is within easy reach. In my dreams, I can eat at each restaurant and not be concerned with my bank account balance or my weight on the scale. The crossover of cultures in California is represented in the menus hanging outside the eateries, competing to lure hungry customers in by the nose and hold them there by the taste buds. An immigrant melting pot of ethnic foods and flavors.

Trapped in the snarl of traffic, I can appreciate the notion familiar to many in this part of California: you are what you drive. There are plenty of examples currently around me to support the theory. A healthy dose of shiny, luxury, high-end European imports idle at the stoplights, impatiently waiting for the short race to the next red light. Eco-friendly hybrids are sprinkled among the seemingly endless traffic, quietly making a statement of their own. Large SUVs tower over other vehicles, many with petite women driving with a lot of empty interior space.

I reflect that this is prime California coastal property of our tribal past, and present. Santa Barbara and Montecito are considered by many to be the pinnacle of places to live. Location, location, location. What's not to like? A mild coastal climate much of the year. The Santa Ynez mountain backdrop soaring above the city, with the Pacific Ocean and lovely beaches waiting below. The area boasts fine homes, a harbor to moor the yacht, golf courses to play, luxury spas for rejuvenation, UC Santa Barbara campus on a premier stretch of coast, dining options aplenty, and vast consumer consumption choices. A perceived perfect world for many. But, Mother Nature has her say, shaking up residents with earthquakes, prolonged droughts, wicked wildfires, and when the rain does return, mudslides tossing rocks and trees down gullies, wiping out anything in the way.

Above the commercial district surrounding State Street, the Santa Barbara Mission is positioned like a castle surrounded by a moat of fine homes. Called the Queen of the Missions, the impressive structure has obviously undergone many upgrades through the years, but still holds a historical look. If only those old thick adobe walls could talk in Native tongue. What history would be told if the Indians of the Spanish Colonial era were asked for their opinions?

At a standstill at yet another red light, patience being tested, I wonder what I must look like to others around me. My truck has a liberal abundance of rust and dirt. One side mirror is cracked like a drunken spider web, making for some interesting, distorted, mosaic-like reflections. With my shovel hanging out of the truck bed, I could be mistaken for illegal immigrant labor, which my cross-cultural appearance might also suggest.

Thoughts of the immigrant culture direct my hungry stomach to take action. The place I seek is authentic inside, the comforting colors of Mexico surrounding the interior in green, red, and white. The music of canned mariachis blares out the door. Nothing fancy in here, just some simple tables leveled with cardboard, and cheap plastic chairs. The overhead wallboard behind the counter lists the basic ingredients of Mexican food all mixed and matched. The rough plastered walls are randomly decorated with large sombreros, Mexican flags, faded posters of bullfighting, Mexican beer and Cinco de Mayo.

I settle into a seat on a stool at the counter by the window. The food arrives quickly. "Gracias." The fresh salsa — the benchmark of any Mexican restaurant — is very good, the chips freshly made, the shredded beef flavored to the edge of the heat ledge, the ranchero sauce homemade. I dip the remaining few chips into the last of the mixed up meal in front of me and push back my stool, pausing to look out the window to the street.

Busy people check the time while hustling to get somewhere. They chat on phones or texting as they multi-task walk, bike, or drive their cars at half attention. Some seem to be talking to themselves while others seem mute thanks to sound systems stuffed in their ears. Everyone on the move, except a desperate looking street person hanging out on a bench across the way. In his outdoor home, he, without a phone, talks to himself. A shopping cart parked at his side is filled with random torn plastic bags stuffed with his worldly possessions. He's dumpster-diving to survive in the paradise of others.

I order a chicken burrito, exit the restaurant, and make my way toward the homeless man, bearing the foil-wrapped gift.

He gives the burrito back to me, unopened. "I don't do Mexican. Got cash?"

CHAPTER 8

City lights behind me, the last colors of the day play against the coastal mountains, the faint glow of the setting sun lighting up the tops of the dimming ridgeline. Traffic is thinning and night is creeping in as I make my way down the two-lane road toward the reservation.

Looking ahead is replaced with the panic of looking behind as bright red lights flash from an emergency vehicle roaring up onto my bumper. He orders me to "Pull over!"

So I do, when I can. Mega-wattage spotlights torch directly at me, it seems like aliens from space are about to beam me up to the mother ship. I glance back through the mosaic of my cracked mirror; the figure approaching me looks otherworldly.

Stepping up to my lowered window, a shadow comes over my mirror as a full eclipse. "Police! Get out of the car!" he orders in English and Spanish as the police radio crackles.

"What did I do?" I ask, in English and Spanish, as he steps up closer to my window and peers cautiously inside.

Apparently he thinks my question is some sort of threat. He pulls his gun, stands back and tells me again, shouting even louder, "You speak English, get out of the car!"

When a loaded gun is pointed at me, I do what I'm told in any language. I exit my truck and come face to face with the man. My eyes go slanted as the lights continue to blind me.

"Is there a problem, sir? I wasn't speeding."

"You have a cracked rearview mirror and one taillight is out," he says with authority.

I laugh, which he doesn't think is funny. "What do you find so amusing? You on drugs?" he asks as he scans my squinting eyes.

"No, sir. It seems ridiculous you have a gun pointed at me because of one cracked mirror and one burnt out bulb."

"I pulled my weapon because you wouldn't get out of your car."

"I was asking you a question."

"I'll need to see your driver's license, registration, and proof of insurance."

"It's in the truck."

"Go in the truck and get it."

"Now I'm confused. After I'm in, do you want me to get out?"

"You stay in. Keep your hands on the wheel where I can see them."

"This all started with a basic question in plain English. By the way, I speak three languages," I inform him.

"I'll be writing you a fix-it ticket for the mirror and taillight, and a notice for non-cooperation with a law enforcement officer."

"Not cooperating? Come on! Cut me some slack—."

"Tell it to the judge," he says, cutting me off. Then holsters his gun with authority and steps closer to me, holding his lethal weapon flashlight while I fumble through my glove box to find my wallet. I hand the official State of California documents to him, hoping they aren't expired.

"Get your hands on the wheel!" he orders.

Hands firmly on it, I put myself in the cop's shoes. Who knows what kind of people he had dealt with today? There certainly are a lot of questionable characters out there on the streets of California for him to be uptight about. Maybe someone pulled a weapon on him not long ago? Plenty of people have guns in gun-toting USA. An abundance of loyal NRA members lobbying for their own personal arsenals, sicko mass-shooters of innocents, deranged terrorists, desperate drug dealers, auto-carbine collectors, hunters of actual wild game, and school children with their parent's pistol for sharing with their classmates. It's a Constitutional right to be armed to the hilt in America.

"Wait right here, Mr. Martinez. I'll need to check your license and registration."

His bright lights are burning into my eyes, intensified by my mirrors. By taking one hand off the wheel and maneuvering the center mirror, I point the blinding light back in the law enforcement officer's eyes while he sits in his patrol car doodling. Apparently, this speeds up his ticket writing.

"I should take you to jail right now for being uncooperative with a police officer!"

"You're messing with my circadian cycle! I'll be up all night!"

"Alright, Mr. Martinez, as you will see by the infringement citation, you're required to fix your mirror and taillight, and you will be required to provide an explanation to the judge as to why you were uncooperative with an officer of the law. Your options for court date appearances are written on the back of the ticket in detail. You may wish to hire legal counsel in your defense. Have a good evening and drive carefully."

"I hope you're calling it a day soon. You're sure uptight."

"Been putting in long hours. With my wife fighting cancer, we're trying to stay on top of the bills to keep from getting buried. Insurance bastards keep working her like she's a number."

"Sorry to hear she's ill. But a cracked mirror and I get a gun pointed at me?"

"For all I knew, you could be a crack dealer."

"And?"

"Your record's clean." He still eyes me with a hint of suspicion. "Without laws and cops like me to enforce them, America wouldn't be the land of the free."

"That's debatable, depending which side of the barrel you're on."

"Move to Somalia or Yemen and see how you like it there."

"I'm not moving from California. We were here first."

I look at the man in front of me standing like an urban warrior in full action-figure uniform complete with bulletproof vest. My mind wanders to the schoolyard of my youth. "Guessing you were a Scout?"

"Eagle," he proudly proclaims.

"I was a Woodcraft Ranger."

"What's that?"

"Native American theme. We didn't wear junior-quasi-military-uniforms, only fake Indian stuff. Our indoor ceremonial fire was four colored light bulbs. I thought it was cool."

"Cowboy and Indian kind of stuff?"

"Only Indian. Anyway, hope my fix-it ticket helps you reach your quota."

"Drive safe out there, Woody Ranger."

"I was driving safely, Seagull Scout. Sir."

The enforcer of the laws strides to his car as I watch in the rearview mirror. The light show ends as he spins an illegal U-turn and guns the engine, speeding off like there's no speed limit. The pupils in my eyes re-adjust, and I see the casino lights glowing brightly behind the ridge in front of me like a full moon about to rise.

Passing the understated reservation entry sign to the subdivision, I pull up to my duplex apartment. No denying it's a dumpy looking place, and looks even grimmer in my headlights. The pre-casino constructions are low budget, cheap, nasty and not built to last.

My neighbor looks like he's still working and all the windows are dark. I fumble with my keys in the blackness, open the door by braille, and make my way through the entry. Flipping on the lights reveals dirty dishes still in the sink. The lonely drum set sits in the middle of the living room looking neglected, and my less-used surfboard collection hangs suspended from rope from the ceiling. The unmade bed and well-lived in couch are the center of my limited furniture collection. My meager apartment lacks the warmth of family history of my grandfather's well lived and loved home. Everything has the air of the temporary here, including me.

Cautiously, I open the hall closet a crack to keep from being smothered by the stuff I've haphazardly shoved into the limited space. I dig down and find my tent, sleeping bag, airbed, camp chair and camping box with the cooking gear. The ice chest is the last to come out and I cringe at its odor. I turn back to the kitchen and open the fridge without a similar fear of its contents spilling out. There's a big shopping trip in my near future as I stare at the almost empty shelves.

I sigh into the silence of the room. Plugging in my tunes, I decide to escape into music. I settle in, flip my sticks, and have a go on my drum set. I build the beat sprinkled with assorted percussion. It's the sound of ages; a primal beat from deep within flowing into my hands from within my soul. I'm one with distant universal vibrations touching me in the moment of Now. The beat of the music casts aside the clutter that's been rattling around in my head and brings me down to Earth.

In the distance, like a spirit calling, a haunting backbeat from another world joins in. A voice echoes from beyond. I stop drumming and silence the skins.

My neighbor pounds firmly on the adjoining wall, shouting filtered pleas for quiet.

In the quiet of the room I hear a text come in on my phone. "Peter, apologize for ditching you at the Museum. Promise to touch down again later. Just got a new job and I'll be very busy and fully focused for the foreseeable future. I'll catch up with you another time down the line for a coffee."

"Linda, Not a problem. I've got fieldwork at a remote location and I'll be away for a stretch too. Until we cross paths again, good luck living life in the present. Peter."

Hope is rekindled. At least I now have Linda's number.

CHAPTER 9

On my computer search, the ENRG entry gate to Rocky Point is difficult to locate, leaving me to consult with the almighty Eye in the Sky. I hone in on the approach road from outer space satellite perspective and find the entry at the end of the pavement. Satisfied, I steer the all-seeing eye for a close-up surf check of Rocky Point. No significant swell to be seen wrapping around the point and keeping Internet surfers unsatisfied. Good. I scroll up the coast to the Air Force base and a nervous feeling comes over me, as if the watcher is being watched. I pause and wonder if the NSA is now tracking me. Scary. I quickly detour and scroll down to the reservation and zoom in on the structure of the casino. It's obvious the photo was taken on a weekend with lots of cars in the parking lot. Scroll over to my subdivision, and close on the driveway of my duplex. I can see Old Red parked in front with my kayak in the rack. I look over my shoulder. No one there. I collect myself. The last of my things in one hand, I shut the apartment door and flee the Internet.

Stepping into the bright morning, I squint up to the sky still wondering about the all-seeing eyes orbiting above. Walk around Old Red and give it a check of the tie downs. I hop in and thankfully it fires up. I give a quick glance in the good mirror, and then watch the reservation shrink away behind me.

Just beyond the off-ramp from Highway 101, I roll up to a service station since I'm about to hit fumes. There's only one choice. The gold lettered ENRG sign taunts me to pull up to the pump and pour in some exploding petroleum product. Forced to give in, I swipe my credit card. In this moment, with my hand firmly on the pump handle, squeezing the trigger, it becomes ironically obvious I'm giving my money to ENRG so I can fuel up and continue down the road to try and stop ENRG from producing more fuel for my truck.

Off the wide concrete expanse of the highway and cruising along the main drag headed for the coastal mountains beyond, an obvious zoning change leads me to the strip malls seemingly birthed from the big box retailers in the distance. Towering in front of me are huge buildings off the scale of anything else around. As I close in on the mega-mall, a monolith signage with towering letters casts its corporate shadow and blocks the sun. I pull into the parking lot and take a deep breath. I am at the doorstep of The Mega Store. I'll need a good supply of food and other items to carry me though for a long stay at Rocky Point, and for better or worse, The Mega Store is a place to stretch the dollars I've been promised.

I extract an oversize shopping cart from the long line of others and wheel it through the large, automated entry doors. A man of retirement age, clad in a vest branded with a corporate logo, greets me, a permanent smile on his time-lined face. I return his greeting, which seems forced and stuff. But not as stiff as mine when I was an entry greeter.

Cautiously I roll into the underbelly of the retail beast. Vast aisle canyons recede in front of me leading to a bewildering number of choices. I freeze, almost panicking with flight-or-fight syndrome as thousands of items covered in bright colored plastic packaging lure me to offer money to competing altars of consumption. Acres of shelves and a sea of aisles splay out to the man-made horizon of the cavernous building. Thinking I could use an experienced isle scout to help me on my shopping journey, I glance back at the entry greeter, hoping for guidance. He's unresponsive, and unlikely to venture far from his post. Onward I continue alone, pushing my transporter as of yet unpurchased goods.

Worn down from the shopping list, I'm soon drained from the emotional toll of too many choices. I stand humbled in The Church of the Consumer, ready to give my offering at checkout. I can see only a few check-out stations with real, live humans manning them, and the lines for them are long, filled with fellow self-checkout skeptics. The self-checkout stations are numerous. My overburdened shopping cart, weighed down with the lead of the new truck battery, many gallons of drinking water and all my other supplies, protests as I give in and wrestle the cart up to a self-checkout. Ready to give my credit card to the unseen deities, peer around and observe others self-checkers having a go. I look back down at the towering pile of food and consumer stuff in my cart and weigh the odds of wrestling with this machine or rolling for the exit door. The greeter glances at me. I sense he's onto me and my thoughts. Number twelve lights up! A real-live-checkout-angel waves a hand my direction! I flee the self-checkout station and race across to her, fending off any other would-be cart-wielding aggressors with grim determination. No one dares to oppose my building speed; the weight of the cart is like a runaway cement truck. I make a split-second decision to check my inertia with a glancing blow of the tabloids rack, but end up sideswiping the low slung, kid magnet candy displays on the way in. The checker looks my way with wide eyes. The corn sweetener residue settles beneath my cart skidding to a stop. Sheepishly, I look up to see the number twelve blinking on and off as it sways from the impact.

"Lost my brakes, then the gearbox. I should have weighed this first at the truck stop," I muse to the cute checkout girl in the very generic, unflattering uniform.

"This place can afford to lose a few candy bars," she says with a glance down at the candy carnage at my feet.

"Appreciate you taking me in."

"You looked desperate."

As quick as I can get my stuff on the belt, she scans it and moves for the next item. Her arm moves in a blur, only slowed by a scan of the beeping bar code. I can't get the items out of the cart fast enough and I'm falling behind.

"Wow, you're fast," I say between grabs.

"Pretty brainless."

"Carpal tunnel test?"

"Not a lifer here, lucky to have a job with all the self-checkout."

"Don't want to grow old at Sprawl Mart, like the greeter?"

"My grandpa."

"At least he's not a robot."

"Retired awhile back, but now he needs the cash."

I reach down and strain to get the battery on the belt. The treadmill slows, then groans to a near standstill. The smell of burning rubber arises.

"You'll trigger the smoke alarm. Put that battery back in the cart and I'll scan it."

"I'm going to wreck this place with my impact."

"Is it credit or cash?"

"Unfortunately, credit."

"Looks like you've got mouths to feed."

"Just me, I'm going to be out in the sticks for a while."

"All good. You want your receipt emailed? Or you want to slash a tree?

"Recycled paper please."

"Very moderately green of you," she says as she peels off a sizable scroll representing my full load along with advertisements and promotional offers. "Well, you have a good day, or a whatever," she says while looking back toward the line stacking up behind me.

The entry doors close behind me with a vacuum-like seal. I've survived the hunt, with some help from the Natives. The beep of the bar code reader still rattles like a robotic bee in my head. I exit the plains of the expansive parking lot with the other urban hunter-gatherers to carry on.

The sprawling suburban growth of track-home-sameness fades behind me in the rearview mirror. The growing smell of fertilizer crinkles my nose as the road narrows and stretches into a straight line, cutting through expansive corporate farm monocultures of grapes, tomatoes and corn. The coastal mountain range rises in the distance, dark specs of cattle dot the hillsides as they graze and search for green grass.

Old Red and I climb out of the valley and into the ranges as the road narrows. Around a sharp corner snaking upward, I drop it into second gear, approaching a turn off with a county road sign for "Pico Road" clinging to a crash-tweaked pole. Still in lower gear, the old girl protests as I keep climbing up the twisting canyon, passing by old-man oaks standing stoutly as sentinels to time. Out my open window, the scent in the air shifts to Nature's perfume, fresh and alive, lacking the hand of man. Bright orange California poppies sprinkle the open clearings, daring me not to look. California quail adorned with stylish tassels on their heads rush across the road on fleeting foot, then leap into flight and dive low into the brush. Busy gray ground squirrels wait until the last second to make the dash of death across the road in front of me, hoping to avoid the same fate as the flattened creatures successfully field-testing evolution.

Around a sharp bend in the canyon, the scene around me is suddenly a harsh reflection of man. The ENRG entry gate to Rocky Point stands out without mistake. The chain-link fence with razor wire wrapped over the hillside joins at the thick steel gate anchored into a very secure looking concrete guardhouse. A large sign, featuring the prominent gold-and-black ENRG logo, answers any mystery as to who claims the land beyond the gate as its own. A familiar black SUV sits parked. As I slowly pull up to the entry, the same corporate militiaman I crossed paths with looks up from his computer screen, then exits his guardhouse. Standing there with arms crossed, he's not smiling.

His backup buddy in the guardhouse steps out and gives me a similarly severe look. They both look at each other. They are taking their jobs very seriously and I'm in their sights.

I feel like I should get out of my truck with my hands in the air. I slow way down and approach the gate, blocked with a car-crunching steel bar.

The ENRG security guard marches up to my window. No warm welcome here. "Feral surfer returns! Two flat tires, asshole!" he growls.

"Don't know what you're talking about," I reply with a grin.

"Get off the property, or I call the sheriff!"

"I've got good reasons to be here. I'm on California State mandated duty."

The letter from Dr. Evans is in the glove box, as I reach for it, the anxious rent-a-cop goes for his pepper spray and points it at my face.

"Freeze!" he shouts.

Being a former professional freezer, and well rehearsed from other authority figure encounters, I know the drill.

"Relax. I'm getting an authorization letter."

"Okay, move slowly, I'm watching you."

He holds his hand anxiously on his pepper spray until I close the glove box and hand him the letter. He reads it slowly, maybe twice.

"How do I know this is legit?" he finally asks.

"Call Dr. Evans if you want, the number is on the letterhead."

The other security guy keeps an eye on me while the militiaman disappears into the guardhouse and picks up the phone. He isn't happy when he returns.

"Okay Martinez, I'll need to see ID."

I hand him my official State of California driver's license featuring my unsmiling face.

"I'll have to escort you to the site. Follow me."

The heavy gate lifts with a groan. I fire up the engine and throw Old Red anxiously into first. Once past the gate, I'm behind the lines in corporate enemy territory feeling like an archaeologist-spy on a mission. The guard jumps in his SUV and stomps on the gas with an angry foot, dust billowing behind him. I don't have any trouble knowing the direction he's going, but seeing is another thing. I'm enveloped in the choking cloud. I back off and pick my own pace as I climb the switchbacks, taking in the unfolding scenery around me.

Cresting the top of the ridge, the landscape falls away to the sea with Rocky Point resting on the water like an imaginary dragon's back. To the south of the point, the deep green of the estuary filled with resting water birds looks like an inviting home to those drawn to fresh water.

A few curves beyond, the SUV sits parked at a pull out, Mr. Security waiting impatiently. Below is a broad vista taking in all of the land to the sea, fence-to-fence, a good place to park and check for intruders with binoculars.

Sticking with his authoritarian attitude, the guard can't help but show his disappointment as he approaches my open window. "Look different from this side of the fence?"

Climbing out of the truck, wide-angle vistas make my head spin. "Really lovely view from up here."

"Wouldn't have been lovely if I'd gone off the edge. This is where I almost lost it when the tire blew."

"Never know where you might pick up a nail..."

"Who said anything about a nail?"

"Lucky guess!" I suggest.

"Lucky I didn't die! Better take in this view while you can, future home of a very large gas station. Remember, you're confined to this area below. You'll see the survey flags marking the development boundaries."

He looks over at the kayak and surfboard comfortably resting in the roof rack of my truck. "Planning on water recreation, are we? Aren't you supposed to be working?"

"Water surveys."

"Hate to have you lost at sea."

"Thanks for your concern."

"Thirty days is what you have, like it says in the letter. Keep that in mind. It wouldn't be good if you stirred up any trouble around here."

"I'll add that to the list of warnings."

The guard walks towards his vehicle, stops and draws his gun. He walks back toward me. I hold my ground. Stopping at Old Red, he fires a single shot. My front tire sputters out of air.

"We're even, almost," he says as he holsters his weapon.

The dust settles from the hasty departure of the ENRG enforcer, leaving me all alone at the lookout. I check my cell phone, no signal. Looks like I'll be weaning myself from the electronic clutter of the outside world. I can see Grandfather smiling.

I dig out the lug wrench and jack for Old Red wondering if the spare is holding air, and if I can free the rusty old lug bolts.

Well, Peter the nail thrower, what goes around, comes back around.

CHAPTER 10

Losing altitude on the hairpin filled road, I creep in low gear toward the estuary below. Rounding the last bend reveals a blue-green lagoon, acres wide, which narrows toward a stream spilling in at the far end. An oak-lined canyon twists down from the mountains above funneling precious water into the estuary. A ring of living water-loving plants clings to the precious liquid with shades of brown at the drying fringes. White water lilies drift lazily in the shallows, floating in a thin tether to the sandy bottom. Clusters of cattails and tulles wave in perfect concert with the sea breeze. Where the lagoon fronts the beach, a natural sandy dam closes off the mixing of fresh water with the salty ocean beyond the dunes. Weeping willow trees cluster around a flat meadow zone, laying down some inviting shade. This will be the place to make camp. Perhaps a spot where others may have come to the same conclusion generations ago?

The road spills out close enough to the estuary for a reasonable approach in Old Red. I roll to a hilly stop and shut off the ignition. I step outside. Quiet. The scent of the sea mixes with all the life around me like a fresh breath of Mother Nature perfume.

I quickly conclude that this place is a ten out of ten on the amazing places to camp scale. All the elements come together.

Fresh water, grassy meadow, big shade trees, sandy beach a stone's throw away, big ocean beyond, and world class surfing potential a walk up the coast. A smile grows on my face and won't give up without a fight.

I scout around and select the ideal position for the tent, considering the amazing views, the wind and the cycles of the sun. A good compromise is to pitch the tent in a patch of wind-beat grass amongst the trees. After staking the corners, threading the poles and tightening the hold-downs, I finish with the veranda and stand back to admire my new temporary home. Inside it, it's time for furniture. I pump up the air bed, then toss sleeping bag and pillow upon it. Fresh water containers are secured, solar shower hung high from a well-placed dead branch, a fire pit area in the open has plenty of room to keep a blaze contained with a circle of stones, and there's plenty of dry driftwood to keep it burning. I anticipate the night with the placement of the lantern and unfold and position the camp chair for a view across the water. Testing the chair to make sure it's comfortable, I note the very handy drink holder.

Drawing in a deep breath, I pause to take in my surroundings. The presence of quiet that comes with the absence of man-made noise surrounds me in peace. Frogs begin cautiously croaking as crickets chime in. Soon there's a pond-wide chorus. Small fish surface between the water lilies, sending purple and green dragonflies into sky dances above the calm water's surface. A very responsible pair of mallard ducks look after a flock of youngsters as they frenzy-feed on water bugs near shore. It's my Walden Pond West.

Small yellow butterflies flutter from bright flower to bright flower, occasionally pausing in their search for sweet nectar. A western fence lizard races from exposed sunshine to shade, stopping briefly for a few push-ups to show me who's toughest, its blue belly flashing like jewels. Sand dunes at the edge of the beach lay momentarily settled in wind-sculpted lines sprinkled with coastal grass, the roots clinging to a precarious foundation. Low-lying sage and other vegetation reflect of the salty location and the regular presence of the wind. Behind camp, the coastal mountains rise up thousands of feet above the lagoon, pocked with green islands of black oaks and Monterey pines high on the ridges, slowly growing twisted away from the prevailing winds.

In the distance, far down the beach, Rocky Point meets the ocean. The high promontory of the point looks like a head of a dragon, snout level with the sea, the water bursting like white smoke against rocky cliffs.

I close my eyes and give reverence to my surroundings with a blessing for all the good that comes into my life. I rise, give a deep bow to Mother Earth, and say a silent prayer to all that have come here before me. What history the area could tell about being alive with the Old Ones, my ancestors. Surely they were here, living life, loving life, laughing in joy, and mourning in despair.

I am overwhelmed knowing that Mother Earth's creations, such as this beautiful landscape and the interwoven cycles of life dwarf anything attempted by man.

As if to show me otherwise, the deafening roar of a neutral-colored military jet slicing over the ridgeline behind my camp rudely interrupts my thoughts. Not content with just one fly-by, the pilot carves a big turn in the sky and comes blazing back toward my former oasis. My fleeting visitor is so low I can see his face as I cover my ears from the jet's thunderous blast.

Not happy with the invasion of my sacred place, I raise my hands and fire a pretend shot with my imaginary gun as the jet disappears over the ridge. In the growing quiet, I feel slightly remorseful for pretend shooting at the pilot, and hope it didn't add me to a list of state enemies. A voice in my head orders me to, *Ignore the armed drone hovering over your head.*

A walk on the beach ends the long day, which melts away in front of me under a sunset show of changing colors striking cumulus clouds floating above the ocean. A backlit halo lines the edges of the water, constantly changing in a slow motion symphony. The light of day finally fades to twilight as I make my way over the last of the dunes and back to camp.

Almost too excited to eat, I remind myself I need to be well fueled for tomorrow. A flour tortilla wrapped around ripe avocado, tomato, onion, and cheese with salsa tastes like a gourmet meal enjoyed from the best seat in the house. The soft light of my lantern mixed with the warm yellow flames of the small campfire lights up the willow trees in a ghostly glow.

The star-filled night sky gives off its own light show of cosmic scale limited only by my imagination in this precious moment of time in my outdoor church.

CHAPTER 11

At dawn I crawl out of my sleeping bag well before sunrise, not able or wanting to sleep any longer. First light of the morning glows as I fire up the stove to get the coffee going. Colors of the new day alight while planets fade away. Fresh morning light striking the distant mountain crests is my entertainment while I eat a bowl of muesli. Coffee disappears quickly and I hydrate in preparation for what I anticipate will be a long, hot day.

Time to load my backpack with a stack of wooden stakes, mallet, survey tape, notebook, pencil and camera. I double-check the top of my shiny new steel water bottle is tight, put my lunch in the top pouch and heft the heavy pack on my back. Reaching down to grab my shovel, I wobble under the load.

I set off toward the spot where estuary meets the ocean, reasoning a pile of cast-off seashells and other tribal village leftovers are likely to be found there. Although probably under thick deposits of topsoil, I'm hopeful they will reveal themselves in a mound.

I'm only a few steps away from camp when the quiet is broken by the sounds of rotating blades beating the air. An approaching helicopter is tracking my way from the south. Coming directly on course my direction, the black and gold motorized humming bird drops altitude, circling low above my camp. Clearly seen on the door of the gleaming machine, a prominent logo depicting planet earth rising above bold letters beneath, ENRG.

The pilot in a seriously polished helmet glances out the side window and surveys the area below. It's clear he's looking to land and it's obvious I'm camped in his destination. The dust starts to swirl around me as he lowers the noisy copter near my quivering tent. A strong blast of air tests the poles, ropes and stakes as they strain to hold my fabric home upright in the manmade maelstrom. I hunch over and cover my face to avoid the debris pelting my body, jamming my fingers in my ears at the deafening sound of the screaming jet engine. The skids touch the ground as my surfboard flies and tumbles through the air, landing in a clump of bushes like a spear. My foul-mouth cursing is unheard inside the man-made tornado.

The rotor blades slow, allowing me to see again. I drop my pack in a heap and run to the bushes to check the damage to my board. Fresh dings line the rail, and a broken branch has pierced the foam and fiberglass of the deck like a dagger. I pull it out while glaring at the helicopter and its occupants.

Surfboard under arm, I stride directly to the door of the helicopter waiting for it to reveal the rude intruders. The door opens on my approach and out onto the skids steps a stout middle-aged man. He grips the handle of the door, revealing a large silver watch around his thick wrist. He steps down out of the aeronautical eggshell, hair as slick as the pilot's helmet, sporting a smile filled with over-whitened teeth. He's about my height, but carries an aging barrel chest. Beefy arms expand his red shirt with ENRG logo embroidered on the broad chest.

The blades slow to a stop and quiet returns. "Sorry about your surfboard," he says with a look of genuine concern.

I hold the board up, turning it over to show him the large hole in the deck.

"It was an accident. You were camped in the best landing zone. You're Peter Martinez I assume? I'm Richard Thorne, Managing Director for New Project Development in North America for ENRG." He reaches into his front pocket and hands me a business card on fine glossy stock.

His beefy hand reaches out and I meet his firm handshake in equal measure.

"I'm Peter Martinez, managing director of, me. I'm cardless."

Thorne looks away and glances around. "Nice place to camp."

My throat is pasty from the prop wash and it feels like a layer of mud earth is stuck to my tongue. I grab my water bottle and clear my throat. "Nice ride you have there."

"With the head office in LA, it's more efficient than wasting time in traffic on the 101. Really nice and quiet out here."

"Isn't this a wonderful setting for an industrial petrochemical facility?"

"Glad you agree."

"Bad joke, a really bad joke."

A lone black and yellow Monarch butterfly casually flutters by my face, and lands on the bill of my hat. I watch cross-eyed as it stalls on the brim. Finding no nectar, it flies on.

"Look, I'm going to be up front with you, Peter. Can I call you Peter?"

"Sure, Dick."

"Don't call me, Dick."

"I think you know how important oil and natural gas is to this country. Without it you wouldn't be driving that antique truck. What you have in your tank could have come for one of those offshore oil platforms out there. Oil doesn't just move that old truck down the road, it moves the economy of this entire country."

"Can't argue about the fuel in my rig. But they say we're on the downward slide of peak oil. The easy stuff has been found and reserves keep dwindling," I point out.

Thorne looks toward the offshore oil rigs in the distance. "Exactly. That's why it's more important than ever to keep fracking and extracting what's left. Get the product to American soil and the consumer as efficiently and safely as possible. Protect the marine life, the ocean, the beaches, you know."

"I've seen the advertisements. ENRG forgot to mention global warming from all those burnt fossil fuels spewing carbon into the atmosphere."

"Warming and cooling of the planet has been happening way before humans. Look at the geologic evidence of sea level rises and falls."

"The dinosaurs didn't survive severe climate change. We may not either."

"They had brains the size of a walnut, and as a bonus, we get their oil!"

"Pretty brainless what we humans are doing to the planet right now. Ever hear of the Exon Valdez and Deep Water Horizon? What about electric cars instead of internal combustion? Conservation and increasing efficiency? We should develop more alternative power sources like solar, wind, tidal and geothermal."

"Accidents happen, part of life. The energy alternatives are all good concepts, but it won't happen overnight. That's reality now. In the meantime we need the oil and gas. Think of our country, this is the economy of the USA we're talking about."

"I live in another country, an Indian Reservation. We don't have oil wells on our res."

Thorne glances down at the surfboard in my arm.

"Maybe you should. What do you think that surfboard is made from? Chemical products refined from petroleum! How about that tent? How about your plastic kayak? Are you being a hypocrite greenie?"

"I get your not-so-green point."

"Anyway, hope you don't mind, I did some background checking on you. Looks like you're 'The Man' when it comes to finding antiquities for the Santa Barbara Museum of Natural History. ENRG needs a smart person like you. I have a better business proposition I'd like you to consider."

"Proposition?"

"As corporate contributors to the Museum, I'm well aware of their current funding shortfalls. I checked the website and read about your discovery at Mission Santos, and the crowd-funding facility to try and scratch up enough money for a proper archeological operation. We at ENRG are willing to make a substantial donation to the Museum, with two conditions. One, the donation is only used for further archeological work at Mission Santos. And two, you'll be on the payroll as the leader of the survey of Santos, for which you will be very well paid."

"How much pay?" I ask as innocently as possible.

"Three hundred thousand for directing the project at Mission Santos. Very good money for your efforts."

"A bribe?" I ask.

"That word is not in my vocabulary. We at ENRG offer more for your services than you're getting now by funding the Museum project. It's a type of business deal that's done every day around the world."

"And I have to do what here at Rocky Point?"

"Have a nice month here, enjoy your camp, put that surfboard to good use, but produce a disappointing survey. No archaeological reason to stand in the way of giving the American people what they need, oil and gas. Then, when you're done with your working holiday here, you can go do meaningful work at Mission Santos." He hands me a cardboard shipping box.

"What's this?"

"A cash advance for you on the Mission Santos project, enough to buy yourself a new truck. You can put that rust bucket of yours out to pasture."

"That rust bucket is part of my family, it was my grandfather's."

"Looks like a major gas guzzler to me. Why don't you recycle it and get yourself an electric hybrid car, it'll make you feel like you're doing your own tiny part to prevent global warming."

The money feels like it has a gravity of its own pulling me toward it. I open the box, take out a single one hundred dollar bill from the stack and hold it in front of me to have a good look. I read it like a script to Thorne. "In God We Trust, Federal Reserve Note, This Note is Legal Tender for all Debts, Public and Private." Holding the bill out as it flutters in the wind, I wave the US government note to its presenter.

"Another American government promise? I'll hold onto this hundred for now, before it inflates away. You owe me for the dings in my board. Come back and show me the same amount in pure gold coins, and then we'll talk. Make it Canadian Maple Leafs."

"If I bring back the Canadian gold, do we have a deal?"

"We have, awareness…"

Thorne's expensive smile grows again. He takes the box back into the helicopter and turns to me with a parting word. "That's what I like to hear, an open mind. Remember, it'll be strictly business, Canadian Gold Maple Leafs. No one needs to know but us. This is a limited time offer. You've got my card. I'll be in touch soon."

I stand eye-to-eye with a rarity in my life, a high-ranking businessman of a major multi-national corporation. "Are you one of those business executives I hear about who makes a fortune even if the business tanks under your watch?"

"The price of a barrel of oil is subjective. Besides OPEC, all about supply and demand. Look, I help provide a product almost everyone on this planet uses, including you. That's the real world I operate in. I work hard for ENRG, I'm good at what I do and I'm paid very well. We employ thousands of people worldwide. My job is to put together the development deals that keep people working and make the company and shareholders a return on investment. Like the deal I'm about to make with you."

"I said, we have awareness," I remind him.

"We'll see how aware you are when you see the gold."

"How much money do you make a year?"

"I'm hoping more than my wife can spend."

"Guessing she's not frugal."

"Frugal is not in her vocabulary."

"Money doesn't buy happiness they say."

"They likely don't have much. You aren't anti-money, are you? Great things are being done all around the world every minute of every day because of money. I help support a lot of good causes with the money I earn."

"It's just what some people do to get cash. How they spend money is another question. How big of a mansion or a yacht does a person need? We're raping the planet to cater to a one-percent handful of rich elites."

"The middle-class gets a leg up in the deal too, what's left of them. Besides, being wealthy doesn't make you a bad person. A guy like you can do good things with money."

"I've never had enough extra money to consider what else to do with it."

"Capitalism at work," he states with finality.

"Capitalism based on endless consumption, endless economic growth and spiraling debts isn't sustainable. How much longer can we keep burning through the natural resources of the planet like there's no tomorrow? All to keep feeding the consumption creature until it all implodes in an economic and environmental collapse?"

"Well, until there's a better global economic system, capitalism is what we're stuck with." He connects with the pilot, gives a thumb's up and turns back to me with parting words. "You might be better off with the gold. It's a good hedge, against… all sorts of unknowns…"

"Hey, Thorne, what the hell does ENRG stand for anyway?"

"Extracting Natural Resources Globally."

"Of course. Well, here's another word option that seems more relevant right now, Enlisting Natives and Rewarding Greed."

"I can keep my part of the deal. Can you?"

The engine fires with a roar and I cover my ears as the blades start to spin into a blur. Dirt blasts me again as I brace my surfboard for the rotor blast.

The helicopter lifts off in a storm. The gold and black ENRG logo on its side fades away, leaving behind the scent of burned fossil fuels.

Sending the corporate Big Bad Wolf on the gold run bought me time to keep working, and to consider options. He will return, and when he does, then what?

CHAPTER 12

After the reality of the mixed terrain I'm dealing with becomes painfully apparent, I need to adjust my initial plan for the first stage of my survey. I stare at large clumps of brush, wondering what creatures might lurk within the shadows. Reduced to a crawl by the dense bush, an unseen rattlesnake gives me a sudden warning with conga-tail percussion. I retreat and back out of the way while branches grab me, holding my clothing until the panic sets in. Breaking back out into the open, I glance around and review what other possible critters might also be my nasty neighbors. I count scorpions, tarantulas, black widows, red ants, ticks, deer flies, not to mention the poison oak that brushes my bare skin as I try to run away from all these critters!

And I still haven't found anything relating to artifacts. I crawl on my belly looking for small chips of stone, arrowheads, beads, fishhooks, or any tiny clues that might lead to bigger discoveries. This close to the earth, I see things in detail that I never would when standing. A beetle's tracks meander back and forth to where only it knows. A lizard's tail drags through the sand as it hunts for what? I see the lovely miniature arrangements of tiny flowers I missed from above. Strands of grass bend to meet the ground in a tickle of original tracks created for the first time with each gust of wind.

Water bottle is empty and I'm down to my last few wooden stakes. Frustrated, I now doubt what first seemed like such an obvious site of an Indian village. Plausible scenarios crop up. Maybe the estuary wasn't there many years ago? Maybe the old village site is now under the estuary? Maybe there was no year round water then? Maybe it was only a seasonal hunting and fishing site without much left behind? Maybe I should take the Santos job and move on, or not?

I'm lured to the shade of a weeping willow standing alone in the green grass, drop my backpack and lay down to rest in peace and quiet. Pulling my hat over my tired eyes, I relax, and the day's events run through my mind. Eyes close. I drift into dreaming.

In my daydream it's night. I'm sitting in front of the campfire near my tent, looking into the dancing yellow flames. Grandfather's greenstone canoe dangles around my neck. I hold it in front of my eyes, looking at its smooth lines in the reflection of the fire. A sudden motion draws my gaze back to the dancing flames. Although I see nothing out of the ordinary, I know I saw something move. Now I have a drum in my hands. I give it a primal beat. Flames dance in the night. Keeping the rhythm, the faster I drum, the faster the flames move, dancing with my music. Frogs join in with a chorus of croaking, crickets add a backbeat, a lone owl contributes a haunting melody, coyotes cry in the dark. I'm a conductor with nature as my orchestra. The full moon overhead lights up my stage.

My eyes pull away from the moon and look back into the fire. Faint silhouettes of the People, the Old Ones, my ancestors, dance in the flames, many of them wearing ceremonial dress of feather, shell necklace and headdress, moving in circles with the beat. Men and women with children and elders gather around to watch the dancers. It's a celebration with the tribe in full ceremonial costume. I suddenly stop drumming, not sure of what I see. Dancers stop dancing and turn to me. I close my eyes. Nothing. When I open them, I see only flames.

Awakening into the daylight, I'm still lying in the grass against my pack. Slowly I get up and spot the last stake I'd hammered in, reminding me to put in my lone remaining stake for tomorrow. I pound it until the stake strikes an object, pull it up, and pound it down again. The sharpened end is coated black. I wipe it off and try a third go. The stake sinks deeper. I pull it out once more and see more black charcoal. My first promising sign—could be an old fire pit below. Driving the stake in again, I wrap survey tape to it and write, "End day one." I make a note in my logbook with the old reliable graphite. I reach down for the comfort of the stone tomol hanging from my neck and honor my grandfather and his Dream Helper gift.

Day fades to night as I stack up driftwood and prepare to light the campfire. I strike the match, thinking it's too easy to start fires in these modern times.

Sitting around the campfire eating a well-deserved meal, I ponder my plan for the next day. I'll return to the old fire area and hopefully find some signs of my ancestors, connect pieces of the mystery puzzle and establish some details on the occupation sites of the village area, if it was in fact once here.

Gathering my lap drum, I settle in beside the fire and pound out a few beats. No real song, just random melodies playing in my head. I stare into the dancing flames of the fire, slowly building up the beat. My eyes close in search of inner-rhythm within my soul. I hear in the distance a sound of nature calling back to me, the coyote. Then the crickets and the owl join in. I open my eyes. Has my Dream Walk come true? There in the flames, the Old Ones, Native dancers dressed in ceremonial finery. They dance to my beat as I build the song to its end. I silence the drum and look at faces gazing back at me, faces from the past. I close my eyes and open them again. There are only flames. All is dead quiet.

Then the earth rumbles beneath me. I'm thrown from my wild, rocking horse chair. I try to get up, but the earth ripples in intense waves under me and won't let me go. I watch the lantern swinging wildly against the tent pole, hoping it won't break. The kettle falls into the spitting fire, hissing steam into the night sky. The earth settles. A distinct reality flashes in my mind as tsunami disaster images roll in my head. I grab what I can carry, jump in my truck, and drive up the rock-strewn road.

I make my way back to camp when I sense it's safe. It's a mess in my headlights, but the earthquake shakes me up in more ways than one. I toss a bucket of water on the dying coals and call it a very disturbed night.

CHAPTER 13

I'm suddenly awakened by the sounds of breaking waves echoing off the walls of the cliffs. When I get a clear visual, I see uniform waves wrapping around the point, offshore winds feathering the swells into soft, fine mist. Early morning sun hasn't hit the point yet, but the swell looks like orderly corduroy lined up to the edge of the blue horizon. Clean lines from far away wind storms, another classic Southern Hemisphere swell, waves pulsing thousands of miles across the Pacific Ocean to cross paths with me.

No other surfers in sight, not even a boat to be seen. Yes! I quickly justify all the hours I put into the job the previous day. By a very simple majority, my one-man committee meeting has approved my request for a surf session as necessary for good morale. The next set of perfect lonely waves roll toward Rocky Point as another unsuppressed laugh-out-loud moment erupts.

I pull a roll of trusty duct tape out of my truck and make a sticky patch for the hole in the deck of my board. Unkind thoughts of Richard Thorne and the helicopter invasion enter my mind only briefly. The smell of tropical scent triggers memory waves as I rub on a quick wax job on the deck of my board for maximum traction. I scarf banana, and take a long pull off the water bottle to top the tank. With eyes glued to set waves approaching the point, I hastily leap into my wetsuit.

The morning sun is striking and lighting up the waves into a glowing temptress. My pulse quickens as I try to calm my excited mind. Breathing consciously brings me back to my center. I find the steep, narrow goat path wrapping down the face of the cliff leading to the small cove below. I focus on picking my way down the trail, staying low, board held down slope in case of a slip. As I get closer to the sea, the waves look much bigger than from above, but a deep channel running out from the cove is mostly void of big waves and a rip tide offers an assisted ride out.

My smile of anticipation dims when I see a large fin cruising the surface in my intended route, a very large fin and no mistaking it for a dolphin this time. The sight of the shark sends chills through me and pulls at my primal fight-or-flight instincts. I'm safely on shore for the moment, and glad I'm not seeing the top-of-the-food-chain next to me in his element, but definitively unhappy that it chose to look for a meal right here and now. Perfect surf calls loudly and I'm stuck on shore weighing my two options that aren't easy to sort out: go or don't go. Glancing down at my wetsuit clad body, how much do I look like a seal?

My desire to surf these waves is so strong I close my eyes and say a silent prayer to deliver me from harm's way. When I slowly open my eyes, I can still see the fin cruising, but in the distance many more fins are coming, rising for air—a fast moving pod of dolphins. They circle the shark as a mobbing pack, keeping at it until they herd it well away from where I stand in awe. Was my dolphin surfing mate leading the charge of these sea faring vigilantes?

At times like this I have to wonder, what causes dolphins to come to the aid of humans? We humans certainly have abused the dolphins. Kill them as bycatch in our fishing nets, pollute their ocean world with our waste, choke them on plastic trash, capture them for shows as our slaves for entertainment and kill them for dolphin burgers in the Land of the Rising Sun. With all the harm we do to them, they seem to forgive us. Minds and hearts bigger than our own. They've lived on this planet longer than us humanoids, with intelligence to rival ours. I jump into the Pacific and paddle out to join my surfer, sea-mammal friends.

Trickles of cool saltwater clear from my eyes and flush my sinuses as I leave behind the last of the turbulent whitewater near shore. Now fully awake, senses heightened and taking in all my surroundings. A lull in the swell brings relative quiet as I stroke beneath the jagged cliffs to the takeoff zone. California gulls glide in circles above me, staring as the scavengers they are.

A set builds on the horizon and it's becoming apparent I could use a longer board to stroke into big swells. Powerful water is pushing in around Rocky Point and I'm under-gunned.

A double-storied wall of water builds toward me, rises up and pitches forward exploding in energy onto the rocky reef. I repeat to myself, *Be patient and pick the best wave of the set.* I dig deep into the third set wave with an extra stroke. In the wave's grasp, I leap to my feet and drive down the moving mountain of water. The speed of the drop sends the fins on my board singing behind me. I keep dropping, the moving mass of water growing down the line in front of me. I hit my bottom turn and lay into it hard, digging the rail in deep and slingshot across the face. G-forces pull at me in the arch of my turn, the wall of water throwing over into a tube.

I enter the sacred space of the reflecting-glass saltwater cathedral. Time seems to slow. Rich golden rays from the rising sun light up the wave like spun liquid gold. I reach my hands out to touch the beaming light coming towards me reflected in the glassy wave, a watery tube perfectly shaped, the energy-filled spinning water meeting the tips of my outstretched fingers. Riding deep inside the wave tunnel on the brink of ultimate surfing pleasure, fully in the Now.

Time warps as I race ahead of the tube leaving the harmony of circular water behind. I carve another hard turn and shoot up high on the face, hitting a big turn at the top, down again and up like a big saltwater roller coaster with just me on the ride. The wave keeps daring me on and I join in the exciting dance. The ride comes to an end as I kick out at the shore break. The long journey of a wave pulsing across the largest ocean in the world comes to an end on the shore of Rocky Point.

Gratitude ripples through me. Grateful for being here, grateful for all that surrounds me, grateful for my healthy body, grateful to be alive. I close my eyes and take in a deep breath of air filled with sea mist, the precious gift filling my lungs with its life force.

When I open my eyes, I feel a calling. I look up the cliff face near the end of the point, and I see something I'd never seen there before—a large slip. A fresh scar of a rockslide has cascaded down the steep rock wall, likely from the last night's earthquake. In the midst of the new slip, a small dark recess of a portal draws me in. I quit paddling and sit up on my board to study the location. Make a mental note on where I can access it from above. About a hundred feet up, no doubt access will require a rope and some sort of solid anchor. Distracted by the discovery, I'm caught inside as a wave rises up and I'm pummeled for my lack of attention. Humbled out of the impact zone, I stroke back out toward the end of the point to see if I can pick up any more detail about the newly exposed earth.

Finally surfed out, wave after wave to myself, many laps paddling up the point doing coastal research, I tear away from the wave playground and ride prone on the whitewater to shore.

With land legs under me, I almost run up the steep path to the edge of the bluff and double-time it along the cliff toward the end of the point. Carefully, I creep to the edge, find the slip, and look over to see a scary pile of rocks far below. There are powerful waves crashing onto the base of the cliff, thundering as they explode into whitewater. It's a no fall zone, beyond vertical to get to the slip zone, and the tide is on the way up.

A quick survey shows none of the rocks around are big enough to make me confident enough to secure a rope. If I can get close enough,

I'll hook a rope to my truck hitch. Walking back to camp, I run down the list of unknown variables of exploring what seems worth investigating.

My wetsuit quickly becomes another ornament on the willow tree, and my board rests safely in the tent, out of the sun and the wind. Grabbing my headlamp, camera and journal, I throw it all in the pack with building excitement. From Old Red's cab, pull out the climbing rope from a tangle of starter cables and seldom used odds-and-ends collected behind the bench seat. I slide sections of it through my hands; it's frayed, but sturdy. The harness is a twisted mess, but intact and equipped with basic climbing hardware.

Amid a pungent smell of crushed sage, I cautiously look out the open door backing to the edge of the cliff. I calculate the distance and leave enough room to get around and secure the rope. I set Old Red's hand brake and leave the truck in gear. The last thing I see when the door closes is the fragmented mosaic of ocean and sky in my shattered mirror. Wedge a couple of rocks under the rear tire, just in case. Carefully laying the rope out in neat coils, I secure one end of it to the ball of the hitch and test it with several hard tugs.

Attentively, I wrap the rope around and thread it through my harness, then try the grip with both hands. I creep carefully towards the edge of the cliff and perch on the brink when I can back up no further. Toss the coils over and glance down to see the end of the rope hitting the rocks below. The tide is coming up, but if I hurry, I can make my way back along the shore without dodging waves crashing against the cliff face. As I suspected, it's beyond vertical.

The tension on the rope is reassuring. I step off into nothing but air. My heart flutters as I dangle in space with the ocean far below. With nothing slowing me down but the friction of the rope, I lower myself until I'm even with the entry of the dark hole in the slip. Dangling too far away from the rocky face to touch it, I shift my weight like a rope swing, closer and closer until I grab a handhold next to the entry. Lowering myself slowly down, I stand on a ledge of solid rock below the gap in the cliff face. Cautiously, I relax the tension on the rope.

I turn to focus on the portal, too dark to see into the depths. Rocks have been piled up by someone, stacked neatly around the small hole, all of it largely hidden. The first rock I try to move holds tight. With a bit more force it gives way and falls inward. A rock at a time, I gently clear the way enough for me to squeeze through what looks like a deeper opening.

A sudden stream of fleeing bats exiting the cave in a panic almost knocks me from my perch. Following the beam of light from my headlamp and crawling through the entry, my startled eyes adjust to what no human has likely seen for hundreds, if not thousands of years.

In the burial cave are human skeletal remains placed lovingly with personal shrines set around them. Bows, arrows, spears, shell jewelry, carved effigies, stone canoes, bowls, grinding stones, crumbling remains of woven baskets.

Creeping closer to one of the skeletons, I note a pendant around the neck resting on the boney chest. Gently I blow the dust away as time peels back to reveal a rainbow-hued abalone shell in the shape of a dolphin. Staring down at this once living, breathing link to my past, the feeling of connection between us is undeniable. My heart races as my mind paces.

I kneel down and say a prayer in Noqoto. "Be in peace in Similgasa."

I take in my surroundings respectfully, and spend time with each of the remains, studying them carefully with my eyes.

My pulse quickens as a shadow passes out the entry portal. A flying ghost of an albino hawk pauses, turns its head and looks into the cave while gliding through the blue sky framed in jagged rock. The white hawk gazes in at me all seeing, and soars away on the spirit wind.

Unsettled by witnessing our tribal guardian spirit, I shift around cautiously, careful not to disturb anything.

I work on capturing close-up images of once living souls. I return to the bearer of the rainbow dolphin and lean in closer until the pendant is reflecting the light of my headlamp. The closer I come, the stronger the feeling of connection. My intuition pulls at me as I reach out and touch the rainbow dolphin and hold it in my hands. The old, fragile cord falls apart. I grip the dolphin in my palm to keep it from falling.

I close my eyes and look inward.

In my Dream Walk: A lovely woman of about my age, wearing only what she needs on a hot summer day, she walks alone on a white sand beach. Dark skin and long dark hair, its length covering most of her face, dark brown eyes that look at me between gusts of soft breeze parting her hair. She reaches out slowly and removes the pendant from her neck, offering me the rainbow dolphin.

Opening my eyes I'm surprised she's not here in the flesh. I look down at her bones, *Are you who join me on my Dream Walk?* I carefully place the rainbow dolphin in my pocket.

I turn my focus to the dark recesses at the back of the cave. Propped up in a pile of earth is a wooden grave marker. In the shadowy light of my torch, a faint wood engraving reveals itself in the shape of a dolphin. Who might be buried there?

I turn at the noise of a few small rocks tumbling by the entry. The rope gives a subtle movement and settles back in place. The wind is coming up. I turn back to work.

I take notes in my logbook and sketch basic diagrams of the position of the bodies and the artifacts. I write a brief verbal description listing all I see, with the date and time noted, as Dr. Evans had instructed me many times. With photos documenting the find in my hand, I'll be back.

Time, I had lost track of it, as the tide continues to rise by the pull of the moon. I gaze out the entry of the cave to the ocean below and see waves crashing further up the base of the cliff.

Time to go. Carefully I position the loose rocks by the mouth of the cave so I can get to them and re-stack them as best as I can to close the entry.

Mixed messages run through my mind as I scan around with my headlamp for a last glimpse. This burial chamber is an archaeological discovery that could change the course of ENRG's proposed development of Rocky Point and shut them down. But, do I really want to reveal its contents? These are my ancestors; if I expose the discovery, what happens to them? Placed into a cold steel drawer at the Museum? Yet, if I don't expose my discovery, what happens with ENRG's plans for Rocky Point? They move ahead with the project and bulldoze our ancestral sacred site? History shows, big money usually wins, but not always.

Conflicted thoughts bounce around in my head as I secure the rope to my harness. I crawl outside the entry, adjust the tension on the rope and work to get the last few rocks fitted into place. Not an easy task with little room to stand, and a long fall looking up at me from the sea.

After adjusting the rope for my rappel down, I pause and draw in a deep breath. What I had just seen and felt in the cave was life changing, a sacred window I was allowed to look into. A peaceful feeling flows through me as I close my eyes to absorb the moments of time shared with once living links to my heritage. A wave crashes against the cliff, bringing me back to the present moment. After a last check of the tension on the rope, I step back and swing away.

Solid tension on the rope suddenly becomes sickeningly slack! I build speed quickly as I twist in mid-air, tangling in loose rope! A quick assessment gives hope I'll hit deeper water! Tumbling in the grip of gravity on a date with fate, I take a deep breath and hit the water.

In this moment, there is no moment.

Peace shattered, I come to below the surface to chaos, rocks and loose kelp surround me in turbulent water. I try and push off the bottom, but the rope's caught in rocks.

A ghostly shape swims my way as I unclip the rope and desperately reach out for the dolphin's dorsal fin being offered. With a surge of power from its tail, we break the surface together, both sucking in air. My sea mammal savior pulls me away from the cliff toward deeper water, directly into a wave just beginning to break on the rocky reef. I hang on as I'm towed out of the impact zone and into the free glide of the wave's face, both of us now body surfing with little effort. This journey is clearly on the dolphin's terms. I'm just along for the ride. The lip folds over us and we're both enveloped in a flowing tube of liquid crystal.

The dolphin dives deep and leaves me alone to surf the wave of my life.

Beyond the curling curtain of water, time races like I've never witnessed. Sun streaks across multi-hew colors of constantly changing sky. Clouds stream through the vision, covering daylight in seconds. A rapid sunset of streaming light shimmers in glassy reflection of dual dimensions. The end of day gives way to the sudden coming of night. Shining planets, stars and galaxies travel in a curved orbital arch of mirrored images reflecting in the spinning wave. A rising full moon disappears under a full eclipse. Lightning shatters the darkness with blinding blasts of electrical power. Deafening thunder rumbles through the night shaking me to the core.

All goes black.

CHAPTER 14

Darkness is broken with a cautious gaze out the opening windows of my soul, revealing a surreal scene of a full-spectrum rainbow of color arching across clearing sky. Shafts of sun burst through lacy clouds on the tail of a passing thunderstorm.

Am I dead?

Lying in wet sand, I roll over and slowly get to my knees. Gazing around in a daze, it's apparent my surroundings are different in bewildering ways. Although it looks like Rocky Point, there's no dried, dormant vegetation from the hot summer. Now, every living plant is in brilliant green palette of peak springtime with colorful splashes of flowers on the rolling hills above the beach where I kneel with bewildered, wide-open eyes.

Down the ridgeline, no access road and no steel fencing to be seen. Scanning the sky, there's a distinct absence of smog or jet contrails in the cobalt blue atmosphere. I turn toward the ocean and see a flock of brown pelicans cruising by in formation, riding an air-wave updraft above waves, their wings skimming the water in flight-feather-fine-tune. Behind them on the ocean's surface, no offshore oil drilling rigs or merchant ships to be seen anywhere.

A lone dolphin plays on a wave directly in front of me, its sleek body visible in the clear water. It pops out the backside of the wave and leaps into the air towards where the end of the rainbow pauses on Rocky Point. Is this a Dream Walk? I check my hands and feel my face. Slowly I rise to my feet and wobble forward, taking first steps into another world.

I sense a presence and turn around. Down the beach a long stone's throw away, a lone figure of an Indian woman stands on a sand dune with an object in her hand. She looks at me as if she sees a ghost. Her hand trembles as she drops what she carries and runs toward shore.

I wonder if I've seen a ghost. I look down to my toes and see nothing but my birth wear. No possessions attached except for Grandfather's greenstone tomol hanging around my neck.

I walk down the beach and find the lone set of footprints where the woman had been, reach over and pick up a basket left in her tracks. The woven patterns are intricate and perfectly symmetrical, the weave is tight and precise, a beautiful piece of hand-made creativity. Holding it in my hand, I connect to her artist soul.

Walking to the top of the dune, my eyes widen again to take it all in. A row of tomol canoes parked in loose formation above high water mark along the shore of the calm lagoon. Beyond the sheltered flotilla of Native craft, a village circle of neatly constructed conical huts fan around a large central gathering area of larger structures. Wisps of smoke spread into the air above the community pouring out of the village and coming my way in a tribal stream.

Leading the way, the woman from the beach purposely strides down the trail at me. Barking dogs enter the growing procession. A gathering of people on a mission to meet the mysterious messiah. Are these the Old Ones I studied in my past? Are these the ones in the burial cave I discovered?

With this crowd of lively strangers gathering around me, I quickly position the woven basket as my fig leaf. I sheepishly smile at the members of the growing audience all looking my direction. As they get closer, I become strangely comfortable amongst them. Despite being out of place and out of time, I feel I am home.

I scan the faces beaming up at me with incredulous stares. Sun-bleached hair neatly arranged, sharp facial features set against skin darkened from outdoor living, woven fiber and animal skin clothing is minimal reflecting the warmth of the day. Dark eyes shine back as clear as the bright sea behind me. Many of the men and women wear beautiful, intricate necklaces of select shells linked to carved amulets. Many of the physically imposing men carry spears, likely unsure of my intentions. Far from any sort of a threat, I feel like a child who had been abandoned long ago, only to find his family again, many centuries later.

To the front of the group steps an elder of presence. The aged man carries himself with straight-posture dignity. His white hair and dark skin set off a stunning necklace featuring a white crystal hawk dangling on his storybook skin. We lock eyes, and I get an immediate sense of a life filled with noble leadership. He steps close enough that we can feel each other's breath. Reaching out slowly, he touches the greenstone Dream Helper hanging from my neck. The crowd behind him goes quiet.

"From the islands?" he asks, his weathered hand pointing to an island far offshore.

"Not sure where I'm from," I reply, as I look around at the tribe of faces staring at me.

He gestures to the basket over my crotch. "You carry little."

The tribe erupts in laughter. A wise man, and a wise guy. I give a quick peek under the basket. "Water's cold?"

He gives a welcoming smile as he extends his hand to shake mine. Instinctively I switch hands on the basket and meet his warm grasp. "Welcome to our village of the Noqoto."

I gasp in lungs of ancient air.

"I am Paxa."

"I'm Peter, or I think I'm Peter..."

He turns toward members of the tribe and announces, "Welcome Pee-ter to Noqoto!"

The villagers close in as Paxa leads me down the path toward the village. To the side of me strolls the woman I first saw on the beach. She stares my way, studying me with curious eyes. Around her smooth neck framed by her hair, the sun glances off a familiar pendant of a bright rainbow dolphin made of polished abalone shell. Like the pendant I once held in my hand...

The path widens at the entry to the village, and the crowd spreads out to places of comfort. The huts are woven domes, high enough and big enough for a family. The central lodge is large, supported with what looks to be a sturdy framework of whalebones and driftwood beams lashed together. Graphic carvings etched in bleached bone featuring designs of whales and dolphins grace the entry. On the fringes of the village, smoke rises from a chimney sourced from a sunken structure; what appears to be the sweat lodge has an earth-covered roof.

Children run away to play as elders slowly retreat to the shade of the trees. A pungent smell wafts from racks of drying fish laid in the sun high enough to be out of reach of dogs. Deer skins lie draped over railings set in the ground, signs of a fresh kill attracting swarms of flies. Some villagers gather together where baskets and pottery are being made, others near them grind acorns and seeds with mortars and pestles, the raw material of their trades neatly organized in various piles in their shaded work stations. Everyone quietly stares as I pass.

Paxa turns and motions to man standing at his side who is a reflection of him in younger years. "Pe-ter, my son, Yaqi. He will show you the guest hut."

I'm momentarily speechless at the man standing before me—the warrior I saw in my vision at Mission Santos…

"I think we've met before," I whisper.

Yaqi stares back with no emotion.

"The language you speak is like ours, but not," Paxa points out.

"Where I'm from, it's a dying language."

He then pauses and again looks at me deeply. "My daughter Talkitna saw you come to us from the sea. She says you ride waves with a dolphin?"

"Riding waves of time," I say, teetering on the edge of two worlds.

Yaqi turns to me with a stone face. "Why are you here?"

"Not sure."

"Lost?"

"Very."

"You travel far?"

"Not sure how far, or why, or even when. What century is it anyway?"

I gaze around at the communal village scene in front of me. I turn my confused gaze back to Yaqi.

He stares at me, even more confused, then raises the woven flap and gestures toward the entry. "Cover yourself, then come tell us more of what you do not know."

The inside of the hut is small, but neatly made up with a low-lying cot covered in furs sitting to the side, a small fire ring in the middle. A shaft of sun pierces through the round hole in the ceiling, lighting up the neatly woven walls of thatched willow frame. I test the bed and stare up at the circle of blue sky framed above. I close my eyes, pause, and open them again. Smiling, I hold the greenstone in my hands.

I hear a gentle voice calling. I open the curtain partially and poke my head out. Against the glare, the silhouette of a woman reaches out. As my eyes adjust, I see it's the woman I first saw on the beach, the dolphin pendant swinging free around her neck shooting me reflections.

"My name is Peter."

"I'm called Talkitna."

"Tal-kit-na."

"Pe-ter, you ride a wave with a dolphin? I have never seen this. You have no tomol?"

I reach for the canoe pendant hanging from my neck and dangle it in front of her. The sunlight bounces off giving the greenstone a glow from behind. "Only this."

She reaches into her woven bag and hands me a bundle through the crease in the door. "Take my husband's coverings," she offers.

"Thank him."

"I wish I could," she whispers, then bows her head and walks away.

I tie on the woven loin cover and slip the soft deerskin cape over my head, sit back on the cot and drink the cool water. Exhausted, I lie down and try to fight off the sleep my body cries for. I don't want this dream, if this is what it really is, to end; I don't want to wake in another time. If I sleep, what will I awaken to? Yet my battle with fatigue is useless. I rub the greenstone, relax and close my eyes. I give in and fade away.

I dream of the future I had left behind, visiting Grandfather at his home. We sit together on his deck looking out to the sea:

"Grandfather, do I Dream Walk into my ancestral past? Or am I from our ancestral past, and I've Dream Walked into the future, only to return to my past?"

"Time is not linear, Peter."

"Yeah, got that. But when will this Dream Walk end?"

He leaves my dream with a knowing smile, but an endless circle of questions remains.

My eyes open, but it's as if they are closed. The hut is drenched in darkness and only the slightest hint of light finds its way inside. I'm reminded of my bruising fall from the cliff as I sorely crawl out of bed and open the curtain. Under the bright stars above, The Noqoto are here, gathered around open fires, outlines in the dark night of a tribe I only just met. Alive.

Talkitna sees me standing at the door, her face reflecting in the flames. She rises up and makes her way to the hut as my heart races.

"Did you sleep well?"

"I had a dream, within a dream…"

"Join us by the fire. You sit with my father as his guest. I hope you're rested and ready to answer his questions. He's very curious about how you find yourself to be here. As are we all."

"I'll try and fill in some blanks, but there are a lot of them."

Her father gestures for me to sit next to him on a log bench seat by the fire. Talkitna hands me a polished wooden bowl carefully inlaid with shells and filled with the meat from a large lobster tail. As soon as the bowl hits my hand, hunger raises its voice and demands I fill my mouth with the rich meat.

Looking up from my meal, I suddenly realize I'm the focus of all eyes. I quickly realize there is much more than my eating habits garnering all the attention.

Paxa kindly lets me finish chewing the last bite before he speaks up. "You were tired and hungry."

"I've traveled a long, long way. Thank you for inviting me to stay in your village."

"You would likely extend the same. Is your village large?"

"You can't imagine how many call California home."

"A peaceful place?"

"Most people are friendly and peaceful, but there are serious troubles too."

"Do you know of white man's Missions and those inside, men in hooded robes, warriors with weapons of exploding fire and the horses they ride?"

"I'm familiar with their history. What have you seen?"

"These days of my old age, I do not venture far. Yaqi went to see with his own eyes the white men who come to live on the land of The People. The hooded shaman and soldiers with weapons forced him to stay. He escaped the first night. What he witnessed was slavery, sickness, death, cruelty and sorrow."

Paxa hesitates, the emotion of his concern for his people rippling through the air. "I've told my tribe to stay away from the Mission."

"How far away?"

"Not far enough. Tell me more of what you have seen."

"I've seen more than I can tell. If you want to try and survive, you're wise to stay away from the Spanish and their missions as long as you can."

Paxa directs his thoughts toward the fire. In this moment, he reminds me of Grandfather with his contemplative way.

"Why have you come to our village?"

"I search for distant family."

"I hope you find them."

"I may have…"

I put down the bowl and lean back from the fire, taking in all the faces that surround me. There is another agenda as they all look toward Paxa with hopeful eyes. Paxa slowly rises to his feet, stands still for a long moment with his head down and eyes closed. His arms spread wide, he opens his eyes. "My people, time for stories!"

The people on the outskirts of the light of fire move closer to Paxa. Wild kids stop running and wiggle to the front with unblinking wide-eyes looking up at the old man as he begins to speak.

"Those from foreign lands who live at the Mission do not understand the Earth Mother. The roots of their tree of life have forgotten how to draw life from the land and the sea. They are troubled with primitive fears. Their consciousness dwells on the perils of their surroundings. They enslave others to herd their cows in this land of plenty. They carry weapons of war to enforce their laziness and greed. They spread sickness. They spread tragedy. Among others, like the Noqoto people, the spirit of the land lives within us. We are one with our Mother Earth. We are one with the Great Spirit. Here where I stand, hundreds of generations of our people have stood before us. Here where I stand, we will continue to stand as the Noqoto. One with our Mother Earth, Father Sky, and the Great Spirit."

I look up from the fire and am pierced by the feral eyes of a man dressed unlike the others. Dark. Mystical. Layers of ornaments around his neck rise toward his angular face. A necklace of bear claws and rattlesnake rattles adds menace to the wild look in his eyes. His gaze shoots into me, through me, leaving me gasping for breath.

His figure is imposing, older than Yaqi, but almost as muscular. "The stories you speak tonight are very much the truth," he acknowledges to Paxa.

He casts me a look that sends me reeling back. "But what is the truth behind this man? He comes from the ocean being led by a dolphin on the tail of a rainbow?" He grabs a gourd of water and suddenly empties its contents into the fire, creating hissing vapors of steam. "Perhaps he will appear from a cloud of steam next?"

Some members of the tribe shake their heads and murmur, wanting an answer to my mysterious appearance. Paxa raises his hand and brings silence to the crowd before he speaks. "Are you questioning the word of my daughter?"

"I don't question your daughter's word, perhaps the eyesight of a grieving widow. What is the true story behind this man here in front of us?"

"This man knows of white men and the Mission. I believe he has knowledge filled with truth," Paxa replies.

"Mostly the white man's version of Mission history." I add.

"You come to us from the Mission, an ally of the Spanish?" he asks accusingly.

The term "Mission" and "ally" brings unanimous looks of concern from the gathered.

"Isqua is our tribal shaman. Meet Pe-ter," Paxa says as he gestures toward him in introduction.

I stand and look at Isqua face-to-face. His eyes are like nothing I have ever seen on a man. I slowly carefully extend my hand. He ignores my cautious attempt to connect our flesh.

"I'm no ally to the Spanish, but I know of missions," I point out.

"He knows of the white man's Mission! Their priests and soldiers bring slavery, sickness and death for our people! We must force them to leave! Kill them if they won't!"

I take in the faces of those gathered around me and divert my eyes away from the shaman. "The priests are devoted to their God and are driven to convert others. History shows their many soldiers, guns and horses give them the advantage over you," I warn.

Yaqi steps forward while raising his hand to speak. "Not even you, Isqua, with your visions and your medicine magic, can fight the sickness the white men bring. I too want to send them out of our lands, but I've seen the sorrows of our people at the Mission."

"When do we stand up to those who invade our ancestral land?" Isqua says forcefully to those intently listening.

"I speak from experience, the Mission is a place of death for our people." Yaqi adds.

The shaman takes a step toward Yaqi. "You turn to fear, Yaqi."

"I have left blood behind the Mission walls. I speak of truth. Not fear."

Paxa raises his hand, silencing Isqua's next words. "For now, we will continue to stay away from the Mission."

Isqua walks away from the circle of light disappearing into the darkness of night. The tension shared around the tribe permeates the air in his passing.

All is quiet in the still evening until the sounds of music vibrate out of the circle of light. A lone wooden flute calls out, joined by the beat of drumming, followed with a percussion of rattles shaking in time. Slow mysterious sounds come together in harmony, introducing a lone female voice. She sings with no lyrics, only the sound of a lovely voice played like one of the instruments. I sit mesmerized by the haunting music, a song without words, only emotion.

The song fades to an end as the singer steps forward into the light of fire and bows her head while closing her eyes. When they open, she looks at me, looking at her. Flames dance in Talkitna's reflective eyes. She turns and walks off toward her hut, momentarily pauses, and glances back in my direction. She glides away into the dark outside the circle of light.

I'm left staring into ancient fire, my mind dancing with mystical mysteries.

CHAPTER 15

My deep, dreamless sleep ends abruptly thanks to a blinding beam of sun on my face.

"Come, Peter," the voice of Yaqi commands.

"Where?"

"To meet our people."

"I just woke up."

"You are last to wake."

He acts like a reluctant tour guide with other things to do than hang out with a suspect stranger. Once again, it seems all eyes are on me as Yaqi leads me through the village.

We approach a group of women sitting beneath a large shady oak, the village's gathering point, and by the looks and sounds of the conversations, a good place to gossip. As we come closer, I sense I'm the prime subject matter for discussion. A handsome older woman with a strong composed presence stands out. Her connection to Yaqi soon becomes apparent as her face lights up at seeing him.

"This is my mother, Alapay," Yaqi says. "Many say she is the leader of our tribe."

"A man's view is not the only view," Alapay points out firmly.

"My mom would love you."

Sitting behind Alapay, working on an amazingly detailed basket is Talkitna. We exchange looks, with her mother very much noticing.

"You've met our daughter Talkitna."

"Yes, briefly."

Alapay looks at her daughter with mother's eyes. "Who does this man who comes to us from the sea remind you of?" Talkitna doesn't answer and looks away.

"What does your heart tell you?"

"In those clothes, he looks like his spirit," Talkitna whispers while looking through me.

"Many moons since he disappeared."

"He may still be alive, somewhere," Talkitna says, hope in her eyes.

Alapay looks in the direction of the ocean. "My love, I know it's hard to accept, but he's gone to Similgasa," she says tenderly, while giving her daughter a well received hug. Both women grow very quiet as the words settle.

"Is there a reason this stranger comes to us from the sea, led by a dolphin?" Both women look at me like they're witnessing a lost ghost.

Yaqi guides me to the shore at the edge of the lagoon where a small fleet of tomols is beached near the water. At a wood-chip-carpeted patch of ground, a group of men stand assembling tomols in various stages of completion. By the look of the physical effort involved, it's no mystery why the men have muscle on muscle.

There's one man, older, more weather worn than others, putting the finishing touches on a tomol that stands out. Its clean lines, high level of craftsmanship and finish work mark it as the finest of any of the tomols being assembled.

The older master stops working and eyes me like a boss sizing up a young apprentice. Yaqi and I move directly through the work party toward him, while crunching through deep wood chips.

"Peter, this is Kasmali, master builder of tomols," Yaqi announces.

I reach out to shake his hand, worn and calloused, the hands of an aging master of his trade. Hands like Grandfather's.

"I've heard the story of your riding with dolphins. Sometime we can talk of your journey in more detail," he tells me with calm intention.

"I'd like to talk to you about what it takes to build such a beautiful tomol," I reply as I get a closer look to his boat.

"My father taught me as his father showed him, and back through many generations."

I look down the bow of this boat clearly built by a highly skilled man with eyes that see every detail, a man my Grandfather would be drawn to.

"Someday I'd like to see what it's like on the water," I say with admiration.

A closer look reveals fine shaping, drilling and lacing at the joining of each plank. The thin cord used to bind them is handwoven, with not a twist out of order. Over the joins, black tar has been rubbed into the lacing. I touch the sticky black sealer and sniff the crude oil.

Kasmali comes closer and takes a long look at the tomol hanging around my neck. "From where did it come?"

"My grandfather."

my hands on the line and free it from my ankle as the fish lunges for the bottom, peeling off-line as it burns through my clinging hands. As it makes a desperate dash for freedom, I try to slow its run without much success.

"Wrap it here!" Yaqi shouts, showing me a well-polished wooden cross brace.

Standing, I grip the line tight as I try to gain length. But the fish has other plans and tears more line through my now bloody hands. I finally get some hard-earned line back and give it a half wrap around the wood, setting the drag, so I can play it out without shredding more skin. Sweating heavily now, hands, arms and lower back straining, I wrestle the creature fighting for its life. Coming to the surface, the fish shows itself for the first time, a yellowfin tuna glistening in the sun as it struggles to break free of me. After a good battle, I turn the tide my way and tire it enough to get it to the side of the boat. Yaqi grabs the gaff and gets ready. I stand, preparing to bring the fish on board, when I see a growing mass of a shark below with different plans. I've fought hard for the yellowfin and don't want to lose it to the latecomer. I pull steadily to get it into the boat. The acrobatic fish hits the surface and goes airborne. The shark follows, chomping into the tuna as it hits the boat on re-entry. Knocked off balance, I grab for the rail, miss and plunge into the churning water next to what's left of the yellowfin, my own blood from my cuts mixing with its bloody remains.

Yaqi almost jerks my arm off as he helps pull me into the boat. The shark bumps the tomol again looking for the missing meal. Yaqi takes up position in the bow, grabs the spear, and waits for the sharks return.

"Leave the shark alone!"

Ignoring me, he thrusts the spear into the shark, driving the shaft in deep. Unlike me, he's well prepared with deerskin wrapped around his hand and the thick cord wrapped around the cross brace. Yaqi plays the rope out expertly until there is no slack. Our boat lurches forward and is tugged along toward the distant horizon. With the bow dipping dangerously low, the shark pulls us into the rolling swells. I turn back to shore to see a wake of white water trailing behind us as we head out into the open ocean. Yaqi doesn't seem overly concerned. I am.

Our forward progress slows. The shark doesn't have much left and is giving up its last attempts to survive. Cautiously we bring the dead weight toward us until its belly-up body comes into view. Yaqi gives a final thrust of the spear. Looping a rope around the tail, we labor together to drag the big fish into the tippy boat. The body of the hunted leaves little room for the hunters.

Yaqi reaches into a woven bag and pulls out a steel dagger. He waves it in front of my face. "Bleed it," he orders. I glance at the blade, engraved in Spanish with a familiar inscription: "Santos." Mission Los Santos I wonder?

Paddling along with hard pulls, the scars on Yaqi's back confront me. "Your scars, Yaqi, how did you get them?"

"At the Mission, the hooded priest tried to make me stay. Many soldiers came with their weapons. I was put in shackles and I could not fight back. The hooded one beat me in front of the enslaved natives. He is a cruel coward."

"He was giving you an unhealthy serving of Divine Justice since you refused to join his Mission and his religion."

"What do you say?"

"He tried to make you believe what they offer is better than the lives you live. To get you to passively follow and obey, so you would become part of their Mission Indian workforce."

"Why would I give up freedom?"

"Everyone should ask the same question," I say.

Yaqi continues his story with heightened emotion. "When I was released, I collapsed. Mission Indians carried me. When I opened my eyes, the shackles were gone. I told them I would kill if they tried to stop me."

"Did you kill?"

"Yes," he states as fact, as he wields the dagger in front of my eyes.

"Soldier?"

"Yes," he says without a hint of remorse.

"You're on the most wanted list."

I return to the laborious task at hand, my arms and back straining to paddle against the drag of the dead shark weighing us down with little spare freeboard. Plenty of meat for everyone in the tribe, and not just shark fin soup. A wave of pride goes through me knowing I'll help contribute food to the tribe, as they have shared their food with me.

We finally hit the sandy shore at the edge of the village as the sun's warming rays make their final appearance of the day. A few of the young ones run to help us pull our tomol up the beach. When they see what's on board, they leap away to the top of the dune, staring down at the monster fish. Their excited yelling and waving brings a crowd of onlookers to inspect the catch.

With the help of a length of stout hemp rope and the combined muscle power of many others, we win the tug of war against gravity and drag the shark carcass above high tide. Out come surgically sharp obsidian knives. Before the sun sets, the shark has been carved into portable chunks of meat, its skin efficiently stripped off and laid to dry on a rack of driftwood. Yaqi and I walk back to the village with a crowd of well-wishers helping to carry the bounty. They seem to soften to me, more grateful and accepting of the mysterious stranger.

The sun is long gone, the sky is still and calm as a large moon rises over the ridge in a mirror reflection off the glassy lagoon. I step into the liquid moonlight and wade out for a well-deserved rinse in fresh water after the eventful day.

Returning to the village common area, I feel like a new Dream Walker.

Talkitna comes toward me with a concerned look. "I hear your hands were cut, let me see," she orders.

In the light of the fire I show her the scars of the novice hand-line fisherman. Even in the poor light they look gruesome. "Remains of your fishing trip with Yaqi," she says.

"What about the one that didn't get away!"

She is clearly unimpressed. "Wait at your hut."

My heart thumps in my chest as she walks away. I watch her silhouette in the moonlight and forget about my wounds.

She makes her way back to me carrying a small woven bag. As instructed, I hold out my hands. "Healing plants will help," she advises.

She gently rubs in the paste, which is blissfully painful. She covers both my hands in a bandage made of leaves and wraps them with light cord.

"You're a special guest tonight given what you and Yaqi have provided for the tribe," she says, admiring her handiwork.

I strike a pose with my bandaged hands. "I feel like a praying mantis."

"What?"

"Don't know what you call them. They're insects that look like they're praying. They say the female eats the male right after they mate," I add without thinking.

"It's true?"

I nod yes. She shakes her head as she turns to walk away.

I move closer to the fire. As I reach Yaqi's side, loud applause comes our way accompanied by smiles.

Music begins with just a few lonely notes, and then builds to spontaneous dancing erupting in the warm, beautiful night. People come up to me to shake my hand, only for me to clumsily respond with praying mantis handshake.

Fillets of fish come off the fire and Yaqi hands me one of the skewered steaks.

"Not sure how I'm going to eat," I say, my club-like hands fumbling.

Balancing the fish in one hand, I reach up to give Yaqi a high-five. He stares back at me, not sure of the meaning of this gesture. Hesitantly he raises his hand up to mine and we slap them together as I grimace in pain.

Paxa approaches, Alapay on his arm. "You have shown great bravery in bringing such a large shark back to Noqoto," he says directly to me.

"I was the chum."

"You are modest." Paxa turns to the assembled and raises his hand.

"My People! Let us give thanks to Yaqi and Pe-ter for bringing us this feast tonight!"

All around the crowd erupts in applause, truly appreciative of the bounty we brought back. Their pleasure is infectious. The music starts up again. I get sucked into a group dance and feel myself being swept up in the celebration. There's no real order to the dance, just mutual feelings of joy. I can't help but beam as the drums beat louder and the tribe joins in a song. My bandaged hands rise above the others in celebration, the stirred dust of dancing feet floats up into the night air as the light of the filtered glow of the moon shines down upon us.

The tribe dances on without me as I slip away into the darkness and stroll in the moonlight to the deserted beach. A low tide leaves my fresh tracks on the damp sand as I walk in the direction of Rocky Point. The tribe's music fades in the distance, masked by the breaking waves as crystal refractions of moonlight dance on the water.

A wave pushes onto the shore and erases my tracks, leaving me concerned about future footfalls of the Dream Walk.

CHAPTER 16

Awakening eyes slowly focus on the sky peering down at me from the skylight. Slowly I stretch out arms and legs, trying to shrug off the aftereffects of the fishing trip.

My bandaged hands are looking worse for wear after the evening festivities. Deciding I'd better check what they look like in the light of day, I bite the cords loose and the wrappings fall away. I see my hands are much better.

I dash out of the hut and glance around, hoping to spot her. I make my way to Alapay who's working on the final trimmings of an otter-skin cape. "Good morning, Alapay. Have you seen Talkitna?"

"Good morning, Pe-ter. She is upstream, gathering. Want me to show you?"

"No thanks, I'll follow the stream."

Reaching the far side of the lagoon, I can see a fresh flow of water from the canyon above pouring into the lake. Fish are schooled around the mouth of the stream, feeding in the cool water mingling with the warmer lagoon. A shadow passes and an osprey swoops down and plunges into the still water with stretched talons and wings open. When it rises from the surface, a struggling fish struggles in the raptor's grasp. Straining to gain altitude in the calm air, the osprey lands deftly in dead snag of a tree housing a woody nest high in the branches. Hungry babies poke up their heads at her arrival and cry out with impatience, ready to feast on the fresh catch of the day.

Dense willows line the waterway along the lower part of the stream. Occasionally I call out to Talkitna, only to hear my own echo in response. Higher into the base of the mountain I ascend to a point where the water tumbles over a sprinkling of boulders, leaping in small waterfalls over rocky ledges into bubbling pools. Overhead the oaks grow taller, spreading shade with their far reach. Green ferns line the watercourse of the damp earth, curls of new growth unfolding in circular wonder. Wild blackberries present themselves in a large tangled patch as I carefully avoid the pricks to pick a handful of ripe ones. I call out again, hearing no sound other than the song of water, a liquid melody that grows into the loud chorus of a cascading waterfall. The canyon pinches tighter the higher I climb. A well-trodden deer trail cuts into the contours of the steep bank, and I make for it.

The unmistakable roar of falling water calls behind dense trees. Stepping up to a bench in the rocks, I part a curtain of fringed ferns. A tumbling waterfall spills from a notch in the cliff high above, splitting into fine mists cascading down into an aquamarine pool. Appearing from behind the lace of falling water is a woman, her eyes closed as she rinses her hair. Stepping back from the falls, she grabs hair in her hands and twists while turning my direction. Her eyes open in surprise when I step into the clearing.

"Talkitna!" I shout above the roar of the falls, as I hold out my newly healed hands toward her. Her look of surprise turns into a smile. Diving into the pool and swimming my direction, she surfaces in front of me, hair slicked back and floating at water level, her dark eyes looking into me like I'm a mirror.

"Talkitna, my hands are healing really well. Can you show me the plants?"

"You're on my coverings."

Oblivious, distracted by the sight of her, my feet are planted atop her neat pile of coverings. Embarrassed, I turn my back and offer them to her.

Her voice rises over the falling water. "You can look now. We'll have to do some walking for me to show you the plants."

"What a beautiful place."

"My mother's favorite place to take me."

"I need to cool down. Is it taboo if I swim?" I ask.

"I'm no keeper of this water."

I dive in for relief from the heat, and when I come to the surface, I catch her slight smile.

I follow as she leads the way down the stream with graceful maneuvers through the mixed terrain, truly one with her surroundings, something she does as second nature. When the water slows, we slow. Surrounded with lush green vegetation growing at its edges of a deep pool, Talkitna pauses.

"Do you see that dark green plant with the broad leaves there?" she asks, pointing. "Those leaves are what I use to wrap your hands. They help to heal quickly."

"How do you know?"

"How do you not know? What do you use for injuries? This knowledge has been shared by my mother," she explains to an adult child who has missed his lessons.

As we work our way down the stream toward the village, the depth of her knowledge of the natural world is apparent to me. The intimacy she shows for the life around us is beyond memorization, a connection on a level beyond surface understanding.

We exit the canyon and cut across an open area until we get to a western facing slope baked in the hot sun. Here succulents grow far apart in the dry soil. Talkitna points to another plant. "This helps to heal quickly, the juice of this I rubbed into your cuts."

"Aloe!"

We walk together across the hillside with me lost in her world of plants, the distant sea framing the land in blue. All around us fields of wildflowers scream out in brilliant color announcing a sweet bounty to the bees, butterflies, hummingbirds and fortunate humans.

Talkitna looks at me with eyes filled with concern. "Hungry?"

"I had a few berries."

"I have food. Come with me," she offers.

She leads the way higher up the hillside into a grove of oaks clinging to the steep slope above. I can barely keep up as she moves effortlessly. I lose sight of her when she disappears into the shadows of the trees. I try to follow her, but there are few traces to be found. Her laughter in the distance reveals her standing high above on a large rock looking down at me. By the time I clamber up, Talkitna has laid out a picnic of venison jerky, wild plums and pine nuts. I try to catch my breath, amazed she isn't breathing hard at all. Behind her is a spectacular view of the village below framed by the estuary and ocean stretched to horizons.

"You're in amazing shape, Talkitna, you could run a marathon."

"Mar-a-thon?"

"A long run."

"To where?"

"The finish line. Where I'm from…"

"Where are you from?"

"A place far away, many moons from here."

"You Dream Walk?"

I reach down for the greenstone tomol resting on my chest.

"I want to hear more of your far away world."

"I want to share it with you, Talkitna. But, not sure of how much I should tell…"

Talkitna looks off the edge of our rocky perch. "Sorry for leaving you."

"At least gravity is with me on the way back."

"Grav-i-ty? What is this word?"

"Since you asked, a tale is told of a white man, who got hit on the head by fruit falling from a tree. It inspired him to come up with a name for a force that makes fruit fall from trees—gravity. It's what keeps us grounded on Mother Earth as we spin on the axis."

She grabs a stone and arcs it over the edge. "Gra-vi-ty!"

Finishing the picnic, we both lay back on the warm rock, resting in the shade of the oaks. Cotton-ball clouds float overhead through blue gaps in twisting branches, billowing into imaginary shapes for dreamy minds.

"Talkitna, do you want to be somewhere else besides here? It's a big world."

"Some who've ventured from our village have never returned, gone to The Other Side."

"Many would call this place paradise. There'll be many famous songs about the name of this place, California." She looks at me puzzled.

Sitting up, she gives a modest bow of her head and adjusts her gaze to look into my eyes. She gives a serene smile. "If this is paradise, why would I want to go somewhere else?"

"Some think the world is greener over the next horizon."

"My father has a word for them. Lost."

"When too many people discover it, paradise is lost. Sometimes you're forced to move on to find a new paradise. This paradise deserves to be sung about."

She looks down toward the village below looking like a shrunken diorama. She closes her eyes and starts humming a melody until words of lyrical music she sings.

Mother Earth surrounds us in love

Precious rain falls from above

Father Sky looks down on all.

For this we are grateful, and answer the Creator's call.

The clarity of her voice is pure beauty, and the words dance around me, bringing me to a higher place that only music can. When she sings her last note, I open my eyes to check if I'm dreaming. "That was really nice."

"Perhaps we can sing sometime?"

"I'll play drums."

"We should go, people might talk about how much time I'm spending with you." She leaps to her feet and extends her hands to me. I take her hands and rise to face her. Both of us smile at each other at exactly the same time, a knowing between us, a connection. Slowly, we release our hands and turn to the village and the tribe below.

She suddenly turns back to face me. "I forgot about your hands!

"I felt no pain," I reply truthfully.

She takes my wrists in her hands and inspects my healing wounds. "It won't be long until you're healed."

"Thanks to you, and the plants."

"To your healing body."

Making our way back down to the village at the edge of the lagoon, I notice a white flowering plant that looks very familiar. "Talkitna, what's this?"

"Moonflower. My mother tells me these came into bloom the day I was born. The sky was clear blue, the sea calm, mother dolphins surrounded her as she gave birth to me in the shallow water of the sea."

"Dolphins surrounded you?"

"In Mother Ocean."

She gazes at the ocean as I look at her, taking in all she has just told me. "I heard the words from Alapay that someone dear to you is missing."

She takes a deep breath before answering. "My husband, he went fishing alone in his tomol and the weather changed suddenly. Fierce winds turned the ocean white with huge waves. I looked to the horizon for many moons, hoping…"

"I'm sorry for you."

"He left behind a precious gift, Little Wave is a growing shadow."

"Your son?"

"He loves the ocean like his father."

We both look to the sea. She turns back to me and looks directly into my eyes. "Is there a woman in your life?"

"Not presently."

A hesitant smile grows on her face. "This place you come from, please, tell me more."

"You wouldn't believe me.

"Try, tell me."

"Well, hard to put into words for you. One example; your ancient knowledge of the healing properties of plants will be adapted into drugs. Chiefs of these huge tribes, called cor-por-a-tions, they'll secure the patents to the drugs, hike up the prices to cover years of research costs, then market the pills to those in need, and often to those who don't. The more medicines are prescribed, the bigger the shell bead currency for the corporation tribe. Talkitna, when you so freely give your medicinal plant knowledge, you're a true healer with a non-profit, heart-based passion."

My take on the future draws a mixed look, almost as if she feels sorry for me, the village idiot rattling on about strange worlds. Clear images of the harsh realities of the future flash in my mind. Fast forward her a few centuries and Talkitna would likely wilt like a freshly picked flower left behind in a car parked in the hot, smoggy sun.

"What I mean is, your life is good here, Talkitna. It's a beautiful place. Your needs are few. The natural food supply is abundant, water's clean, air's fresh, you're free to do what you want, when you want. You have time between tasks to explore art, recreation, music and laughter. Your tribe seems to be really good people to surround yourself with. Supportive. Community minded. No casinos to get fired from. Free from the calendar, and the clock. Other than real fight or flight, not much stress. You live by the changing seasons, the tides, and the cycles of the moon. Your world is wonderful in many ways, except the impending invasion of your traditional lands, and the genocide to come. Maybe I should shut up…"

She looks at me, her lovely browed furrowed. "You speak many words of your world I do not understand. Maybe I don't want to… I'm going back to my village of Noqoto, Dream Walker," she says as gathers her things and walks toward her people.

I'm left alone to contemplate the tragedies that will come to the people of Noqoto I'm growing to respect and love. My heart and soul weep as I watch her walk away.

CHAPTER 17

The joy of children's laughter draws my attention away from the beach as I follow the excited sounds to the far side of the lagoon.

Duck decoys shaped from tulle reeds bob on the surface. One is suddenly struck dead by an arrow to the sound of loud hoots, and rolls over from the weight of the arrow. On shore, a group of boys playfully lower their heads in respect to a smiling boy balanced in a small dugout canoe floating offshore, bow in hand.

The successful marksman paddles back to shore, climbs out of the boat and hands his bow and just one arrow to the next contender. The boy paddles out, carefully stands up in the canoe, positions the arrow in the bow and lines up his one shot. He holds his breath, releases his arrow and just misses the floating target. Disappointment is all over his face as he retrieves the arrow now bobbing on the lagoon's surface, and paddles back to the gathered young hunters in training. The two contestants shake hands.

I walk over to the group to congratulate the victor. The boy takes a step back, not sure of my intentions. "Well done. My name is Peter, what's yours?"

I reach out my hand to shake his as he modestly looks up at me.

"I am Little Wave," he says as he reaches up to shake my hand with hesitation.

"I like your name. Your mother is Talkitna?"

"Am I in trouble?"

"Should you be?"

"I hope not," he says as he looks toward the village. Turning back to me, a slight smile grows on his face. "Do you want to try the hunting game?" he asks.

"Sure," I say with more than a bit of hesitance.

The boys erupt in enthusiasm at the prospect of the full-grown stranger joining them in their game of skill. Little Wave hands me his bow and gives me the single arrow.

I carefully sit in the tippy little boat and stroke out into the lagoon with my hands. Once I get in position, I slowly get to my feet and put the arrow in the bow. Memories of my youth appear as I see Grandfather instructing me how to shoot at target on the hay bale behind his house. I return to the present, and concentrate on keeping the dugout as steady as I can, pull slowly back on the bow, line up the decoy in my sight, and get ready to release the arrow. Suddenly, the boat rocks to one side, throwing me off balance. The flying arrow arches high overhead as I hit the water with an awkward splash.

I find Little Wave suddenly next to me treading water, a mischievous smile on his face.

"No duck for Pe-ter!"

The boys on shore howl with laughter at my unintentional slapstick performance thanks to Little Wave and his tippy underwater stealth mission.

Trailing a splashing wake behind him, Little Wave takes off swimming for shore. I throw the bow in the canoe and swim after him. Just as I'm about to catch him, he submerges in the murky water and disappears like a sinking frog. I stop swimming, tread water, and look around, trying to spot where he'll surface. When he comes up, he's close to shore, frantically swimming to get away. I sprint after him and make land just behind him as he runs as if a wild animal is after him. He's really fast, but with longer strides I'm gaining on him. I reach out to grab and stop him mid-stride, but he changes directions like a rabbit. I follow, he fakes a right, I adjust, he cuts left, and I fall for the fake and tangle up in my own feet, going down on the wet sand.

The boys love having a sand-coated clown. Little Wave pauses to look at me over his shoulder with a big smile. I break into a laugh at myself. I dive back in the water to rinse off the sand as he jogs off to the village, likely to spread the word of his latest triumph over clumsy Peter.

I scan the sculpted sand dunes for a nice, warm place to lie down and dry off from my latest circus act. I find just the right one, a nice natural spinal curve fitting for a lounge in the sun. I pile up a perfect sand pillow headrest and lay down to soak up a few rays. My chill quickly falls away thanks to the warmth radiating from the sand below and sun above. I fall off into the luxury of a mid-day snooze with nothing pressing on the agenda. I drift into daydreams.

CHAPTER 18

I awaken from the nap with a contented stretch and no idea how long I'd slept. Looking up to the sun, I dig my toes in the warm sand and stroll the dunes to the white sandy beach that curves in a crescent toward Rocky Point. The sand beneath my feet is pristine, lacking any sign of the vast assortment of plastic litter bearing down on the planet. Above the high tide mark, driftwood pushed by storms mark out a huge wooden tangle above the storm surge, trunks of once living giants taken for a ride with nature's flushing of the land without concrete dams to get in the way.

Studying the large pile of wood in front of me and imagining what my Grandfather might do with a few special pieces at the top of the pile, I see a large piece of driftwood worn into a rough shape. I clamor up and drag it clear of the stack, laying it on the sand. With a pointed shell, I scratch the surface of the timber. Streaks of red appear on the dry redwood. Flipping it over, I see it's without large cracks or knots, clean-grained, old growth with tight rings showing many years.

Dragging the dead weight down the beach is a back breaker, but I'm determined to get it over to the boat builders. When the kids see me dragging it, they all come running to help. With three on one end, and two of us on another, we lift it up and carry it the last stretch to the lagoon. With relief, we drop it in the water; a big splash sends rippling waves across the surface. I get a running start and leap on like it's a surfboard, but it rolls over and dumps me in the shallows. Coming to the surface, I hear the boys howling again. Clambering back on the log, I knee paddle it across the lagoon toward the boat building yard. Once again, I'm the source of the boys' amusement. Coasting distance from shore, I drag the wet log up out of the water.

I present it to Kasmali for his advice. "Good wood?" I ask between gasps of breath.

The master brushes sand from the wood and reads the grain. "Very good wood. What will you do with it?"

"Better to show. Any tools I can borrow?"

Kasmali nods in understanding and reaches into a large net bag, pulling out an ax made of iron. I'm delighted, and shocked, when he hands it to me. Carefully, I run my finger along the edge, nearly drawing blood given its sharpness.

"Where did you get this?"

"Yaqi took it from the Mission."

"Did he grab a power-planer too?"

Kasmali gives me another of the confused looks I'm getting to know too well. "I hope it helps you create what you see in the wood."

I sink the ax deeply. I'm stoked to start making a custom shaped surfboard by my own hands! I try to pull out the axe with one arm, but it holds tight. I wrap my other arm around the handle, and it still holds. I climb up on the log, straddle the ax and leverage it free of the wood.

As Grandfather had shown me many times, first thing to do is set up a proper workbench. I wander back to the beach to look through the piles of driftwood for the right sized pieces to build a waist-high stand. Under the shade of a willow, I bury what will be the legs of the workstation in the sand until I have the proper height. I go back to Kasmali to get hemp rope to tie a tripod arrangement together.

I have both looking level and sturdy, ready to handle weight of the redwood plank.

Looking from what will be the back of the future board hiding in the driftwood, I sight down the lines of wood, visualizing where the surfboard will take shape, following the grain in an imaginary straight line from nose to tail. After tracing front to back, I outline the shape of the board down one side.

After a bit of rummaging, I find a crude yardstick in the scrap pile and start to mark increments along my tracing, measuring the distance from the center to the outside edge. Once I have a series of marks, I trace a connecting line between them. I take a step back and eye it again, satisfied with the finished outline of my future wave-riding vehicle. I turn around to grab the ax perched in the bench legs. Many sets of boat-builder eyes are looking my way.

This redwood is soft, and I remind myself to work carefully to keep from taking too much away. The wood will also take on water, making it sink and get even heavier unless I can get a waterproof seal around it. I'm still unsure what I can seal it with. Perhaps beeswax? Stealing beeswax from a hive of bees ready to defend their nest perched high up in a tree isn't something to look forward to.

I chip away with the ax as wood chips build to a thick layer at my feet. I'm becoming regular entertainment for the tribe. Everyone can see it's too small of a piece of wood to be a dugout boat, and too thick to be a plank for a larger boat. As the pile of wood chips grow, my hands are going numb with the effort.

Once I have the basic shape roughed out, it's time to fine-tune the rocker and rails. Yet all I have to go is the memory of what I've surfed on and from having watched the ease with which Grandfather created free-form woodworking pieces with no formal plan, no exact dimensions, and only an experienced eye. If only I had his experience.

Missing a power planer, and electricity, I turn to the local wood workers to see what they're using to fine-tune the shape of their projects. I'm shown very sharp-edged stones and sharpened bones they use as hand planes to peel wood away. They have different degrees of rough stone shaped with a handle grip to serve as coarse grinders to remove rough edges. The fine-tuning is done with fine-grit sandpaper made from dried sharkskin. I think of the dolphin, tracing an outline of its dorsal fin on some outcast redwood creating a fin for the surfboard.

The muscle testing exercise to the extreme slows down and I'm finally at the stage where I can sand the redwood smooth. The shape is now what I had envisioned, and I'm really excited to test the board in the water. But my excitement is tempered by an unpleasant task looming—I still need to get the dreaded beeswax.

I see Little Wave and his buddies cruise by on one of their regular rounds, checking out what I'm up to. I excitedly show them what I'm up to and preach my sermon of the seas to the youngsters. "When I'm done with this, you can take turns riding it on waves! It is the most fun you can imagine!"

Their eyes grow as big as the smiles of anticipation on their faces.

"But first I need you to do a little task for me," I say.

As their leader once again, Little Wave steps to the front of the group. By his enthusiasm, I can see he wants to ride the board as much as any of them, and now I'm hoping he'll help me get there. Perhaps even a repayment of sorts from his earlier practical jokes?

"Little Wave, I have a job for you. This job is one of the most important parts of making this board."

He nods excitedly, ready for the task.

"I need you to help the boys find beehives. You can have the honey, but I need all the bee's wax you can get."

His confident look dims a bit. I have to test his commitment.

"Can you do it?"

"When?" he asks, clearly trying to mask his concern over the task ahead.

"The sooner you get me the wax, the quicker we can have fun on the board. In fact, I'll give all you boys this board to play on, if you get me the wax."

I watch the Bee Boys run off toward the forest on a mission from me. I start to feel a bit guilty about sending them on such a hazardous chore. Hopefully they know more than me about how to find, and deal with a hive of wild bees. Their reward will be two-fold: the joys of boarding on waves, and honey.

With hard work, the board of my dreams sanded smooth and finally ready for beeswax, but the boys haven't returned. My worry is justified when I see Talkitna marching toward me with a stern look. "The young ones have so many bee stings on them they can hardly move! They are sick in their stomachs from all the honey they've eaten! Little Wave told me you sent them!"

"They volunteered. Did they get the wax?"

"Not without pain! You promised them fun!"

"Their pain will soon turn to fun. Where's the wax?"

"Little Wave has it in our hut, he's protecting it like a sacred object. He wouldn't give it to me, and he is in no shape to bring it to you."

"I'll go to him. Do you have something I can heat the wax in? I need to rub it into my board when it's really hot."

"You should have come to me first instead of little boys!"

"Sorry about that."

"You can apologize to the boys."

As I make my way to the huts, I can hear some of them moaning and groaning. When I open the flap to Little Wave's hut, I find him splayed out on his bed, looking like an overinflated red balloon, swollen red stings all over his face and up his arms, sticky honey covering his face. But there by his bedside, lies the sacred ball of wax.

"Got your wax," he moans.

"Good work, kid. Sorry about the negative side effects, I figured you knew what you were doing. Cheer up, you'll have such fun when you get ride the board!"

"I hope so. It was not fun getting the wax."

With swollen hands, he hands me the large ball of compressed wax. By the size of it, I think I have enough for the surfboard and a belly board.

Returning to my treasured surfboard with melted bee sealant, rubbing wax into the redwood brings out deep richness in the wood, revealing the tight growth rings reflecting hundreds of years of history. The next chapters of this tree's story will be told as a surfboard, no longer a piece of lonely driftwood, about to bring pleasure to those who ride waves.

Kasmali wanders over to check on me as I'm rubbing in the second coat of wax. The board looks good, something so beautifully handcrafted that a collector might hang on the wall as art. For a moment, I think of all the hard work I've put into it and don't want to risk dinging it in the surf. Sanity returns and I decide wall art is no contest.

The master boat builder stares down the lines of the rails while rubbing his hand gently along the soft rounded edge. I can see his reflection in the buffed gloss of the wax. "You must mark your creation with your animal guardian totem," Kasmali says. "You should be proud, it's a fine shape. Only one problem, your boat is too small, it will hold almost nothing."

"It's for only one person, Kasmali. We call it a surfboard. Have you ever seen anything like this?"

He pauses and considers. "I have traveled far by land and sea, and I have never seen a thing as you have created."

"It's like a wave dance."

"You are wave dancer?"

"I'm a surfer."

With a breeze hitting my face, I look across the choppy lagoon as warm winds blow from high on the ridgeline where trees bow to gusts. A warm offshore wind shapes the long grass into concerts of motion—favorable winds for surfing. Now all I need is a nice swell.

CHAPTER 19

The sound of waves lures me to consciousness and I happily leap out of bed. In the first light of dawn, I see what I'd been dreaming of. A nice set of waves roll across the dim light, breaking crisply and cleanly in offshore winds.

In the cool fresh air, I jog through the quiet village and call out at Talkitna's door. "Little Wave!"

"Peter?" comes the sleepy young voice.

"The waves are here! I'll see you on the beach, hurry!"

Talkitna's sleepy face peers through the flap of the door.

"A life changing moment is about to happen for Little Wave!" I plead before she can admonish me.

The buzz of excitement led by Little Wave's enthusiasm is spreading through the sleepy huts of Noqoto. The long process of making the surfboard has given plenty of time for the tribe to speculate about my motives, and now they will see what's driving me to the sea. An understanding that something special is about to happen pervades the village.

As the sun strikes the waves, the entire tribe gathers together on the beach. Offshore winds feather the peaks of the waves, holding the faces of the breaking swells briefly aloft. A perfect wind, and a sunny, blue sky day. I wrap my hands around my new surfboard, gently feeling the rails like the curves of a new lover. The engraving of my animal totem on the board's deck makes me smile—the little dolphin is about to enter its element. I slip the redwood board under my arm and trot down the beach to the edge of the surf.

Talkitna steps out of the gathering crowd toward me.

"Can you handle the big waves in your little tomol?" she asks.

"Saltwater in my blood," I assure her.

"Hope it won't be your blood in saltwater."

"I'll be more than fine. I'm stoked!"

Little Wave runs up to me. Ready and full of youthful impatience he asks, "Time for fun?"

"I'll show you how first, and then we'll go out together."

I wade into the cool water, hop on the board and start paddling out past the white water. Once out beyond the breaking waves, I sit up on the board and turn to shore. Lining the beach are most of The Noqoto, curious about what I'm up to. Turning back to the horizon, I see the long awaited set of swells rolling to me as I adjust position to meet the waves. Spinning the board, I paddle hard.

With one last stroke, I'm up to my feet and dropping in skimming my hand along the rippled surface of the water as I set my line across the face of the wave and hold it. Stalling, I shift my weight back on the board, then cross-step to the nose, matching the speed of the breaking wave behind me. The ride is coming to an end as a closeout rapidly approaches. Stepping back to the tail, I turn and smack off the lip into a re-entry on the way down. As the white water closes in around me, I ride it to shore. Hitting the sand, I casually step off the board and bow to the clapping and cheering tribe.

Kasmali is the first to step forward. He knows more than anyone how much time, effort and soul I put into the making of this surfboard.

"I can see now what you saw in a piece of wood. What you have shown us is a gift."

"Thank you for your help, Kasmali."

To my delight, Talkitna walks up with a smile and a nod. "You are Wave Dancer!"

"Wave Dancer?"

"Your tribal name is now Wave Dancer!" Talkitna insists strongly.

"Wave Dancer sounds sort of… New Age, in an olden way."

"Meet Wave Dancer, everyone!"

A spontaneous ovation bursts out from the crowd, clapping, hooting and whistling.

"Talkitna, will you wave dance with me?"

"Yes, I want to try."

Our conversation is cut short by Little Wave, who runs up, anxious for his long-awaited fun. "That was great, Peter! My turn!"

"You heard your mother, I'm Wave Dancer now."

"Wave Dancer is my new hero!" Little Wave announces to all.

He disappears into the crowd and soon comes sprinting back, surrounded by the other boys, the little belly board I made them under his arm.

Together Little Wave and I work our way out through the white water until we're in position. He shivers from the cool water, his eyes locked on the horizon. "Now wait until I tell you to paddle, take off at an angle and lean on into the wave face," I instruct.

"Tell me when!" he replies without breaking his concentration.

"Be patient, watch the waves come to you."

A nice set is building as we both paddle further out to meet it. The gift from the sea is upon us. "Ready? Here it comes. Turn now, paddle hard!"

I give him a push and help send him on his way. From behind all I can see is the faint outline through the back of the translucent wave of the path he's traveling. Suddenly, it looks like Little Wave is getting barreled on his first ride as he disappears! I don't see him again until he runs up on shore, leaping around as his friends share his excitement and joy.

I catch a wave and ride it, this time I give the board more of a workout to see what it can handle. The shape and the polished finish give it plenty of speed and maneuverability. I drive the board up high on the wave and drop back down in near free fall, again and again. When the wave picks up, I respond by trimming the fastest line across the face and stay just ahead of the whitewater. The wave matches me and throws over into a tube as it hits the shallow sand. Now with only tunnel vision, I crouch low and skim my hand along the face, slowing my speed just enough to keep me in the tube. Exiting the tube into the open, I hear a chorus of excitement from the tribe.

All eyes are again on me as I walk up the beach. Little Wave comes running up, and I fail at a low five, finally connecting with water flying from our hands.

Talkitna walks our way down the beach, beaming pride and joy. As she comes to the nose of my board, her joy switches to bewilderment.

I turn and follow her eyes toward the ocean.

A Spanish galleon sails at full mast, leaving a tumbling white wake. Flying from the stern, the flag of King of Spain. Sailors line the rail, staring at our tribal village.

All goes quiet on shore behind me, the stunned silence of my tribe telegraphing concern. I'm unable to keep my thoughts to myself. "Shit, there goes the neighborhood," I say under my breath.

The ship sails on by us and disappears from sight around Rocky Point. Talkitna turns to me looking very frightened and asks in a scared whisper, "Who are they?"

I hesitate to say what lies ahead. I stand alone in front of Talkitna, knowing the truth of the disaster the Europeans are about to bring to these peaceful people of my past. My heart sinks with sadness as I look into her eyes. "Spanish flagged, likely a supply ship from Mexico making a run to the Presidio in Monterey."

"What do they want?" she asks with concern.

"You don't want to know."

"I do want to know," she demands with harsh eyes against me.

"I'm afraid you are about to find out for yourselves."

Staring toward the distant horizon of the sea, questions roll at me like waves. Can I help my ancestors? Am I an avatar traveling back in time to warn them of their future? Armed with the knowledge of time passed, what can I do to change the course of history unfolding now? And this beautiful lady standing in front of me peering deep into my knowing eyes, what do I tell her?

CHAPTER 20

Life moves on to the concerns of daily existence for my tribe after the Spanish ship's passing, although the threat of the coming of the Europeans hangs over the tribe like a threatening thundercloud.

The Noqoto busily prepare for a coming trade fair with neighboring island tribes with a flurry of work and organizing. I learn that the islanders across the channel serve as the reserve bank of the region. They find and refine the rare shells that serve as the regional currency. The women and men of Noqoto are well known for their artful skills. Our tribe would be able to trade to other tribes for what they held in abundance, and they with us.

Kasmali proposed to our tribe that I be the chief of surfboard making. The unanimous support I receive, even from the shaman, made me proud. Little Wave helps with the sanding and the beeswax waterproofing; he's really into it and doing a fine job. I hope a surfboard might be of great value after I have a chance to show the trade fair visitors my first venture into early, early California surfing retail.

On the day of the fair, I'm putting some final touches on my latest board when one of the boat builders shouts. I look out to the ocean and see a growing fleet of large tomols sitting low in the water filled with paddlers coming our way, their island home far behind in the distance.

"They're here!" Little Wave shouts as he drops what he's doing and sprints to the beach.

I count seven big boats with many paddlers. The women and younger children ride as passengers, the ladies acting as navigators pointing toward shore.

The People of Noqoto stream by me, running excitedly to the edge of water to greet them. The passengers crawl out of the tomols and I help others pull their boats up onto the beach. The tomols are very heavy, but our wood workers place rounded driftwood underneath the boats to help ease the burden. Their boats bear loads of trading commodities, baskets holding unknown goods, and stacks of sea otter and seal fur bundled up and serving as seats for steersmen.

On the beach, I seem to be the only outsider, as everyone appears to know everyone else. The women hug and laugh with the joy of old friends meeting again. The men shake hands and slap backs, sharing a story or two of their exploits. A few older kids and teenagers look around with wide eyes at their peers, adjusting to each other's growth and changing hormones.

Little Wave runs with his belly board under his arm to meet a friend. "What's that?" the island boy asks.

"I ride waves with it!" Little Wave proudly informs.

"Can I try?"

"Let me show you!"

Together, the boys carry the board to the water and leap in with the enthusiasm of kids with a new toy and sharing a new adventure.

The women get down to business, proudly displaying items of trade—clothing, jewelry, baskets, hats, food, and unique art pieces. As I walk by Alapay, she gestures for me to come over. "Wave Dancer, I want you to meet my dear friend, Limuw."

I reach out to shake the hand of an older woman with long graying hair, a wide smile and a lively twinkle in her eye—a beautiful reflection of her earlier years. "We are old friends growing wiser together. It is nice to meet you, Wave Dancer. Alapay was just telling me how you came to be here. You have found a very well respected tribal family. I hope you know how lucky you are."

"I feel very fortunate. You come from the islands?" I ask.

"Yes, a long boat journey away. I was once worried about that crossing, but after all these years, I now trust. You should visit us. We love to have visitors like you. We have some nice ladies looking for a man."

A nerve is struck in Alapay. "The latest member of our tribe will not be wandering so far so soon, Limuw."

"Maybe someday I'll visit."

"Perhaps you can catch a ride with a dolphin?" Limuw looks over at Alapay and winks. Alapay smiles and stands behind her story. "Alapay tells me you recently saw a very large boat filled with strange men. What do you know of them?"

"Spanish. I'm afraid there's many more coming your way."

"We too recently saw a large boat coming to our island village. Strange white men signed they wanted to trade for sealskins. The men smelled worse than dead seals rotting. When we refused to trade our skins, they became abusive. One of our women was dragged onto their boat. She escaped her captors by leaping into the sea."

Both women look at each other as Alapay gives a hug of support. "We are not safe anymore on our beautiful island world," Limuw says gravely.

"I am very afraid for the future of the People," Alapay responds, a note of sorrow in her otherwise graceful voice.

In the distance, a gathering of men around my surfboards indicates potential buyers. "Excuse me, I've got customers."

My display of surfboards against the base of a large fallen willow trunk has drawn a crowd of men. As I approach, I can see Kasmali acting like a salesman trying to explain what the strange wooden shapes are for. The men intently listen and study the boards, and I'm unnoticed as I join the crowd. Kasmali's sales pitch is something he had apparently practiced many times before with his own boats; he is drawing the men in with his enthusiasm. His land-based pantomime of my surfing display is rough and over-acted, but helps to get the point across.

Kasmali notices me in the back of the group. "Wave Dancer! Explain to the others what you do with a surf-board!"

All eyes are on me as I step up and face them. "I'm Wave Dancer, the newest member of the tribe. As you can hear from Kasmali, he's very excited about what you can do on a surfboard."

The men nod with obvious respect for the master boat builder.

"Allow me to show you what a surfboard can do. Please come with me." With a surfboard under my arm, I lead the curious toward the ocean. Once I get to the edge of the wet sand, I turn and look back at my audience, which now includes nearly the entire visiting tribe. Word had gotten out quickly once again, and I was ready to surf the demo model.

Small waves peel nicely near the mouth of the estuary, and the sandbank still in good shape. When a set wave comes in, I spin around and stroke into a head-high wave with little effort. The shallow bottom throws the wave into a nice speedy little barrel, daring me to stay in front of the whitewater. With a bottom turn and a stall to match speed, I pull into the mini tube and disappear from view of those on shore. As the wave slows, I throw in a hard cutback, changing directions, only to turn to race the wave again. Rising toward the lip of the wave, I crest the top into a free-falling floater, riding the whitewater to shore. For the grand finish, I step off onto the beach while grabbing my board in one move. Applause spreads through the rapt audience.

Haven't seen the shell currency yet, but I'm sure I just made the first sale, of the first surfboard, in the first surf shop in California.

CHAPTER 21

Privilege is bestowed on me when Paxa invites me into the sweat lodge to join the other men. Crawling through the small, covered entry, I'm immediately hit with hot, moist air filled with the potent scent of human sweat. Heated stones lay piled like a hot rock volcano in the center of the lodge; water splashed onto them issues eruptions of steam. A few animal oil lamps of shell send light dancing onto the walls of the earthen floor. The only fresh air comes through an adjustable vent in the roof that keeps most of the warmth in, but provides enough fresh air to breathe.

I sit beside the other men on low driftwood benches. Sweat begins to bead up as my body adjusts its thermostat. All is peacefully quiet. Closing my eyes, I allow the heat to sink deep into muscles, I relax and let the hot steam do its therapy.

A tapping on my side brings my eyes open in response. Yaqi hands me a smoking pipe carved into the shape of a snake, the burning bowl its mouth, which is darkened by much use. Rising from the pipe is sweet smoke. I inhale lightly and the mouth glows like a fire-breathing snake. I exhale, take in a bigger puff and pass the pipe on. My lungs are at their limit, and I burst into a loud coughing fit. Everyone stares as I disturb the former peace.

Kindly diverting attention away from me, Paxa turns to the island elder sitting next to him and asks, "How is life on your island?"

"Hunters in large boats keep coming. When these white men arrive, we live in fear."

Heads turn as the impassioned shaman Isqua rises to his feet. "These invading white men will keep coming! Let us join our warriors together and force them from our traditional lands!"

Paxa responds with calm, measured words. "We are peaceful people."

"I've seen our futures in Dream Walks. If we fail to drive these white men away, we will never have another chance. Now is the time, or it will be too late to turn them back! We will die!"

"Are you willing to die for what you see in your visions, Isqua?" Paxa asks.

"I will not sit here like a frail elder and let them destroy our lives!"

"Any man you kill will bring more to kill us. You see the wisdom of this, frail elder?"

"I don't fear white men. Without their cows, they would die of starvation in our abundant land. Without them forcing our people to do the hard work they are too lazy to do, their missions would not stand. Only their guns give them power."

Many of the men nod in agreement. A murmur begins and rises to a chorus until Isqua raises his hand to speak again. "Wave Dancer, you Dream Walk. What do you know of our future?"

The men look at me, awaiting my words. Quiet hangs as thick as the hot humid air around me. My head is spinning from the pipe's contents and the intense heat. And then, the smoke in my mind clears. I'm here as a Dream Walking avatar to warn them!

None of the men move as they stare at me, concern lining their faces. I break the silent questions hanging over their heads. "Here is what I see in my Dream Walks of the future. I'm not going to hold back.

You're just now getting a glimpse of the first waves of the Spanish who seek to control your land. They send Franciscan missionaries to manage the building of their mission basecamps, under the guise of Catholic conversion of the Natives, backed up by many soldiers with weapons. These men come to establish the mission operations, forcing local Native labor to build the buildings and support the food and goods production. But their real goal is to claim the land as theirs, to plunder natural assets and fill the treasure vaults of the King of Spain. Treasures gained at your expense, held under the barrel of a gun. Even if you stop the Spanish now, years later the Mexicans come north and claim your lands as their own. They conquer California and sweep over the few struggling Natives still clinging to what's left of their traditional ways. The Mexicans give massive land grants to their own elite, creating private land with their paper laws of ownership. Not long after, another human tide rushes in, searching for California gold. Stopping men with gold fever is futile! They want the gold! You're in the way! And in a cruel twist, you'll be lucky to survive all the new diseases they bring—venereal, small pox, flu, measles, and the common cold. Just when you thought it couldn't get worse, they'll drive in silver spikes and connect train rails across the continent. Then more masses of people will flood into California by steam train from across America! Isqua is right about what he sees in his Dream Walks. In only one generation, tribes of Natives like you will wither away, leaving only scarce pockets of scattered souls, the survivors without land to call their own. As a minor concession, the United States Government will eventually grant the desperate few Natives some spare bones of land. They call them Indian Reservations. I live on one, or I did live on one."

I take a deep breath of sweaty hot air while scanning the incredulous faces staring at me. Then it dawns on me—there's an upside to the downslide. "But there could be silver linings for our tribe's future. A few days walk up the coast from here stands Mission San Jose. Somehow, someway, acquire as much land around San Jose as you possibly can. In the future, it will become a place called Silicon Valley and fortunes will be made there. Put this into our tribal lore. Write it in stone. Mark my word, there will come a time of opportunity for positive change for our People. Play your future moves right, and the tribe can buy all of Rocky Point back, and much more of our traditional lands in California!"

I grow weak in the knees as I stand up too quickly. Sweat drips into my eyes as I sway in one place. Dizzy, hot, stoned on who-knows-what, my lights go out.

When I awaken, I'm on my back looking up at a circle of concerned men staring down on me. Yaqi clears them all back, and reaches for a gourd being offered. He holds it above me, tips it with a smile and I watch a small waterfall hit me between my eyes.

"You are a freak," Yaqi confirms for the nodding audience.

The heavy flap closes behind me as the cold night air rushes against my hot sweaty body. Moonlight leads the way to the ocean's calming waters. I stand on the beach at water's edge, looking up into the cosmos, knowing what will come. I dive into the shore break, staying under cool water until I have no more breath.

The refraction of the moonlight on the glittering surface of the water dances in my eyes. I dip below the water again and open my eyes to see the moon that shines down through clear water. A small school of baitfish cruises by, leaving well-lit phosphorescent trails. Bubbles of air float toward the moon, their round floating orbs bursting at the surface.

I stroke toward the shore. Light from a distant bonfire in the village calls me to the comforting warmth of The People of Noqoto and the visiting islanders, whose world and traditions are about to change forever.

CHAPTER 22

Yaqi's intense energy forces my eyes open. With an excited low whisper he impatiently calls me to attention, "Wave Dancer, we hunt!"

Crawling to the door of the hut with my blanket still around me, I peer out at a grin that glows in near darkness.

"Hunt? Kill something?"

We are barely out of the village when Yaqi breaks into a double-time trot. I have no choice but to mimic his speed or I'll be left behind.

Early morning sun is on the rise, lighting up the natural world around us in rich colors. Birds call to one another announcing our presence, or ignore us and keep singing their songs. We follow a narrow trail at the foot of the mountains as it folds around undulating shapes of the land. Morning mist sinks down the valleys, meeting at the bottom of the canyons, leaving the oaks standing like ghostly creatures enshrouded by dense fog. Armed with bow, arrows and spear, I'm on the hunt to kill what I still don't know.

Up ahead the trail forks, and I pick up my pace to make sure I'm on Yaqi's bare heels. When he reaches the fork splitting our path, he freezes and gestures for me to follow him and take cover behind the trunk of a broad oak. I can hear something coming our way through thick mist as the earth vibrates with the footfalls. My heart races in anticipation of what's to come as the creature approaches. Yaqi silently places an arrow to his bow.

Down the trail, the ghostly shape of a Native man appears in the mist. Yaqi puts his bow down and steps out approaching one of The People.

"Peace, brother. Where are you from?"

"Peace, brother. The Mission. You would not believe what I have seen!"

"I have seen."

"But have you seen these?" The man reaches into a satchel and pulls out a handful of bright, shiny, glass beads looking like a brilliant rainbow of almost every color. "Look at the colors! I think they are more valuable than any shells!"

"You are a fool! Tell your people never go near the Mission!" Yaqi warns.

"You are the fool. With these beads I can trade for everything I want."

Yaqi knocks the satchel from the bewildered man's hand and pushes him to the ground with a forceful shove. The colorful glass beads spill to the earth as the visitor rolls with the shove, smoothly leaping to his feet to defend himself. Yaqi faces him, a force to be reckoned with. Both have tense hands on sheathed knives ready to draw.

"Tell your tribe to never go to the Mission!"

The man staggers a step back, turns and scoops up a meager handful of beads as he flees into the woods.

Yaqi angrily kicks a hole in the soil, grabs the remains of the bag and throws the beads in. With a final sweep of his foot, Mission bait disappears into the earth.

"Bury them deeper," I suggest.

"He will bring his People death." Yaqi concludes.

The long silence of Yaqi's contemplation ends, his face a reflection of the deep inner scars of his encounter with the Mission.

Faced once again with a choice of which fork in the trail to follow, I assume Yaqi will lead, but he stands without moving. "Which way?" I ask.

"You choose."

I close my eyes, open them, and point to the right hand trail. "That one?"

"No."

"The other one?"

"No."

"Back the way we came?"

"No, we split. You go one way, I'll go the other. Both canyons lead to the ridgeline. When you can climb no higher, head my way and we'll meet. Stay on the ridge."

"Why are we splitting up?"

"Animals will flee toward me when they hear you."

"What if I can't find you?"

"I'll find you."

At a loping coyote pace, he disappears up the trail, following the left fork in the canyon. I hustle across the creek up the opposite fork.

The canyon narrows quickly, the creek tumbling over rocks squeezed between small cliff bands blocking my way. If there are any deer around, I remain ignorant of them as I keep my eyes locked on small handholds and footholds. Getting too close to the creek is a mistake as the mist makes the rocks slimy and slick. Farther up, the creek narrows until it disappears entirely along with anything resembling a trail. The brush grows thicker and tighter, reaching out and grabbing any appendage that presents itself. It's a bush thrash, I'm being swallowed in living obstacles and, as Yaqi predicted, making a lot of noise.

Untangling myself near the top of the ridge, I finally get a good view of the expansive ridgeline in front of me. Much easier cruising on the exposed crest amongst the windblown, low -lying shrub. I gaze down the ridgeline and see in the distance where the left fork meets the ridge. Sprinkled along the crest are speckled grey granite outcroppings looking like old man's worn gap teeth; weather-twisted oaks and Monterey pines are stuffed in the crevices, clinging to survive.

I clamber up onto a large chunk of rock sticking out like a monolith, and sit down, tired legs dangling over the edge into the rising wave of warming air. Dense fog works its way up from the ocean filling the canyons below me like a river in reverse, flowing with damp gray mist. The rolling sea of clouds like a soft blanket below me, the bright morning sun above bathing me in warmth, I lie back on the cool rock and adjust my bed roll for a pillow. Deep-blue sky looks down on me, a fading moon bidding good-bye to the new day. Quiet envelopes me. Calm, no wind, not even a bird to be heard. My mind meditates on the peacefulness all around me. I close my eyes.

Like a soaring bird, now I am looking down on my body lying on the rock. I soar above the earth and fly down the crest looking for Yaqi. I spot him below, sitting cross-legged on a rocky ledge, meditating with eyes closed. Next to him, a lone sun-bleached skeleton of an ancient oak clings precariously to the cliff.

My eyes open, I'm back anchored to the earth on my rocky perch. Father Sky looks down on me. But who am I? Peter? Dream Walker? Wave Dancer?

Working my way carefully across to the crest, I find the same twisted oak of my Dream Walk, the rock outcropping familiar. I climb up the vertical rock face with a few critical moves and peer over the edge. Yaqi sits cross-legged on the granite shelf with his eyes closed in meditation. Rays of morning sunlight burst through the branches of the twisted oak alighting him.

Without opening his eyes, he speaks. "Wave Dancer."

"Any deer come?" I inquire meekly.

"A herd."

"I wasn't that loud ... was I?"

I clamber up to stand upon a high point in the coastal mountains pushed up by great forces of Mother Earth. Beyond diminishing hills in the distance, inland valleys lead to the great central valley visible in the flats, the dense green of the floodplain not yet divided by geometric grids of drainage canals, dams, aqueducts, powerlines, roads, towns, cities, factories, fences, and farms. In the far distance, beyond the lushness of the valley, the jagged mountains of the Sierra Nevada range still hold a mantle of white winter snow.

I struggle to express what I see. Only one word finds its way from my mouth. "Beautiful."

"Worthy of a prayer to Mother Earth," Yaqi says.

We both bow our heads in silence. The blessings of life we share not taken for granted, a gift of life, an appreciation for the miracle of Mother Earth surrounding us.

"Where to?" I ask, breaking the sacred silence.

Yaqi stands, turns and points down to a meadow in a clearing below us. "We will work our way down to the edge of the grass, and wait in hiding until dark. Deer party."

Looking down at the meadow, I doubt my commitment to take a life. I had a go at archery practice with Grandfather behind his house, aiming at a hay bale. I later shot a rabbit and truly wished I hadn't.

Cautiously peering over the edge of the vertical rock band, I try to get a bearing on the route we'll be taking to reach the meadow below. There's no trail in sight and the terrain looks steep.

"I brought you to this peak so you can see clearly, like the hawk soaring."

"This is an awesome place, huge views. Worth the climb to see it all. I need water soon."

"Below is the sacred spring."

It's as if he can smell the water of the spring. Visually, there are no clues to its location until we creep through a challenging wall of bushes and come to a lush clearing. There, the breeze carries comforting sounds of running water. Coolness envelops me as we break out of thick vegetation into an oasis of spring water cascading down the rock face into a rippled pool below. A miniature garden of green ferns and bright colorful flowers clings to the soft mossy face. The pure notes of water falling into the pool below are music to my thirst.

Clear, cool water tumbles from the side of the cliff, almost at the underground source of its journey from land to sea. I drink in the sweetness long and hard until I can drink no more. "That was the best water I've ever had," I say as I splash some on my face.

"Not many know of this place, it is sacred." Yaqi takes a moment, deep in thought.

He leads me away from the coolness of the grotto up a rough game trail. We head steadily toward a large mass of rocky crags above the spring. Sweating once again, we work our way closer to the dark, shadowy entrance in a cleft of the cliff face. Yaqi disappears into the dark of the crack, seemingly swallowed by rock. I peer into the darkness until my eyes adjust and I can see the dim outline of his body. Entering the chamber reveals a natural stone cathedral filled with pictographs, the swirling patterns of circular shapes like starbursts surrounded by the abstract paintings of inner journeys. Yaqi reaches up with his hand and holds it on the tracing of another hand from long ago.

"I touch another," he says.

"The artist touched you with his soul."

"The dust of the Old Ones lies deep."

Yaqi dips his hand into a pouch at his waist and produces a smaller pouch along with a deer-hair brush. Emptying some of the contents on the rocky floor, he spits into the dark, dusty powder in his palm and mixes it with his finger until it's the consistency of thick paint. "We leave our totem signs."

I watch him carefully trace an outline of an Orca figure and fill in the blanks with a dark color.

He hands me his brush. I pause. Slowly I reach over and dab the brush in the paint. My drawing takes shape as I fill in the outline of a leaping dolphin, leaving behind my totem sign. Not quite done, I draw an outline of an apple, minus a bite. A symbol of temptation, and perhaps a hint of future investing.

We make our way back to the spring for a final drink before working our way down to the meadow. The wind calms and the water turns sleek as a mirror. I come closer to the water's edge, pulled in by the reflective surface drawing me in. At the edge of the pool, a white petal reflection of the Moonflower calls out.

"Moonflower, the Spirit Guide," Yaqi's voice breaks the silence.

"Spirit Guide?"

"Are you ready for Moonflower?"

"I'm not sure what you mean."

"For the Spirit Journey with Moonflower," Yaqi answers with intensity in his eyes.

"I'll pass for now, I've been tripping since I got here."

Dropping down in elevation, we approach the outskirts of the meadow, finding many deer tracks in the dust at our feet. More moderate going and the terrain opens up, and the evergreen scent of pine prevails. Wind-strewn needles carpet the ground, mixed with cones tossed here and there. Yaqi reaches out for a green branch and grabs a handful of fresh pine needles, puts a wad his hands and rolls them together. Rubbing them all around his body, the aroma of the pungent pine scent takes over.

I follow his motions, rubbing my own wad of needles together, stroking them on my skin as a gust of wind sends the pine boughs waving. Yaqi observes its direction carefully. "We need to be down wind. Follow my steps, quietly."

With me two steps behind, I intently follow his every move, concentrating on seeing and feeling everything beneath me to keep from making a sound. We descend down toward the meadow as the sun disappears behind the ridge and leaves us in growing shadow. Yaqi stops in front of me, looking down where two deer trails cross. Kneeling close to the earth, he reads the tracks. Rising slowly, he looks at our surroundings until he swings around.

In a low whisper, Yaqi directs, "Fresh tracks, headed to the meadow, we walk downwind to the far end and wait in hiding. We will not be alone."

"Not alone?" I whisper back.

"Another hunter."

He takes a few steps ahead and points down to another unmistakable track, that of a large cat walking the same direction as us. I kneel close to the predator's very impressive calling card; a lump grows in my throat followed by streams of adrenalin rippling through my body. My handprint is no contest. Although I try to whisper, my words sound like I'm just breaking puberty.

"That's a big mountain lion!"

"Shhh," Yaqi hisses sharply.

"Sorry."

"I watch ahead, you watch behind," he calmly directs.

Watching our backs, trying to keep quiet and trying not to lose sight of Yaqi becomes all consuming. Once we reach the meadow and pull in behind a large oak, I relax, knowing our backs are covered by thick wood. Yaqi crouches down on his haunches and signals this is where we will wait. From this angle, much of the meadow can be seen with just a slight peek around the oak. Yaqi readies his bow and arrows. I follow his example, but struggle as images of a large cat quietly sneaking up behind us cloud my mind.

A tug at my arm shakes me from my mountain lion doom-focused contemplation. Following Yaqi's line of sight across the meadow, I see what has caught his attention. A deer with prong antlers steps into the clearing, cautiously looking around before lowering its head to graze. Appearing like dark stealthy shadows, others cautiously appear, graceful females, larger males, and spotted fawns with anxious eyes peering out from behind protective mothers. Patiently directed by Yaqi, we let the herd settle into concentrated foraging. They slowly work their way our direction, closing the gap between us, increasing our odds of a kill shot.

Yaqi gestures for me to load the arrow. My heart races as I try to stay calm. He lowers himself down to the height of the grass and I follow his lead. In what becomes an unspoken conversation between us, we work together. Our wooden bows strain taunt against the tension of the stretched sinew. My sights are set on a pronghorn standing to the side of the herd. I strain to stay steady and focus my whole being into sending the arrow straight to the heart of the animal. As I aim the arrow, I give respect for the life I'm hoping to end. I release and my arrow cuts through the air at the same moment as Yaqi lets his arrow fly.

Yaqi's shot hits true, his animal drops. My shot hits low, only wounding the animal. A sickening struggle to live ensues. I quickly ready another arrow, but before I can fire again, another arrow finds its mark sending the animal tumbling to the ground. Yaqi springs up and races to the fallen deer while drawing his knife from its sheath.

Pulling up next to him, my heart is pounding in my chest with primal instincts. With Spanish knife at the ready, Yaqi stands looking down as life fades from its brown eyes.

"Thank you, brother deer, for the gift of your life so that we may live." He kneels down and cuts deep into the throat of the dying animal, stands back and watches dark blood pouring into the earth.

"Wave Dancer, finish your kill," he instructs me out of respect for the animal.

I make my way to the deer, still struggling to live as it lies on the grass. Blood dribbles from one of the arrows, my arrow sticks out of the animal with little sign of blood. I look down into its eyes and it stops struggling, as if knowing the outcome. I pull my obsidian knife from its sheath, tears filled with emotion spill for the death of this beautiful creature.

"Thank you, brother deer, for the gift of your life so that others may live." I mimic Yaqi's motion with the knife, cut deep and watch life fade from the eyes. With a final shudder, the lovely animal moves no more.

I sense the stalker is being stalked, I swing around to see the outline of a snarling mountain lion coming my way in a low crouch, the predatory eyes locked on the deer, then shifting to me.

From somewhere deep within, my fear is replaced by courage as I rise up high with my arms filled with weapons stretching into the air. I shatter the quiet with a primal scream, which echoes back at me off the canyon walls. The cat spooks, looks nervously around and sprints away across the meadow. I quickly spin with the sound of a breaking branch.

Yaqi smiles his glowing grin. "Where did you find such a wild cry?"

"I have no idea."

Looking back down at the deer at my feet, remorse comes flooding. "I blew my shot."

"We work as a team."

"I wanted a clean kill."

"It is in the past. Getting late, we must gut these deer."

"Sorry, you have to do it. I haven't a clue, my meat came pre-wrapped."

In the fading light, Yaqi makes precise cuts to lay open the deer exposing the entrails as he goes. He works his way through the skin, the incision from back to front, his finger delicately between the blade and the skin cutting near the stomach. Working from the groin to the throat takes him no time as darkness continues to gather around. Reaching into the animal with both hands he pulls out the contents of the entire cavity, the deer now free of internal organs. He stands up with hands like a surgeon, looking at me like I'm some sort of orderly. "Help me get this one hung, then I go for the other."

The animal is fresh-kill-warm as we drag it to the side of the meadow towards a sprinkling of boulders. Yaqi makes a cut behind tendons in the knee joint and finds a nearby branch big enough to support its weight. Stringing the branch through the cut, we both pick up each end of the pole and carry it toward two stout trees. Yaqi pulls a cord from his bag and wraps it to his end of the pole. Throwing the rope over an overhead branch, he then gives tension to the line and starts pulling until he can prop the end of the pole into the high cross-section of the branch. He repeats the steps on my end until the deer is hanging out of reach.

Working our way back to the other deer in the near darkness, I flash on the sight of the mountain lion still lingering in my mind. My eyes grow wide as an owl looking for any available light to fill panicked pupils.

Thankfully, the field dressing of the deer is complete with Yaqi's great efforts. He is truly one with the land. Even in the dark, fire comes with his skillful spinning of the fire starter. Yaqi soon has flames of burning oak warming our bodies and cooking our meal of venison. My contribution is modern-man-minimal.

"In time, most people won't know how to make a fire as you've just done. The fire comes easy with a simple flick of a switch, lighter or a match," I comment.

"What other magic do you see in your Dream Walks?"

I'm punchy with exhaustion, so I let it fly. "Well, where do I begin? How about right here? Tonight we sit under the stars watching the flames of a wood fire dancing above the glowing coals cooking our freshly killed deer we hunted with bows and arrows made from natural materials. Hundreds of years in the future, a modern man hunts a pre-packaged frozen meal that comes from food raised on corporate farms. The water to grow the food comes from dams, aqueducts, pipes and electric pumps. The meal features chicken produced in conditions no living thing should endure, fed corn that is grown from genetically-altered seeds, raised in soil fertilized with chemical nitrates. There's a sparse sprinkling of vegetables to accompany the dish. Those vegetables are trucked cross-country to the food-processing factory to be mass-manufactured with the machine-plucked chicken. Flash-frozen in industrial grade freezers to be shipped cold store by eighteen-wheel refrigerated truck hundreds of miles to a distribution hub. Shipped once again to a supermarket hundreds of miles away. In the supermarket, the pre-packaged meal is placed in a rolling steel cart by the modern guy who takes it to the self-check counter and swipes his loyalty card adding to the digital database of his spending habits. He pays with a credit card using unseen electronic money loaned at high interest by banks that borrow the loaned money at much lower interest from The Federal Reserve, which is a private banking cartel that loans money created out of banking-thin-air. What a deal! He drives the frozen meal home rolling down fracking-induced oil-paved roads in a car manufactured from a Japanese company that assembles the car in a factory they own in America, using American labor. He drives home in his personal transport device, burning of fossil fuels spewing carbon into the atmosphere and choking off the life of the planet. Not thinking long-term, he adjusts the air conditioning for comfort and increases his speed with slight movements of his foot on the accelerator. His left hand casually taps to music played by unseen musicians recorded in a mixing studio manipulating sounds that play across the whole world. He arrives in his driveway and opens the garage with press of his soft, pasty-white finger on the remote. He steps into the kitchen, removes the packaging on his frozen meal and sets the timer on the microwave as it cooks creepily with mysterious bouncing molecules driven by unseen electrons created by a power generation plant hundreds of miles away that burns fossil fuel and spew carbon into the night sky. Like magic the food heats in less than three minutes. He sits down to eat his dinner in front of his favorite electronic entertainment." I take in a big breath.

Yaqi looks at me as if I've totally lost it. "You are a freak."

"Yes, you are freaking right I'm a freak. A Dream Walking freak!" I confirm.

Back to the scene in front of me, the granite boulders make a nice hearth with the heat reflecting from the rocks giving us comforting warmth. The deer from the hunt hang near the edges of our circle of light. Large piles of dry pine needles are the bed calling to me after a day filled with adventure from sun up to sun down.

Savoring the taste of the cooked meat, I fight back the urge to eat too fast. My hunger is telling me otherwise, but I won't let it win as I savor each bite with a blessing for the life I had helped take so that we can survive.

"If it weren't for you, the deer I wounded would have suffered."

"Your arrow will fly true, someday."

Maybe I didn't have it in me to be a hunter. Maybe it was something that has faded away from my connection to my ancestral past, and I would never learn to kill. Staring into the flames, I wonder if I'd ever have it in me to kill men as Isqua was intent on doing to oust the Spanish occupiers at the Mission.

"Isqua speaks of killing men. Do you, Yaqi?"

"I do not hunt men."

"But men hunt you."

"How do you know?"

"You killed a Spaniard at the Mission."

"White man's weapons make it easy to kill. I want guns, not rainbow Mission beads."

"Guns are just the beginning of weapons you cannot imagine."

"In Dream Walks?"

"It is insanity you don't want to know."

"I do."

"There will be nuclear weapons with the power to end all human life."

"How?" Yaqi asks.

"Ironically, it's called MAD, short for Mutually Assured Destruction."

"I do not understand."

"That makes two of us."

I pick up a small stone and toss it in the fire, sending sparks floating up from the flames driven by the rising heat into the night filled with an enormous sky of brilliant stars. The glowing embers dance with the light of the universe until drifting into blackness.

"I'm done for the night, I'm exhausted," I say with half-closed eyes.

I lie back in my bedroll and stare up at the night sky until sleep takes over without any argument. Suddenly, my deep sleep is disturbed as an earthquake enters my dream. Yaqi shouts and shakes my shoulder. "Bear!"

Opening my eyes, dwindling flames give enough light to see a huge grizzly bear standing on its hind legs as it reaches up for the hanging deer. Yaqi's cry of warning calls its attention to us, and it flashes a menacing display of teeth ready to defend its next meal. Leaping up, I scramble for my meager weapons, which are long steps away.

Yaqi lunges for his bow and arrows, looking very small against the massive beast. The bear goes for him with surprising speed, not giving him a chance to get to his bow. Leaping away from the bear, he lunges forward to scramble up boulders. No handholds to be found, he slips down to the ground.

I grab the closest weapon I can find, the sharpened wooden pole that once held our dinner. I spin around toward the huge bear as it closes in on Yaqi. My primal scream echoes across the canyon as the beast turns to face me. I raise the pole high into the air as calm confidence replaces fear. The king of the animal food chain rises up on hind legs and shows every bit of teeth and claws.

Calling my bluff, the bear lunges after me closing the gap in a fraction of time. I quickly jam the end of my makeshift spear in the ground and crouch down low with the sharp end pointing toward the massive hairy chest rapidly closing in on the small human cowering before the mighty beast. Its outstretched daggers of claws and a mouth full of fearsome fangs fly at me as I hold the spear tightly aimed at its flexing chest muscles.

The bear's momentum is powered by pure brute strength and its massive bulk drives the spear deep into its chest. The bear stops in its tracks with a sickening howl as I spin away and scramble to flee from beneath it. It rises once again onto hind legs and stands tall for a moment, the spear stuck deep. Blood pours rhythmically with each beat of the heart. Mortally wounded, the great animal drops to the ground in front of me with an earth-shaking thud.

After a few tense moments, Yaqi joins me as we slowly approach the animal with spears ready for any signs of life. The great bear takes its last breath of life and moves no more. I drop to my knees, no longer able to stand, overwhelmed with the taking the life of such an animal.

"You give me back my life," Yaqi says, while reaching out to grasp my hand.

Shakily, I return to the fire and toss in more wood to feed the dwindling flame. Sleep is a lost cause as I have adrenalin flowing to keep me up for a long time.

"I didn't want to kill it," I comment.

"You didn't have a choice."

"Guess not."

"We are brothers now, Wave Dancer."

Wood on the fire helps to warm the outside of my body and the brotherly blessing from Yaqi warms me inside. Looking over at the furry mountain that was once a living bear, I scan across to the hanging deer.

"How are we going to haul all this back to the village?" I ask.

"You are now a man of great honor having killed the mighty bear, the protector of the land. You will carry none of the burden."

"I can carry some of it."

"You will not. At first light I will run back to get the help of others. You go to where I showed you the spring. Now is the time for you to seek your Spirit Guide."

"Spirit Guide?"

"Your heart is filled with many questions only the Spirit Guide can answer."

"True, much of my life is still a mystery."

"The Creator is the Great Mystery."

"The Great Mystery?"

"The Great Mystery is the Creator."

"You speak in circles."

"Life moves in circles, like the soaring hawk, the changing seasons, the passing moon, the changing tide."

"Sometimes it's hard to see clearly."

"The Spirit Guide will show you the truth. Time?"

I look deep within the well of my soul. "Yes," I affirm.

"You must go within." Yaqi draws from his pouch a small package wrapped in leaves. Unfolding it in front of me, he reveals the pressed white of Moonflower fading in the light.

"The Moonflower, a gift from me, as it should be. Take this with you to the sacred water of the spring and when you are ready, swallow it with a long drink of water. Soon you will follow your Spirit Guide down the path to understanding."

"Thank you for all you've shown me." Serenity fills me as we watch the new flames dance from the glowing embers.

"You must travel with your guardian totem animal."

"A long way inland."

"The tattoo of a dolphin I will create for you."

When I awake at first light, Yaqi is gone and the dwindling swirling smoke of the fire twists into cool damp air.

The fresh tattoo on the back of my shoulder throbs with a pulse of its own. Stiff and sore, I pry myself up and walk around camp and cautiously making my way to the massive hulk of the bear. In the light of day, it's even more fearsome. Huge claws stretch out from massive feet attached to more pure muscle than I'd ever seen. I fear it as it lies dead. Approaching the once mighty animal, I kneel down close to its head and the dense smell almost overwhelms me when I pull back the mouth to reveal huge teeth. Tragically, this mighty species of Grizzly bear will not survive the California of the future. And I helped its demise.

Gathering my gear from camp and bundling it together, I take a final look back to see what's left behind. With very little in my possession, I'm treading lightly on the land. Grandfather would be proud.

CHAPTER 23

Familiar landmarks are few until I spot the rock outcropping on the ridgeline. Clambering through dense growth, I descend to where my natural instincts lead me. The well-hidden grotto reveals itself through a gap in the trees, the falling water sounding like familiar notes of a song.

Sitting at the edge of the pool, I place my hand on the gift of Moonflower. Gently unfolding the package, I hold the flower in my hand, close my eyes and place it in my mouth. The taste is bitter. I chew until it is mush and then swallow it down. I rise and lean against the rocky face, drinking deeply from the trickle falling past my lips. The water is sweet and soon erases the taste of the bitter flower.

High above me, the rock outcropping with the twisted old oak beckons. The higher my body climbs toward the summit, the higher my spirit climbs as the Moonflower rises up in me. As I stand on top of the rocky shelf, a smile of blissful joy grows on my face. From this promontory, everything below becomes indistinct, as if painted by the wide sweeps of an Impressionist's brush. This is where Spirit Guide and I will take our journey together. Sitting down in the shadow of the old twisted oak, I cross my legs and face toward the sea.

Shut-eyed in quiet meditation with deep breathing of life-force air, I close the curtain to one stage of being, opening my mind to the infinite universe.

In my Dream Walk, I enter a widening cave filled with pictograph drawings from the ancient Old Ones, my ancestors. I see the visions of the artist's eye in their creation, and I'm entering their spirit world. Dancing pictograph animal totems and sacred symbols float around me, spinning together in cosmic concert like the stars and planets orbiting in the night sky.

A powerful rush of love rises up in me. Love for my tribe. Love for friends and family. Love for Mother Earth. Love of peace. Love for Yaqi. Love for Talkitna. Love for myself. Tears of joy pour out of me in pure streams of emotion.

I open my eyes and look up at the blue sky; a white cloud floats directly overhead. I close my eyes once more. Like the cloud, I see from above, looking down on me sitting on this rocky perch. My body is earthbound, but my mind is traveling like a great bird soaring across the sky. Down the ridge at my side is a hovering golden eagle, feathers ruffling as it soars on the wind. The eagle turns an eye to me, acknowledging my presence. My vision is now like his, the ground takes on frightening detail as I see all that the mighty flying hunter sees. A clarity I've never seen, colors brighter and intense, each leaf alive with veins of green life, individual blades of grass stand distinctly as the wind stirs them, bees gather sticky pollen, a snake slithers into a dark hole in the ground. A gust of wind sends oak leaves soaring, until they float gently down.

Banking towards the sea, a brilliant sunset bursts in a kaleidoscope of color. The sun's rays peek through gaps in the clouds, and one brilliant beam aims directly at me. The surface of the ocean shimmers in the fading twilight of a palette of red-orange colors giving way to night.

In the dim light, the village of Noqoto appears below me. Members of my tribe walk toward the fire— a gathering of my ancestors. On the beach across the lagoon, a lone woman walks at the edge of the sea. She pauses, looks up to the twilight sky, connecting with no words spoken. Talkitna returns her gaze to the moon rising.

In the far distance, the dark, jagged edge of a mountain calls to me as I soar across a broad valley to the next ridge. Rising on a warm thermal, I climb higher as I approach the rocky peak. Cresting the silhouette of the summit, I just skim the tops of the rocks. Glowing in the distance through a hazy horizon, an inland sea of lights stretches out as far as I can see, the man-made grid of modern lights of the City of Angels, Los Angeles. I pick up speed as I descend toward the bright lights like a moth drawn to flame. Slow moving rivers of red and white lights pulse in starts and stops along paved roads leading to orderly, linear, geometric subdivisions. I look down into windows of homes and see more than I want to know. I turn away.

I soar closer to a steel and glass cluster of high-rises buildings, the downtown civic center pulsing with man-made light at the end of the electricity grid. Above me are no stars to be seen; they are lost in the night sky flooded with artificial light glowing in a dense urban haze. I rise higher and see in the distance the glow of the HOLLYWOOD sign on a ridgeline looming over an audience.

At the edge of the sprawling lights, I steer toward the darkness at the meeting place of land and sea. Looking down far below at Los Angeles International Airport reveals planes on the tarmac heading toward waiting gates. At the ends of long, bright runways, planes line up, anxiously burning their fossil fuels. The gunning of jet engines sends a long-winged, pressurized tube full of humans up into airborne highways.

Down to the edge of blackness I dive like a falcon toward lights cutting across the sand on the beach like a brightly lit ruler. A smell of the sea mixes with the scent of industrialized man. Expanding below me, a sprawling petrochemical plant stands as a monument to man's addiction to oil. Lit up like day, a mysterious maze of twisting pipes goes every which way. Neat rows of petrol storage tanks surround tall stacks spewing disguised acrid smoke into night air. I pass between the choking smoke stacks, holding my breath and closing my eyes to the dose of toxic waste. I soar on into darkness.

As my eyes open, warmth comes streaming back into my physical body. The new day's sun ascends from the horizon, striking me with its golden beams. Birds sing out in their joy to be alive. Where I sit is cool and comforting, grounding me to my Mother Earth. I'm physically in the same place I started my inward spiritual journey, near the curling branches of the weatherworn oak. My body is stiff, my mind wide awake as I rise to greet the morning. I stretch out in yoga, lean back in pose and look to the cosmos. I breathe deeply. My surroundings begin to cloud up in a watery haze. A flow of tears wells to the surface, sorrow for my tribe's impending genocide. From deep within my soul, a cry rises into depression. A lone tear breaks free of my face and falls towards Mother Earth, landing on the granite.

I make my way back to the precious spring to drink deeply again. Splashing the cool water on my body reminds me of the simple pleasures that make life wonderful. I sit in the cool shade of the grotto feeling blissful again. Looking up at the cascading water, a gust of wind sends it swirling into a misty rainbow and wraps around me in a cool, colorful cloud.

I'm alone, hungry without a desire to eat, tired with no desire to sleep, my mind wide open to all my Spirit Guide has revealed. I take time to savor the lessons.

I shift to the very edge of the calm pool of water. My reflection in the mirrored water looks back with clear eyes. I see deep within my soul to the heart of my truth.

CHAPTER 24

With a deep breath, I say goodbye to the sanctuary of the grotto. I step away from the shelter of life-giving water and know there is no turning back from my spiritual journey.

The meager path soon gives way to the main trail well worn with the tracks of The People headed back to Rocky Point carrying the bounty of the hunt. I'm ready to come back to join the tribal fold of the villagers of Noqoto, a place I feel at home.

The first person I see is Little Wave in the distance, with his friends hunting on the fringes of the oak grove, their gazes locked on the branches above. I give a bird whistle. All eyes turn to me. They charge down the trail with bows slung over their shoulders and dead squirrels whipping around wildly, tails gripped in the boys' hands. My best little friend races ahead of the others, skids to a stop in front of me and gushes his greeting.

"Wave Dancer, you return!" he cries out.

"How are the mighty hunters?" I ask, with a glance down at the small prey.

"Not as mighty as you! What a bear! Were you scared?"

"It's good to understand fear," I say from experience.

"We will tell the tribe!" The young hunters are gone in puffs of dust.

Yaqi is the next one I see, smiles growing on both our faces as we approach each other on the trail. He reaches out to grasp my hand as we stand eye to eye.

"Your journey?"

"Rewarding"

"You saw the Great Mystery?"

"I witnessed the Great Mystery."

"Good to have you back in the village, brother Wave Dancer."

"Brother Yaqi, I thank you for the dolphin tattoo."

Behind him the village filters through the curving willow branch tunnel, and it is obvious that the news of my return delivered by the speedy young messengers has spread rapidly.

"There will be a feast and celebration in your honor tonight. Very few men have taken the life of a great bear with only a green spear of wood," Yaqi says with a serious look as he motions me to lead the way.

On the outskirts of the village, The People of Noqoto gather in front of me. What starts as a few hands clapping grows into a loud ovation. The tribe shifts to line up on both sides of the trail, all eyes on me as I approach. Yaqi steps to the front of the chain as I pause to take in the hallway of humans and all the grateful attention directed at me. I give a humble bow. Yaqi turns to me and, with a gesture, indicates I should enter the corridor. I'm not quite sure what to expect. He raises his hand high in the air as others follow, making a line of outstretched arms across the human hallway.

I raise both my hands, step forward, and give adjusting degrees of high-fives to each of The People as I walk toward the village, my smile returned in kind with bursts of thanks.

The best comes last as Talkitna gives me a slow motion, double high-five as our eyes lock. "Welcome back to me, Wave Dancer."

"Good to be here with you," I answer very honestly.

"Big celebration in your honor tonight."

She shyly turns her head away. I turn back and look to the long line of faces, an abundance of knowing, beaming smiles.

Walking into the village, Paxa and Alapay stand waiting for me like proud parents. Paxa steps up and clasps my hand in his. "Welcome back from your spiritual journey."

"Glad to return to you and the tribe."

Alapay looks at me with the same familiar smile and a big hug. "Yaqi told us what happened, we are grateful."

"He would have done the same for me."

"Tonight we feast and celebrate you, and Yaqi. The bounty you two have provided the tribe is greatly appreciated by all," Paxa proclaims.

"The tribe has shared so much with me."

Paxa asks a question I can see welling up. "Wave Dancer, do you return from your spiritual journey the same man?"

I feel a lifetime has passed since I'd left the village, but the question has a simple answer. "My soul connects with The Great Mystery."

"You are at peace?"

"I am at peace."

Returning to my hut I confirm that life is good, and about to get better as I pause to look across the lagoon to the ocean beyond. I drop my hunting gear, grab my surfboard and run toward the ocean baptism that calls to the born again surfer.

Cresting the dunes, a brilliant sunset lights the backs of the waves, turning them to coils of blown glass. I wade into the holy water, dip my head under, and purify my soul in the Church of Mother Ocean.

Paddling into a set breaking in front of me, I look into bursts of liquid stained glass color curling my way until I'm forced to close my eyes and push my redwood beauty through the face of the wave. The saltwater bath runs the length of my body, streaming off me with each stroke of my arms. Sitting up on my board facing the last of the day's sun, my legs dangle into Mother Ocean and the tips of my fingers stretch to Father Sky closing together as if in prayer.

One wave is all I ask, one wave. Gliding into the pull of the magical gift from the sea, I push to my feet and dance with the swell of energy wrapping across the sandbank toward shore. Down the line in front of me, a lone dolphin cruises into our wave bodysurfing the shoulder. I pull up side by side, drop-knee the stance and reach out to touch my totem animal guardian. The dolphin and I connect physically and spiritually. She calls out in language I can't understand, but the emotion of the sound she makes is that of pure joy. With a flyaway exit into sunset sky, the dolphin disappears beneath the Pacific. Riding in on a wave of pure joy, I surf to the beach and call it a wonderful day. Board under one arm, I turn to see the last rays of the sun on another lap around the cosmos.

Pumped up with post-surfing bliss, I step out the curtain of my hut towards the tribe gathered by the fire. Before I get there, Talkitna swoops in and takes me aside, leading me to the edge of the firelight. "Wave Dancer, I have a gift."

From behind her back she produces a headdress artfully laced together with strings of shells in precise patterns of intricate beauty adorning a headband of deerskin festooned with flight feathers woven into the impressive creation. She reaches out and presents it to me with pride. "I made it, just for you."

Honored, I bend down and allow her to place it. Rising up carefully, she shifts it firmly in place as she gazes at me, looking satisfied.

"Thank you, Talkitna. It's lovely. What feathers?

"The great Condor, the highest honor."

"I'm not done," she says. From a small pouch she pours out dark powder, spits into her hand and mixes the dark red color with her finger. She steps up to face me, so close her body touches mine. Turning me toward the light of the fire, she carefully draws lines on my face, her finger slowly marking my clean skin with patterns of connecting swirls starting from my forehead and wrapping down my neck. All the time she's using my face as a canvas, I stare at her face as a portrait I'm falling in love with.

"Now you are ready for your place of honor with the tribe. Tonight you sit with Paxa and Alapay," she says, stepping back to admire her work. "You are a brave man, Wave Dancer."

"Instinct, not sure about brave."

"You stood your ground and faced fear," she says as she gestures for me to lead the way.

Approaching the circle of fire, the stretched skin of the great bear hangs out to cure, our two deer skins looking very small on either side of it. Meat cooks on pointed green wood poles, delivering instant flashbacks of the memory of the animal charging toward me with claws bared.

Paxa and Alapay rise to their feet at my approach. All is quiet as he raises both hands before speaking. "My People! We are blessed to have the safe return of Yaqi and Wave Dancer who have risked their lives for this abundance. For this we are grateful!"

Once again the tribe breaks into applause. Hoots of joy and a few high-pitched whistles lace the sound of clapping hands. Drums pound loudly and rattles shake, stirring the vibrations into a rising mood of celebration. Paxa once again raises his hands to quiet the tribe. "Tonight we celebrate the man we call Wave Dancer who saved the life of Yaqi from the Great Bear."

This time, more respectful clapping along with solemn looks reflecting thoughts of almost losing Yaqi. Paxa raises his hands once more. "Tonight we celebrate with a feast, music and dancing. We honor Wave Dancer for his bravery. We honor the Great Bear and brother deer for their lives once lived so that The People of Noqoto may live on!"

Music arises from the back of the circle of fire. Instruments drive the beat into the hearts of The People, lyrical flutes float on the whispering wind as food is passed around. There are beds of gathered watercress and wild onions under thin slices of venison steak with wild mushrooms sitting on top, and flat bread of ground wild grains to use as a wrap. I fold mine and bring it to my watering mouth. It has been, a long time since I've nourished my body with food, and the fulfilling meal I'm about to eat, I hunted myself.

The food disappears and is replaced by the quickening tempo of music. My feet tap with the beat as the musicians stop in front of me to play a joyful tune. I'm drawn in to join them without argument, and I take a drum offered me. The primal beat rises from within me, joining the group linked with musical vibrations as individual instruments coalesce into one. Each player takes a turn to break away into a solo. I go last, playing the drum like never before, my hands pounding with the discovery of ancestral sounds. All around me dancers spin in unison, caught up in the tribal beat. The pure joy of creating music for others lifts my spirits even higher than the sparks of the bonfire that fly above the dancers, rising into the night sky. The crowd is in my hands as I wind down to a final few beats and quiet the skin to happy applause.

The loud ovation asks for more, but I'm too drained to continue. Rising up, I give a humble bow. Returning the drum to its owner, I make my way back to my seat by the fire.

"You play with a drum beat from another world," says Paxa.

"Another world is right. That was my take on some classic old Dead."

"The death of a Great Bear is an omen of change to our land."

In the background the band starts up again, this time in a slow melody. The curved outline of Talkitna takes shape out of the ring of light and enters the glowing warmth of the fire. She steps up to me as if her parents weren't there.

"They play the dolphin song, Wave Dancer."

Rising to my feet, I take her hand in mine. I turn to Paxa and Alapay looking up at us both and give a respectful bow.

"May I dance with your daughter?" I ask.

Both of them nod approvingly, their hands coming together as one. "You dancing with Talkitna would bring us joy," replies Alapay.

Talkitna reaches for my hand and leads me to the edge of the warm fire. I pull her close, our bodies pressing together with her head nestled on my shoulder. Our first dance flows together as if there is no time between us. We circle in slow spins around the fire, lingering into the night as most of the tribe slips away.

Talkitna whispers in my ear. "The moon is full."

Taking her hand in mine I lead her away from the fire into the light of the moon. In front of us the ocean glimmers with moonlight bouncing off the sea's surface in dancing displays of lunar light. We slow our steps to a stop. All is quiet except for the sound of breaking waves and my pounding heart.

"Wave Dancer, I have another gift."

From around her neck she removes the dolphin pendant, the moon's glow glancing off its polished rainbow surface. Placing it slowly over my head, she lowers the dolphin to rest against my chest. A beaming smile shining in the moonlight shows her approval. My moonbeam smile joins hers. Gently I hold the dolphin like a sacred and rare treasure.

"Talkitna, it's beautiful."

"The dolphin you wear is my Story of the Rainbow."

"Rainbow story?"

"The rainbow bridge the Earth Goddess stretched across the sea for our people to cross from the islands to the mainland. The People who fell from the rainbow turned to dolphins. You came to me from the sea being led by a dolphin, you are my Rainbow story."

My turn to give her the only object I came ashore with. I lift the greenstone Dream Helper over my head.

"My only possession, a gift for you."

I gently brush aside her thick wavy hair and lay the necklace around her smooth neck. The greenstone settles gently into place amongst her natural curves. "Talkitna, I hope this Dream Helper brings us together again, no matter where and when."

She holds the precious pendant in her hand and steps within a breath of me, wrapping her arms around me. I meet her in my arms and embrace in a heavenly hug.

"I still mourn my husband, I haven't let him go."

CHAPTER 25

The morning fog is beginning to clear from my head as the sun clears the fog from the coast. Pulling the door curtain aside, bright sun filters through the damp mist receding in swirling clouds returning to the sea. The village has no hints of the previous night's celebration except for wisps of smoke rising from the ashes of the great fire. Looking around for a sight of Talkitna, my heart skips beats, anxious to see her again. But she is nowhere to be seen.

I head for the beach. Cresting the dune, I see small playful waves rolling to shore and two people bobbing in the water in the distance. I walk toward them, the surge of the shore break tickling my feet in retreat as sand crabs scurry away from my steps. As I get closer, a set of waves comes through onto the sand bar of the lagoon. Standing up on my surfboard is Talkitna, her huge smile lighting up the immediate universe. Next to her, Little Wave rides his belly board prone, hooting, his hands waving. I run down the beach to meet them as they ride the whitewater toward shore, drunk on pleasure. Talkitna goes down with an awkward splash and comes up laughing, water dripping down every bit of her. Little Wave spills onto shore and flops on the sand. Talkitna's grabs me in a hug, giving me the most pleasant soaking I can imagine.

Little Wave can't contain his contagious enthusiasm for riding waves. "What about my mother wave dancing!"

"She's great. You are too. You need a big surfboard, Little Wave."

"I'll make it!" my associate board builder shouts.

"Talkitna, you're a wave riding natural."

"Wave dance with us!" Talkitna requests, with eyes that can't be refused.

From the water I observe Talkitna's physical strength and sense of balance. She takes a few spills, but still, a very impressive effort. Little Wave is equally impressive with his ability to stay in the pocket ahead of the whitewater, riding the fastest part of the wave, and how quickly he returns to the line up to catch more. I occasionally share the boards with both of them, giving them a few tips on their positioning and the art of reading waves.

With a fine collection of goose bumps, we carry the boards up the beach to the sand dunes. Finding a sheltered area, we flop down in relief to bake our bodies like cold reptiles soaking up hot sun. Wet salty hair, grins on our faces, closed eyes, shared contentment at the simple pleasures that riding waves in the ocean bring. If the feeling of this moment can be contained in a bottle, there's a fortune to be made from our surfing pleasure tonic.

"I'm hungry," Little Wave proclaims.

"Run back to Alapay. I want to stay and warm up," Talkitna says, hardly lifting her head from the dune.

"Take your board with you," I instruct surfer-boy. Little Wave does and heads off over the sand.

Lying on our backs, an arm's length apart, curving into the clean white sand, we're peacefully lulled by the sounds of the ocean lapping on shore. Streaming from far across cosmic time, the sun's warmth radiates to my core. I look over and catch a glimpse of Talkitna's blissful face. My eyes close. I drift off to edges of distant dreams.

Woken! Talkitna suddenly rolls over on top of me, pinning my waist with her muscular thighs. I'm held down by her strong arms grasping mine as she smiles into my wide-awake eyes. "You bring me out of mourning. I'm in love with you, Wave Dancer," she whispers.

I look deeply into her eyes. Inner joy spreads, along with inner conflicts. "You loving me is a dream come true. I love you too. But I'm not sure how far we should go with our relationship…"

"I'm free to love again," she sings, as she releases me.

"I'd love to take our relationship further, but I'm not so sure it's a good idea. Who knows what may happen in the future? We've got a big gap in centuries. We could be blood relatives of some sort. We don't want to mess with the future tribal gene pool. Do we?"

Talkitna pushes up off my chest, stands above me in her minimal coverings. I lay on my back watching this striking natural beauty towering over me, a lovely perspective for me to witness her wonderful attributes. She looks down at me, and smiles a smile of open pleasure. "You talk of a different world. I'm here for you now."

My loincloth rises. "I better swim, I need to cool down."

Suddenly, she freezes, and frantically looks up to the ridgeline high above, her body language doing a one-eighty. Panic grows across her face and vibrates all the way down to me.

I get to my feet and my attention shifts to her line of sight, glimpsing outlines of mounted horsemen looking down toward the village. It's tragically clear they're armed Spanish soldiers in body armor leading the way for a priest in a hooded robe. A tidal wave of worry surges up in me.

"Spanish?"

"They look Spanish, at least from what I've seen in history books."

"Are they who you speak of from Dream Walks?"

"Yes."

On the ridge, riders spur their horses to descend into the oaks, until one by one they are out of our vision.

"What now?"

"Find Little Wave. Take him to the waterfall and hide with him there."

"You?"

"I'll warn Yaqi, he's a marked man. I'll ask Paxa to gather the tribe."

We race across the shores of the lagoon to spread the word. Sprinting into the village to help raise the alarm, I find all is pleasantly normal without any sense of danger. It appears only Talkitna and I have spotted the approaching Spaniards.

I find Paxa socializing with the older men and pull him aside with urgency. "Paxa!" The Spanish approach on horses, soldiers with weapons! Tell the tribe to hide, run!"

"This is our home, we do not run away."

"You'll be sorry if you don't keep your distance from the Europeans. Where's Yaqi?"

"Hunting."

"They will be hunting him."

Paxa gathers the tribe quickly. Everyone knows it's a serious gathering and the concern in his voice spreads through the crowd. Isqua waits until Paxa has finished speaking, then again voices his desire to pick up weapons to defend the village from the Spanish. The debate carries on as time runs short. With horses at full gallop, The Outsiders flood into the village, the armor-clad soldiers, dressed for full battle, their lances raised for anyone who might resist, escorting a dusty priest.

Paxa steps fearlessly up to the front of the tribe with an anxious Isqua by his side. Behind them stand the strongest of our warriors, with a show of spears and bows to the lances, swords, daggers, muskets and pistols of the Spaniards.

The Outsiders rein in their sweat-lathered horses, some looking down on us as others scan our village in the settling dust. The priest in the hooded frock lowers himself carefully from his horse until he touches terra firma. A dusty hood peels back to reveal a man with a scraggly beard framing a crooked smile. The soldiers stay mounted high on their horses, lances at the ready, tarnished metal helmets and thick vests of body armor looking well used. The priest steps forward stiff legged, stumbles and catches his swinging crucifix in his hand. Recovering, he lifts the silver-chained pendant to his lips and kisses the symbol of his faith.

"You are chief?" the Friar queries in a broken attempt at our Noqoto language.

Paxa sizes up The Outsider. "Who are you to ride into our home with weapons drawn?"

"I'm Friar Juan Fernandez, Franciscan priest at Mission Los Santos. I've come in God's name to offer you these colored beads as a gift," he says as he fingers a pocket in his robe and pulls out a leather bag. "And you are called?"

"Paxa."

Fernandez opens his grimy hand to reveal colorful glass beads gleaming in the sunlight. A few in the tribe gasp at such never before seen beauty. The priest pours the beads back, pulls the draw cord and tosses the satchel to Paxa, who shifts away as it hits the dirt.

Paxa stares down at the satchel without moving to pick it up. His eyes shift back to the priest as he extends his hand. Paxa slowly extends his hand. Their fingers nearly touch when Isqua leaps in and pulls Paxa away.

The soldiers ready their lances and move into defensive positions.

The priest gives our shaman a serious glance, the look on his face showing his contempt for the averted introduction. Isqua glares at the soldiers and the priest with the look of the otherworldly shaman ready to fight to the death.

Paxa looks directly into the eyes of the missionary invader of his Noqoto people's home. "We want nothing to do with you and your beads. Go back to from where you came."

"If you won't take my gift, please come visit our Mission Santos. We have much more to offer, including love, mercy and forgiveness for those who have sinned."

"Why did you beat my son?"

"At Mission Santos? Maybe you are mistaken? Can I ask him? We did have an incident awhile back…"

Behind Fernandez and the soldiers, a slight movement catches my eye. I can faintly make out the hidden features of Yaqi high in the willow tree. A gust of wind sends the curtain of lace branches swaying as I pull my eyes from Yaqi toward the priest and soldiers. A light breeze carries the rank smell of the unwashed men in front of me, testing my patience.

Reaching his foot beneath the bag of beads, Isqua flings the satchel and hits Fernandez square in the chest, and he staggers back. Yet he remains intent on getting his recruitment message across.

"Please, come to the Mission and see how devout believers of Catholic faith and civilized people of the Spanish Empire live."

"Go away from Noqoto, priest. Take your soldiers and weapons," Paxa orders.

"For now, we will go in peace."

The priest bends down to gather the satchel. Replacing the bead-filled bag in his robe pocket, he withdraws a small metal container, opens it and takes a pinch of its contents into his fingers. Holding it under his nose, he snorts the snuff and his eyes flutter with the blast of stimulant. Preparing to mount his horse, he hikes up his robe to reveal swollen, gout-reddened feet, pushed into leather sandals looking ready to burst. A burdened sigh from the horse as it staggers to adjust to the substantial load.

Fernandez composes himself, straightens his robe and looks down upon us. He suddenly sneezes. As if in slow motion in the backlight, I see the airborne transmitter of disease riding the breeze our way. I hold my breath and turn to warn the others.

The tribe gathers together in shock from the visit of The Outsiders who look nothing like anyone in Noqoto. At the base of the tree I meet up with Yaqi, grateful to see him safe. "Was that the priest?" I ask.

"Yes, he is the coward."

"Your sister took Little Wave to the waterfall."

"The farther away from the priest and his soldiers the better," Yaqi warns.

Setting out to look for Talkitna and Little Wave, I track the horses. The heavy beasts are not hard to follow as they lead away from the village, back in the direction they came. Disturbed earth points toward the low point of the ridgeline until two sets of tracks break away, heading to a stream. I pick up the pace as I work my way as quickly as I can. At the base of the canyon the tracks change to boots. Further along, barefoot signs of a struggle. My heart sinks. Drops of blood lay sprinkled on the dry dust. I look all around for other signs. I feel sick. A faint noise above draws my attention as I imagine someone whispering my name.

"Wave Dancer."

There, huddled high in the branches of an oak tree, is Little Wave shaking with fear.

"I'm here, Little Wave."

"They took her," he says as tears run down his face.

I've never seen anyone in such need of a hug as the small boy making his way to me. I lift him up in my arms and hold him tight as he sobs at the second greatest tragedy of his young life. His father taken by the sea, and now his mother taken by the soldiers.

"I'll try my best to bring your mother back."

Guilt for having sent Talkitna and Little Wave away from the village tugs at me severely. She would be safe now if she had stayed at Noqoto. Her son, whose hand I now hold, would still have his mother at his side.

In sight of the village, Little Wave runs at a sprint to the hut of his grandparents. The concerned looks on their faces tell me they now know. With labored breath I tell them my intentions. "I sent her away, I'll bring her back."

Alapay looks at me with even greater concern. "You are not responsible for her capture! You must not hold that within you! It is The Outsiders who are holding our daughter against her will! You understand, Wave Dancer?"

Only part of the burden I'm carrying lifts from my shoulders. "Thank you for your words, Alapay. I will bring her back."

"You will not go alone," Paxa speaks in the commanding voice of a leader.

"I should."

"Yaqi will go with you, he knows the Mission."

"Let Isqua come with me. Your only son should stay here," I point out.

"Isqua stays here with me. Her brother Yaqi goes with you. He and I will have it no other way."

Little Wave sinks back deeper into Alapay's arms as she gathers her grandson to her. His big brown eyes connect with me, filled with hope for what I promise.

"Yaqi can show me the Mission, but I need to go in alone."

"You must both decide what will save Talkitna. Bring her back to Noqoto."

A quick circuit of the village and I find Yaqi. I say only three words. "They captured Talkitna."

A shift moves through him, anger rising up, his whole being changing in front of me into a hunter in search of those who hold his sister against her will.

My thirst for revenge is much like Yaqi's as I frantically assemble my bow, arrows and spear. Little Wave runs to me, looking determined and prepared to join in the rescue. Bow and arrows at the ready, a fierce look on his face, he says, "Wave Dancer, I go."

"You're too young."

"I can outshoot any of the boys!"

"Rabbits don't shoot back."

"She's my mother."

"Little Wave, The People of Noqoto need you to stay here. Who will lead them in the future should something happen?" I ask.

The look on the boy's face changes from a warrior looking for a fight to one of pride. "I will stay and look after my tribe."

"You're wise beyond your years."

I look up to see the present leader of the tribe limping toward me. Paxa carries with him weapons and the look of a man who would not hesitate to inflict his own idea of justice.

"First the young warrior, and now you. There won't be any leaders left in Noqoto if you come too," I say with concern.

Paxa hands me a bow and quiver full of arrows. "This bow is the strongest, the shafts straightest, the flint heads the sharpest. I want you to send many arrowheads deep into the captor of Talkitna. The man who steals my daughter deserves to die many deaths."

"Hopefully I'll bring her back without firing any arrows."

CHAPTER 26

Horses' tracks, broken branches and turned up soil provide clues to the kidnappers' passing. Yaqi sets a grueling pace. With my thoughts of rescuing Talkitna, I don't let myself fall far behind his marathon pace strides.

The coastal mountain range looms behind us as we drop further in elevation. Lowering into the valley, we cross paths with a well-worn trail and head north, following a watershed lined with dense green growth clinging to the creeks and wetlands.

The light of day fades and with it, my scant energy reserves. Leaving the trail, Yaqi cuts his own path to an isolated ridge. I stumble after him, refusing to stop even though my legs scream for rest and I'm parched with thirst. Stopping just before the crest, Yaqi turns and waits for me to scramble to his side. He gestures with an outstretched hand for me to keep quiet.

"The Mission," he quietly instructs.

Signaling me to stay low, he and I creep up to the ridgeline.

Mission Los Santos materializes in the valley below. The familiar main structure of the adobe building stretches the length of the compound. A wooden scaffold is being erected high above the rising walls of a new building at the far end. Frames for making adobe bricks lie stacked next to it in neat lines; bricks, straw, and piles of clay and sand are ready to be mixed with water. Iron kettles of animal tallow sit on stout frames, their fires tended by slow moving shapes in the fading light. Nearby, racks of wooden poles string tight like skin drums from stretched hides of cattle. In the paddocks, herds of penned cows await slaughter.

On the fringes of the compound are clusters of crude structures—the Indian outposts of meager, stick-built housing, scattered randomly and insubstantial looking compared to the mission's main buildings. A few armed soldiers with lances at the ready ride the perimeter of the low-slung buildings. At the far end of the complex, the chapel stands out, its three large bells hanging from arches high above. Near the church, a few headstones mark the graveyard of the Europeans. In the familiar distance, an open field with earth disturbed by the creation of unmarked graves. On the outskirts of this field I saw the Dream Walk vision of the mystical warrior—Yaqi.

"The prison," Yaqi replies to my unasked question, pointing to a smaller separate structure near the church.

"She's caged," I comment, imagining what it might be for Talkitna to lose precious freedom.

"We wait until first light," Yaqi commands.

"Agreed, but I go in alone without weapons, as an innocent."

"And I stay behind? No."

"I speak their language, and I know their customs."

"I know the Mission, I've been there."

"You need to stay away, Yaqi. You are a marked man for killing one of their soldiers. You will not help your sister if you are dead. I'm trying to save both your lives, believe me."

End of day comes rolling like an evil shadow leaving the Mission grounds in dark shades of bleak gray. Thoughts of the coming rescue filter through my mind as I silently chew our rations of jerky and wash it down with the dwindling water supply. After such a marathon day of travel, I lie my exhausted body down on a bed of oak leaves. I'm stressing with anticipation for the coming day and sleep is elusive, until I can't fight it back anymore.

When I wake, the first light of dawn is erasing the diminishing stars of the night. My body is post-marathon beaten. I look over towards Yaqi who stands partially sheltered by a madrone as he scans the valley below. I silently join him and we watch the quiet buildings. A lone accolade walks the courtyard of the Mission, then pauses at the bells and reaches for ropes. Calm shattered, clanging of iron crashes with brass.

"Time for me to free her."

"Can you kill a man?"

I hesitantly reply. "To save Talkitna."

"Stay alive, and bring my sister out alive."

"Give me until the moon rises."

"I'll be watching you like a hawk."

Leaving Yaqi and the safety of the cover of trees, I step into the open valley and walk towards the Mission with only a small woven satchel over my shoulder. I look unarmed and exposed, an innocent in search of shelter at the Mission.

Deep magenta of early daylight bathes the whitewashed Mission walls. A crew of Indians makes for the fields in the cool morning of the barely risen sun. Riding close behind, soldiers with lances on duty. Another arid swelter of a summer day is descending on the Mission. Heads turn from the Indian workers as I make my way closer to the entry gate. I give a slight smile their way, but they don't return the gesture. In the fields beyond, sheep graze the hillside beneath the watchful eyes of Indian herders with dogs, the herders in turn watched by their Spanish weapon-bearing masters.

Everyone slows their work as I approach, staring blankly at what must be the rare sight of a volunteer coming to the Mission on his own. The looks I receive reflect pity. The crack of a bullwhip shatters them into compliance. A mounted guard follows with shouted threats of abuse.

In the entry grounds, I slow to a stop and peer upward at the towering wooden cross planted deeply in the earth. Splintering shafts of sunlight split the crucifix with beams projected from the heavens. I say a silent prayer for my deliverance to Talkitna.

The main door of the building opens as Friar Fernandez steps out from cool, shady darkness into the warm light. A salesman's smile erupts across his face. I step up to the priest without emotion. Nearby soldiers rush to his side, weapons drawn. I hold my hands high in the air, and then bring them to my side. The soldiers stay posted, but lower their weapons.

"Welcome to Mission Los Santos," Fernandez announces in my Native tongue.

I say and do nothing as I stare at the man with the dangling crucifix.

"I am Friar Juan Fernandez, head of Mission Los Santos."

"My name is Peter Martinez," I inform in Spanish, breaking my silence.

"You do speak our language! That partially explains your European features, but why do you dress as an Indian heathen?"

"I'm a half-breed, I live in two worlds."

"A bastard child? Martinez is certainly a familiar name in the Kingdom of Spain."

"I'm familiar with this place."

"Mission Santos? That must have been awhile back, I do not remember you."

"Awhile forward."

The priest stares at me without a ready answer. "Do you claim to be a mystic?"

"I have vivid dreams of the future."

"Then I hope you see the future as I envision it, generations of Indian converts to our Christian faith dutifully bound by the Bible and following the footsteps of Jesus Christ our Lord. A pathway to Heaven for the heathens is my spiritual calling."

"There will be very few Native Indians surviving your Missions a generation from now."

Fernandez seems unfazed by my portents. "I'm following in the footsteps of the great Father Serra, I'm trying to help the heathens see the light of God. I would like to show you the light too. Let me show you our island of spiritual sanctuary in the godless wilderness. See what the will of the Lord and industrious neophyte workers can accomplish."

"I look forward to seeing this place again."

"We will start with the new building!" the priest cries with proud delight.

Walking side by side toward the construction site, we draw all eyes but this time, no one stops working.

"Here is our latest building project. It is where oak barrels of wine will be held. It needs to be cool and these walls are twice as thick."

"Who drinks the wine?" I ask.

A puzzled look grows on Fernandez's face. "Most goes to the military garrison at the Presidio in Monterey."

"What do you get in return?"

"We gladly accept what the Lord provides, and sometimes what I request."

"The administrators and soldiers drink the wine, what do the others get?"

"The others?"

"The Indians, the workforce, what do they get in return for their labor?"

At first it seems he isn't going to answer, the truth not easy for him.

"They are blessed with daily meals and a roof over their heads. The ones who stay to accept the Lord are baptized. They become children of God once they accept the Bible and the Christian doctrine. This is their greatest reward."

"Once they're baptized, do they get freedom to leave the Mission?"

"We do not encourage neophytes to wander away from their new home at the Mission," he replies, as if looking to change the subject.

The proud priest leads me into the main building through the huge oak doors of the front entry. Fine furniture graces the reception area, including an old world hutch filled with precious bound books. Featured on a wall for all entrants to see hangs an ornate golden frame featuring a painting of lofty angelic figures floating in heavenly clouds peering down upon mortals in a fiery depiction of hell. Two chairs upholstered with striped cloth of European manufacture await the travel weary. A wrought iron candelabra swings slightly in the drafty entrance. Following the priest's lead, we begin our way down a long hallway of lime-plastered adobe broken with a series of doors.

Fernandez approaches the first door; it groans squeakily against the push of his palm. Inside, rows of Indian women spin wool into yarn. None of them lift their eyes from their work. Most have hair cut short and dyed black in mourning. The room is filled with the gloom of a squalid factory, the assembly workers going about tedious jobs in a stupor. Only one window sheds daylight into dark corners.

The next door opens to reveal a series of looms for weaving cloth. In a trance, none of the women, whose deft hands sweep across the looms, give a glance. In one corner, bundles of finished cloth are stacked to the ceiling, the results of unknown hours of tedious labor.

Another door pushes open, unleashing the stench of melted animal fat. Young Native boys dip candlewicks in and out of a vat of hot lard, building the candles until large enough to hang from an overhead rack to cool.

Further down the hall, the intense smell of tanned leather grabs my nose and won't let go. In this workroom, older Native men form leather into bridles for horses, saddles, ropes and bull-whips, their hands matching the color of the leather, their tanned skin almost as tough.

Muted sounds of pounding wood lead us to yet another door ahead. A woodworking shop filled with stacks of rough-milled lumber neatly organized and leaning against the walls. There are large hand drills, saws with big, crooked teeth, an assortment of hammers, hand planes, square nails, a pail of wooden dowels, and wood chips thick at our feet. In the corner lean two coffins waiting patiently for the next European to die. In the center of the room are the oak staves of wine barrels ready to be banded together, the final shaping of the wood done by Indian labor.

The cool building grows warmer as we approach the last two rooms. Peering through the doorframe, I see pottery being created by delicate fingers that guide the clay into useful shapes, spinning of pottery wheels powered by quick feet. The finished pots, bowls, plates, goblets and mugs sit on shelves, some of it kiln dried and colorfully hand-painted with Native designs. A kiln in the corner is hell hot, the intense, glowing coals bellowed by sweaty human power. Perspiration pours from the pores of the keeper of the kiln as he adjusts the pottery to match the intense heat.

As we approach the last room, the unmistakable sound of metal on metal rises to a din. Heat infused with sweat pours from under the door. When Fernandez opens the door, I see soot-blackened men sending sparks flying. A blacksmith at work at an anvil swings his hammer and repairs the glowing hot metal tongue of a plow. In the chimney dominated corner of the room, intense heat comes in waves from the blast furnace as the foot-driven lungs pump air raising the extreme metal-melting coals. A scattering of finished hand tools stacked on a workbench wait for wooden handles to be attached. Hanging from the wall by iron pegs, metal hoops ready to wrap around the oak shaves of the barrels. Over the exit door, an iron cross hangs above all who pass through this hellish prison of forced labor.

The door at the end of the hall opens into welcoming daylight. My eyes strain to adjust from the dark gloom of the workstations.

Fernandez looks over at me bursting with pride. "What do you think?" he asks.

"Well-organized labor."

"Idle hands are the devil's playground. The Mission provides a useful sanctuary."

"A sanctuary guarded by soldiers with weapons."

"I do not encourage the use of force unless needed."

"I'm guessing most of your converts haven't come here as a matter of choice."

"Some follow, others need to be led to their salvation."

The Mission bells ring again. The Christian converted Indian bell ringers are dressed in clean European wear, shirts and pants unsoiled by physical labor. "The acolytes call my flock to the chapel!

You will stay to hear my sermon? Today I am blessed to baptize a little pagan girl into the arms of our Lord."

"You get them young."

"Our Savior smiles on all ages."

"Nothing disturbs your faith?"

"Religious faith is the foundation of devote, and a foundation must be strong!"

In the chapel, the ceilings soar overhead supported by impressive beams of hand-hewn wooden trusses carrying the roof over the wide span of the expansive room. High on the walls is a band of colorful painted designs mixing Native and European arts. The nave is devoid of pews, making the room seem even more cavernous. At the far end, the altar raises behind the bema, its religious trimmings highlighted in red and gold. A statue of the crucified Jesus dominates the space, his limp depiction hanging from the cross, painted blood dripping from the spikes driven into his hands and feet. The Virgin Mary with hands held in prayer and a silver halo above her head occupies an alcove set into the wall at my side. No shortage of candles being lit by two native boys in crude robes who make their way from one end to the other. Animal fat scented smoke twists up, to gather at the ceiling, a dark cloud descending onto us as the candles grow shorter. To the right of the church altar, a series of steps lead to a pulpit cantilevered from the wall perched above those gathering below.

Fernandez stands at the door greeting each of the Natives with a mumbled blessing. None return his gestures with any sort of acknowledgment other than an occasional glance. Without pews, everyone who filters in takes a place, sitting cross-legged on the hard adobe floor.

The light of day pours through the entry doors, shrinking to a thin shaft as two acolytes pull closed the escape route. Above the altar, a lone stained glass window comes alive, throwing a mosaic of color across the dim room. In front of me, a little girl slowly stands and stares with wonder at the sun streaming light through the symbol of a cross.

The chapel is quiet. Friar Fernandez steps up to the pulpit in his tattered garments of faith. "With God's blessings I have returned safely from my trav—" He stops short.

He glares over our heads as the door slowly opens. Slightly ajar, a cautious set of eyes peers into the chapel. In limps an old, beaten down Indian man, the shaft of light setting him aglow as he drags his way across the room. Looks of concern grow heavy on faces.

The priest's face twists into anger. "You're late!" he roars, his voice echoing off the walls. "Did you not hear the bells?" he scolds, motioning with his hand for the tardy neophyte to come forward. The old man shuffles to the altar. "Come to me! Pray to God for forgiveness for your lack of respect in the house of the lord!" Fernandez bellows.

Climbing down from the pulpit, he pulls out a thick willow branch from behind his back. The old man stops at the steps of the altar, drops to his knees and mumbles a prayer. With willow cane at ready, the priest takes up position in front of the man. The man finishes his prayer and remains kneeling in front of the priest, awaiting his fate.

"God forgive this heathen," Fernandez mumbles in Spanish as he spares the rod.

Back to his pulpit he climbs, composing himself in front of the gathered flock of Indians. "Before we start today's sermon, we have another baptism welcoming a young child into the arms of the Lord. Bring her forward."

The priest climbs down from his pulpit with arms opened wide. A native acolyte makes his way into the crowd and grabs the arm of the little girl who still stares at the stained glass. She pulls against him, but is too small to resist. Dragged up to the altar to face Fernandez, she tries to sprint away, but the priest grabs her arm and firmly pulls her to him.

"Hold still, child."

Still the girl struggles to break free of his grasp.

"I won't hurt you."

She punches him in the stomach. The priest doubles over, wind knocked out of him. He won't let her go. Even more fear in her eyes as he slowly rises up and gasps in a breath of air. "You little savage!" he wheezes as he drags her over to the stone basin filled with holy water and proceeds to give the struggling girl a condensed version of salvation. "With this holy water I welcome you into the house of the Lord. Amen."

He dips into the water and splashes it in her face. She screams shrilly, then stomps on his foot. Fernandez screams back in baritone.

Slipping away from his grip, she runs off to join others as they encircle her at the back of the chapel. The zombies have arisen from their stupor, having gathered strength from this feisty child with a mind of her own. The wounded priest limps over and grabs his willow stick. As he approaches the little girl being shielded by others, the door opens and she sprints outside.

The priest limps back up the steps of the pulpit, gathers himself, and looks out over the congregation. His eyes lock on mine. "Another convert to our faith joins us under the watchful eyes of our Lord," he says, adding to his tally count.

Fernandez's sermon delivered in Spanish, laced with Latin, is dull and uninspiring. His attempts at preaching a catechism of what he calls, "The Essentials for Salvation," leave me and others fighting to stay awake. Even on a hard brick floor with no padding, sleep is the preferred option. How can this angry man with a pious attitude talking down to those gathered beneath his perceived lofty heights expect to bring followers to his belief? And in Spanish and

Latin? Doubtful there are few, if any, in attendance who understand him. As I look around, I see only people in desperation here, the ones gathered around me with no smiles, no laughter, with their hair cut short in mourning at the passing of loved ones.

When the service ends, the muted crowd of Indians slowly shuffles out again, leaving the chapel in a shroud of silence. Father Fernandez stands alone at the altar looking up to the window of stained glass projecting the cross beaming down. He drops to his knees in front of the statue of Jesus and prays. I stand alone in the cavern of a church as a silent witness.

"Thank you, Heavenly Father, for delivering me from my latest quest for converts to our faith. May you help me with pagan children to see the wrongs in their lives and see right in the eyes of you, my Lord." Fernandez rises up from his knees with a grimace and crosses himself.

Slowly he turns to face me.

"You have a way with children."

"She's a fierce fighter. Did my words of the sermon ring true for you?"

"History is working against you."

"I pray for the souls of those in my chapel, they are painfully slow in learning the ways."

"Painfully is right, you certainly had their attention with that cane of yours."

"I am a shepherd; the willow branch is but a tool, in this case a symbol."

"I couldn't help but notice most who attend your church have their minds elsewhere. Could it be they follow their beliefs and don't embrace yours, even if they knew what the hell you were preaching?"

"Hell has no place here in the house of the Lord! Conversion of the heathens takes time and patience, especially since they cannot read The Bible."

"They aren't heathens, they're Native people. They answer to a higher calling, the Great Spirit of Creation. The Heart of Everything. The beliefs they hold are unwritten in a book, passed down from generation to generation by the life they live and the stories they tell."

"They are lost souls until they embrace Christianity. And what are your beliefs? You speak with the eloquence of the gentry, but you stand before me looking like a pagan."

"I'm still sorting out my beliefs."

"And like the pagans, you dress almost as Adam, but your skin is fairer and your language is excellent. What am I to imagine? It appears you are more civilized than crude Indians with their utmost repugnance to give up their own tongue."

"I walk in both worlds, but I'm ready to come back into the spiritual comfort of the Mission," I say with fingers crossed.

"You are welcome here at Mission Santos, Senor Martinez."

We walk toward the shaft of light coming through the doors of the chapel. Opening the door, the bright beam blazes on my bare feet, hitting me with cosmic warmth.

"I'll tell the guards you're free to wander the grounds. I encourage you to see what civilization brings to those who toil in the fields and give their lives to the Lord. I must get to my logbooks to make an entry of the newly baptized and give her a proper Christian name. The business accounts must be balanced as we have visitors expected any day from the Presidio. One of them is Father Cabo, who will be joining me here for his ten years. At last a replacement for dearly departed Father Gregorio. You are welcome to stay with us overnight if you wish; I would very much like you to join us for dinner tonight in my formal dining room."

"Yes, I'm very hungry."

"Very good! Come into the main entry at the ringing of the late afternoon bell and I'll show you your room to prepare for dinner."

"One question, I've lost track of time in my travels. What is today's date?

"Ninth-day of August, 1787."

"Holy shit!"

"Respect! Do not use profanities here in the house of our Lord!"

"Apologies, Padre, time flies. I've been traveling awhile on old El Camino Real."

Thoughts of rescuing Talkitna before the impending devastating earthquake race through my head as I make my way around the back of the church to the prison building. On closer approach, it's an imposing one-room prison with thick walls, heavy door with an iron deadbolt and a stout lock. The only other opening a small window high on the wall closed off with bolted iron bars. A soldier stationed at the door suspiciously eyes me as I keep walking by.

Around the corner, a man-sized grinding stone turns with the help of crude wooden gears. Driving the wheel forward, a one-donkey-drive being guided by a gaunt Indian man with his leather strap offering painful encouragement to the burdened beast.

Near the intense pressure of the grinding action, an Indian woman hand-feeds wheat kernels from her basket while brushing them quickly into the crushing stones path, only a finger away from the grinding rock.

Walking further down the side of the main building, I spot a high wooden pergola holding up the spiraling vine of plump purple grapes dangling down to the paved courtyard below. I reach up, grab a handful and gratefully munch. Wooden bench seats surround a stone birdbath, its water trickling into a small fountain. Mourning doves scatter as I move in for a thirst quencher. At the back of the courtyard, I make my way through an entry door propped open, I spot Fernandez's desk with a large open book. Quietly unobserved, I silently move close enough to see the book contains hand-written entries neatly categorized in orderly rows. Columns for heads of cattle and sheep numbering in the thousands, bushels of wheat, corn, tallies of candles, hides, cloth, olive oil and barrels of wine. An inventory of multitudes of trading items produced by slaves.

Another book at the end of the desk lies open with lists of European names. A baptismal record with neat columns chronologically listed. The latest summary for the year to date shows reveals "'9 baptized," the ongoing tally next to it stating, "51 deceased."

Exiting the business office and leaving the courtyard, I glance back toward the prison. No guard in sight. I head to the jail with a zombie stare, trying to blend in with the majority. Closing in, I slow to a crawl and note the walls are thick, the reinforced roof lashed down, dense oak door with huge iron deadbolt held closed with a heavy gauge padlock. Beneath the high barred window, I pause.

"Talkitna," I call in a low voice.

"Wave Dancer?" her trembling voice answers.

"I'll be back after dark. Be ready."

"I'm ready now."

"Wait until dark."

"Is Little Wave safe?" she asks with a break in her voice.

"Safe at Noqoto, waiting for you," I answer to her unseen relief.

Muted sobs turn to a whimper as I regretfully pry myself from her presence and walk toward the graveyard. Wandering amongst the grave markers, I note that all feature European names. A formal headstone rests above a more recent weedy burial mound, inscribed "Father Gregorio" and the year of his passing, 1786.

I keep walking to the unmarked graves in the distant field, fresh signs of recently dead lying beneath upturned soil. Looking back to the Mission, I know where the Native Indians are buried. I drop to my knees and lower my head to the ground. I touch the Earth. "May you find peace in Similgasa," I whisper to the victims.

Continuing with my self-guided tour, I walk to the far side of the Mission following a small, tile-lined aqueduct, its water flowing toward an orchard.

Across a nearby paddock, the overwhelming smell of boiling fat in iron cauldrons sends me in a wide circle away from those unfortunate enough to perform a job no one would do voluntarily. At the end of the main building, the new construction area is buzzing with activity. Adobe brick making operations are tended to by a large gathering of Indians, each with their tasks along the mundane assembly line. Reinforced by mixed straw, the dried bricks are stacked near the walls of the structure.

I carry on toward a tree-lined path thick with olives growing in the sun. I plunge into the shade of an orchard of trees, drawn to the sweet perfume of ripe fruit. All around me, trees hang heavy with oranges, lemons, limes, plums, apricots and figs. I eat warm apricots bursting with sweet flavor, and toss pits into the aqueduct.

The aqueduct flows to a wider junction as I exit the rows of trees. Following the growing volume of water, I come upon a well-tended flower garden surrounding a basin of water, which tempts me to lie down and cool off from the heat. Below the basin is another catchment, below that, one even larger. At the edges of the lowest basin, Native Indian women string out like beads around the rock lined pond. On their knees, they wash clothes against flat stones, rubbing them against the coarse surface. Some are the clothes of soldiers, there's a hooded robe of the priest, and mixed clothing of others piled high. Clean laundry stretches out on hemp rope lines like flags waving in wind. No one looks away from their task, and no one talks. A soldier keeps his half-closed eyes on the workers while leaning against a tree.

Leaving the spring behind, I work my way out to the fields of wheat blowing in waves directed by the wind. Mounds of wheat are piled in the distance as workers swinging scythes slicing into the grass with bored repetition. Two soldiers on horseback look down on their progress, guarding against any who may try and escape.

In the adjoining field, two dirt-crusted Natives walk beside obedient oxen plowing rows of topsoil peeling from blades with each labored step. Flocks of white herons swoop in behind fresh furrows, feeding on food opportunities newly revealed.

Turning back toward the Mission and the surrounding hillsides, I visualize brother Yaqi, watching me like a hawk.

CHAPTER 27

Mission bells peel across the valley, sending those in the fields running toward the Mission building complex.

No need to run like others, I'm not one of them. I stroll at my chosen pace, taking in the summer scents of orchards and fields baking in the sun. A thunder of hoofs gallops up to me like a coming storm and a soldier reins his horse to a dusty stop. I hold my ground. "Get moving!" he demands. The cracking of his bullwhip gets my attention, so I do what I'm told and pick up the pace. I run toward the workers assembling together in straight lines, prodded into place by soldiers with an occasional kick of a boot and slap on the back with a lance.

At the far end of the valley, a line of pack horses approaches, led by soldiers with lances pointing sharply to the sky. Well-armed military representatives of the Spanish Presidio send dust billowing into the air to mingle with hot wind. As they get closer to where I stand, sitting atop one weary looking mule, an equally weary looking man clad in a frayed, dust-plastered robe of the well-traveled. He struggles to dismount as if fused to the saddle, and finally pries himself free. He attempts to lead the sweat-soaked creature behind him until the mule refuses his efforts. The man relents and drops useless reins.

"Bless you God!" he cries out to the heavens with hands raised in jubilation.

Gathered in the main courtyard at the entry to the Mission, all eyes turn to the new arrivals. Quietly I slide into the orderly line of natives, not quite sure how the introductions will play out. Father Fernandez steps forward, ready to meet the pack train head on.

Saddle stiff, the other visitors lower themselves from their horses and hand over the reins to the Indian stable boys waiting. A hardened man clearly in command shakes the hand of Fernandez.

"Captain Portillo! Welcome!" Fernandez gushes with excitement.

"Good to see you have survived, Father."

"Bless Father Gregorio, may he rest in peace in Heaven," Fernandez says piously while bowing his head. "Thank you, Captain, for your words of my survival. They are life affirming."

The host turns to the man in the tattered robe. "You must be Father Cabo, welcome to Mission Los Santos."

Dust billows from Cabo as he tries to smooth out his robe before moving to shake Fernandez's hand. "Thank you, Father Fernandez. When the Franciscan brothers who return from Alta California said this was a world away, they were right. I've lost count of the days, the weeks and the many months," he points out, looking like he needs a long bath.

"Not Madrid," Portillo says with an embellished sigh.

"Yet it looks like paradise to me," Cabo comments, his eyes scanning the courtyard.

"Like you, I remember standing there for the first time as if it was yesterday, young and full of vigor, fresh out of Franciscan College, ready to save the world in Jesus's good name. I feel like I've aged double my lifetime these past ten years," Fernandez reflects, trying to call back some distant memory from beyond this hot afternoon.

"I want you to know, I am fully prepared for my Mission duty here," Cabo says as he offers his services to the almighty and Father Fernandez.

"Fully prepared?" Fernandez says with a suppressed laugh. "Don't be so bold."

"Perhaps not fully prepared… My condolences on the untimely passing of my predecessor. It is rumored he was poisoned? "

"We do have new kitchen help," Fernandez says, seeking to console. "Where are my manners? Allow me to introduce our commander of the guard, Lieutenant Zalvidia," he says, regaining his composure.

The rough looking solider moves forward, stops in front of his superior and fires off a brisk salute. He's unquestionably a frontier warrior with years behind him, skin littered with scars, sun-creased eyes, uniform worn down at the edges and a long sword at his side.

Zalvidia steps up to the new priest. "Welcome to your mission from hell, Padre."

"Ahh, thank you, Lieutenant."

Gently guiding Cabo by the arm, Fernandez brings him over to a barrel shaped man with close-set eyes and chasms in his teeth. Dressed as a civilian in European clothing, he carries an air of authority. He closes his lips while sizing up the new arrival. "I want you to meet Miguel Cuesta, our majordomo in charge of administering the neophytes."

"Welcome to my Mission Santos."

"Thank you, Senor Cuesta."

"Call me Master Miguel."

Cabo nods oddly before turning to look over the natives lined up neatly in front of him, standing at attention, their attention lacking. To the other side stand orderly ranks of the uniformed military guard looking, contrary to the natives, very much at attention. "I am greatly looking forward to being with you all here at Mission Santos. I thank

God for my safe delivery into your midst and know the Lord will help guide me to help you to embrace the Catholic faith," he passionately orates as the assembled Indians stand mute.

At Zalvidia's command, the ranks of the Indians and soldiers file away while Fernandez escorts his guests to their quarters. I take the opportunity to head to the stables to see how the horses are kept. There are no soldiers in sight near the barn, just two young Native stable boys brushing down the lathered horses, pouring water from buckets to cool them down. I grab a bucket and join in.

"My name is Wave Dancer."

"I am Joseph, and this is Samuel," the taller of the two answers shyly.

"My Christian name is Peter. What are your tribal names?"

"I am Reqam, and this is my brother Sepka. We are brothers, with no mother."

"Or father," the smaller one adds.

"That's why you're here?"

They both nod with far-away eyes.

"What about the rest of your tribe?" I ask.

"A few survived," the tall one says while looking past me with a hollow stare, "The man with the cross and his soldiers came to our village. We needed food."

A shuffling of feet behind me grabs their attention. I turn to see an elder Indian man entering the cool barn, seeking shade. Startled, he eyes me, not quite sure what to think. "Who are you?" he demands.

"Wave Dancer, my tribe is Noqoto."

"I am Cuta, my tribe is gone."

"Is that why you're here?"

"Why would a man stay in his village when there is no future?" he asks, pained.

"Sorry to hear of your fate."

"Why are you here?" he asks.

"Missing a woman. I've come to bring her back to Noqoto."

"The woman in prison."

"Her name is Talkitna."

"Not many Indians leave here alive."

I glance to the back of the stable buildings out to the fenced paddocks leading to the edge of the clearing. Looking from the stables across to the far side of the Mission, I investigate the soldier's quarters. Uniformed men gather in front of the building. With the new arrivals coming with the pack train, I estimate there must be at least twenty armed men, not including Portillo and Zalvidia.

"The Indian acolytes, are they to be trusted?"

"They have left our traditions. They do the bidding of the priest. These are men who torment us from their privilege."

A sudden clanging of the bells sends some of the newly arrived horses into a panic as the stable boys scramble to get out of the way.

"I must go," I say while glancing back at the Mission building.

The bells go silent as I walk across the grounds to the front entry. Fernandez is waiting for me with hands crossed. "How was your tour?" he asks with pride. "You missed the introduction to our visitors."

"I saw them ride in. This is quite an operation you have here, impressive in scale."

"With direction, persuasion, God's love, and a great deal of patience for the ignorant, progress can be achieved."

"From all the fresh graves, looks like you need a full-time grave digger."

"The pall of death visits often. Many of the newly arrived do not last long, bless their souls. Most die from even a simple cold or the disease of the Devil's lust."

"Devil's lust has another word, rape."

"The seven deadly sins of the Devil follow man wherever he lives."

"Don't blame the Devil."

The priest goes silent, laced with guilt, as he turns to walk away. I don't let him.

"You must keep recruiting more local Indians to keep this operation growing."

"Most of the neophytes do not come like you have. They need encouragement... food, gifts, trading material, glass beads."

"And if they don't want what you offer?"

"We have options," he says without elaborating. Come with me; let me show you the room where you can clean up and sleep tonight."

We head to the right through the formal entry and down a long hall. Compared to the hall to the left filled with workers, this looks to be the retreat for those of higher ranking. Paintings come aglow under the light of the open door, Christian overtones of salvation the central theme. Carved wooden crosses are securely attached to every door we pass leading to an arched entry to the dining room at the far end. The priest opens the fourth door. Inside is a tidy room with simple furnishings, a basin of water on a nightstand, soap, comb, straight razor, towel and clean clothes laid out on the single bed. Dim light creeps in from the partially shuttered window overlooking the courtyard beyond. "You may stay here tonight. On the bed are clean clothes for you to wear. I think you will find them more appropriate at the Mission's formal dining table."

"Are all new arrivals treated with such hospitality?" I ask.

"Most are not civilized. Dinner will be ready before long. Please join me and my guests when you hear the bell. Follow the sound to the end of the hallway."

I give myself a clean with the washcloth in the basin, the water quickly turning dirty. I stare at the clothes on the bed. As I pull on the woven cloth pants, they feel alien and stick to me. Near the basin are a comb, scissors and razor with sharpening stone. I shift over to a small mirror hanging from a spike on the wall. The face I haven't seen for a long time comes into focus, the look of an Indian who is living in the past. My hair a long tangle after the marathon run, and I struggle to pull the comb through it. I tie it back and stare in the mirror. Long stubble on my face gives way to the razor. Getting ready to pull the shirt over my head, I glance back to the mirror, turn my shoulder and look at my guardian spirit tattoo.

The sound of a dinner bell rings. At the end of the hall, the dining room opens up. I'm the first to arrive. The room has a formal European look. The large table and chairs must have come by ship; made of black walnut, they feature great detail of old world craftsmanship. A silver candleholder, set gracefully in the center of a table covered by a starched white cloth with hand-stitched lace, burns bright with a small forest of candles. Earthenware pitchers of red wine have been placed at either end. Silver goblets and cutlery marks each formal place setting. Through an open door, I smell the wonderful scent of food cooking in the kitchen.

The first guests filter into the room. Curious eyes glance at me, unsure who I am. My shave along with my new clothes feel like a disguise I'm hiding behind.

Fernandez enters through the kitchen door, sweat beading on his red face. He does a double take when he sees me, also not sure who I am. A smile grows as it dawns on him that it's me with a heavy polish. "Welcome, gentlemen. Excuse me for being so rude. Let me introduce you to another guest here tonight, this is Peter Martinez. He has come back for a visit to the Mission after a long absence. Peter, this is Father Cabo, he's here for his ten years to help look after the Mission faithful, and the pursuit of the salvation of converts."

Across the long table, I bow my head. Cabo seems clearly interested in my presence as he reads me further. He's cleaned up too, silver cross dangling from his neck, dark hair neatly combed with beard cut short, looking like a ladies' man in priest's smock. "Nice to meet you, Senor Martinez. I anticipate hearing stories from you, perhaps you can help illuminate me as to the comings and goings of Alta California and this Mission world we find ourselves in," he says with warmth.

"Your future here is a blank paged book still to be written," I tell him while looking over at the others standing in front of me.

"Yes, yes of course, it is an open book of my own spiritual calling," the priest says with belief as he folds his hands together and raises them to his chest.

"And this is Captain Portillo, head of the guard of the Presidio in Monterey. He is often my savior with what he brings on his visits. And what do you bring our way this time, my good, Captain?" asks Fernandez with hope in his eyes.

"Not nearly what you request. There have been... complications. We have much to discuss," he informs Fernandez. The priest's smile fades to a frown of uncertainty.

"Senor Martinez, what has brought about your return?" the Captain asks.

"I want to put a fresh new picture on my fading memory," I counter.

"And here next to the Captain is, Lieutenant Zalvidia, head of the guard here at Santos," our host says, carrying on with the introductions.

Zalvidia stares me down like a suspicious enforcer. "Where did you come from, Martinez? Likely you would have seen the Captain and his men coming down from the north."

"The first time I've met the Captain. I come from a long way south."

"And what is it you do, 'way south'?"

"I build boats, fish and hunt as a free spirit in this great land of Alta California."

"No one is free here, the King of Spain lays claim to this land, and to all the riches extracted from it to fill the Crown's coffers," Zalvidia cautions.

Fixing my eyes on Zalvidia, I notice that fresh red scratch marks streak down his cheek. "Looks like you had a recent run in with a wild animal."

"It was an unfortunate encounter with a wild female of the human variety. She is no longer in a position to draw blood."

Anger fills me, wanting nothing more than to kill the man in front of me. With great difficulty I hold in my rage.

Fernandez turns to his right as the introductions continue.

"And this is Miguel Cuesta, our Majordomo and administrator of the neophytes, a very important man to keep order in our civilian ranks."

"Those out of order might think for themselves," Cuesta muses.

"Gentlemen, please be seated. Dinner is about to be served. You all must be starving after your long journeys."

Fernandez gestures toward the table, picking up a dinner bell. Almost immediately two Native Indian servers wearing matching smocks step into the room, a gangly teenage girl and a squat middle-aged woman carrying heaping bowls of food to the table. Diligently, and silently, they serve.

With Zalvidia on one side of me, and Cuesta on the other, I'm bookended between two men I'm least likely to have ever picked as dinner companions. Glancing to each man, I give a slight mask of a smile.

At the head of the table, Fernandez raises his glass in a toast. "Gentlemen, I would like to give thanks to our Lord for bringing into our midst Father Cabo. May his long stay here at Mission Santos be filled with good health and spiritual reward in his duties."

Cabo beams broadly as all raise their glasses. The two frontier soldiers remain seriously soldierly, but they raise their glasses and guzzle wine.

"Father, if I may say grace," Cabo requests, as he clasps his hands together and closes his eyes. "Thank you oh Lord for seeing me here to the wonder of Alta California and Mission Santos. I am blessed to have found such a spiritual home to serve you in the name of the Catholic faith. Guide me to guide others in seeking the wisdom of The Almighty. Grateful are we for the food before us. Amen."

Cabo picks up his utensils and prepares to dig in, but suddenly pauses to look up at all around the table staring at him. "Have we not finished grace?" The Franciscan asks, not quite sure of himself. "Am I to be the official taster?" he continues, still not taking a bite.

"Gentlemen, let us all take our first bites together. On the count of three, one, two, three," Fernandez directs the others to follow as he sticks his fork in mouth.

After the bite has been team chewed and swallowed, Fernandez seriously scans the guests and waits for signs. Cuesta suddenly rolls his eyes back and slumps over until his forehead drops in a dull thump on the table. Cabo leaps to his feet and rushes to his side. Pulling the victim upright by the hair, a mischievous grin grows as his eyes roll back to normal.

"Joking!" he blurts, as Cabo releases the newly arisen.

"You are a sick man, Miguel, mentally sick. I think we are all in agreement that the mutton is wonderful and free of harm," Fernandez assures.

Fernandez turns to Portillo as he settles back into his seat. "So, Captain Portillo, you were saying we need to talk about the supplies we've requested?"

"Yes, Father, there are a serious lack of supply ships coming our way from Mexico and Spain. In the very near future, Imperial Spain will be fighting yet another distant war. Resources are wearing thin, and I need not remind you that we are a very remote outpost, and one far from Madrid. I'm afraid we have become low priority. I have a letter here for you from the Viceroy."

Portillo reaches into his jacket and pulls out a beaten envelope still bearing a red wax seal and hands it to the priest. Fernandez breaks the seal and opens the letter, his eyes shifting back and forth with growing concern.

"It says here we at Mission Santos must produce more to satisfy the Presidio's needs. I do not see how we can produce much more. We have the converts working as efficiently as I can get them. I can only do so much with what I have to work with."

"Bring in more converts to carry the extra load, Father," Portillo says. But his suggestion is a thinly disguised threat.

The panicky priest briefly puts his nose in the letter again. "Not easy to bring in converts these days. The closest Indian villages to the Mission have few who are willing to come, the ones who are still alive. They die of diseases as simple as a common cold. A sad reality."

"Perhaps more colorful glass beads will persuade them," Portillo hints.

"More bait does not always help capture the prey. Have a look at the baptismal records, you will see that we have reached a plateau in our numbers and they keep dropping from deaths every week," Fernandez says with defeat in his voice.

"I think we're too easy on the diggers. We could have rounded up more heathens, but kindly Father Fernandez settles for strays," Zalvidia says, clearly happy to offer the use of his warrior's skills.

"They are God's children, not pack animals, Lieutenant. You can only push them so far or they will push back, as happened with the unfortunate food poisoning incident. It would do us no good if we want to get work done here and remain alive," Fernandez sighs. He leans back in his chair, picks up his glass of wine and drains it in one long pull. When he raises it high into the air for a refill, the attentive young teenager comes shuffling to his side and tops off his glass, but pours a bit too much. Wine spills on the table, a red stream pouring onto the priest's lap. His passion for Natives vanishes as he pushes his chair back and jumps to his feet.

"Get me a cloth to clean up and another glass of wine, you clumsy foolish child!" he scolds. The scared server sprints away to the kitchen and rushes back with a cloth, trying frantically to soak up the wine from Fernandez's robe.

"Father, everyone has accidents, especially when learning," Cabo says in support of the stricken teenager.

"I was as innocent as you when I first came to this Mission. Look around you and see all that has been accomplished. The Mission would not stand here without the Natives Indians. The food in front of you would not be here without their working the fields and tending the livestock. Do you think they would even stay here without threat of punishment hanging over their heads?"

Cabo looks over at the frightened girl. Taking it as signal for service, she dashes to his side and refills his glass, very careful not to spill a drop.

Looking to Captain Portillo, the timing seems right to change the subject. "Captain Portillo, do the soldiers stationed here at Mission Santos fall under your command as well as those who ride with you?" I ask.

"Zalvidia is in charge of the men here, but he answers to me," Portillo replies with authority.

"Their arrival here at the Mission must be a reunion for some."

"Most contact with their kind is welcomed, I can assure you."

"Must be hard duty for them, so far from home."

"Hard duty for all of us here. The luxuries of civilized life are very few."

"Only a dedicated solider would sign up for such a remote tour?"

Portillo laughs loudly, clutches his glass and gulps down more wine. "Dedicated? More like desperate! Being stationed here in Alta California gives them hazard pay with extra money to piss away on booze and women. Why else would anyone want to be here?" he chortles while holding his glass.

"Sounds like they need a libation on occasion," I hint.

"Well into it already," he states from experience.

"Keep the lagging morale up," I suggest.

"All these questions of being a soldier, Senor Martinez, could it be that you are interested in joining our ranks? Are you in need of some silver in your pocket? I am sure the Captain would consider your interest, as a half-breed Indian scout perhaps?" Zalvidia inquires, while looking at me and then to his superior.

"I do have an interest in the ways of the military, more from an outsider's perspective. I'm a curious person by nature, which is why I've returned here to the Mission."

"And when you were here before, what was it that brought you?" Zalvidia interrogates.

"I first came to this Mission in search of a higher calling."

"It seems that Peter is a visionary of some sort," Fernandez adds.

"Visionary?" Zalvidia asks.

"Visions of the future he says, like a prophet."

"My vision right now is me standing outside a brothel in Mexico City with a big hard on and silver coins in my pocket," Zalvidia says, smiling.

Momentarily at a loss for words, Cabo regains his composure and speaks his truth. "Lieutenant, you speak of lustful sins in the presence of devoted men of the church. Perhaps you should think twice before showing your weakness for the Devil."

With a huge laugh, Zalvidia almost breaks into tears at the conservative man of the church in front of him. "You are the one who takes a vow of celibacy! Some of us here are not ashamed to follow a vow of procreation!"

"So what do you suggest, Lieutenant? My commitments to my personal beliefs are wrong and yours are right? I suggest you look ethically deep in your mirror and ask yourself where you will end up when death comes knocking."

"The only reason I'm here at Mission Santos with Friar Fool is silver in my pocket."

"I see, so greed, sin, and lust are your priorities in life. Do I dare ask about killing of your fellow man?"

"Wake up Padre, I am a trained killer, trained to keep passive men like you alive. Without me, my soldiers and our weapons, you would not be sitting there with that smug look of righteousness on your face. We could try a little experiment if you like. I'll take all the soldiers and weapons away from the Mission for thirty days and see what happens to you and Father Fernandez. Want to find out your fate, passive priest?"

Cabo, looking as if he might explode in anger, gathers himself, bows his head and closes his eyes while clasping his hands together in silent prayer. When he raises his head and looks at Zalvidia, his calm has returned.

"We each have our roles to play in life, do we not, Lieutenant? You would not have your silver coins without me, and I would not be here to save souls without you."

"Simple," says Zalvidia.

"Complicated compromises we make to spread the word of God," Cabo notes.

"Who were you before you became a Franciscan, Father Cabo? Here you are, far from home, no one knows who you are. Is there something in your past you escape?" Zalvidia asks the man who is becoming noticeably uncomfortable.

"Few will reach sainthood. Now I give myself to my Lord and help share the word of the Bible, spreading the Catholic faith to others," he answers assuredly.

"Are you a man who sees not everyone is suited to your beliefs?" I ask.

"I see the world day-to-day. I can predict no outcome. We do the best we can with what we have, right, Senor Martinez?"

"Some try to impose their will onto others, even if they must force them to obey. I hope you don't take this attitude with you into your new job," I say locking eyes with his.

"I'm new here, we shall see how each day unfolds," Father Cabo replies as he looks back over to Zalvidia and silently shifts his attention back to the food in front of him.

"Would you care for another plate?" Fernandez asks the new priest.

"I don't want to appear as glutton, but I could eat a mule."

Fernandez nods to the server and points to the empty plate. She dashes in, grabs the empty dish, and in a brief moment another full plate arrives. "Gracias," he says to the server. "She's a lovely child," he adds.

Fernandez rings the bell. The arrival of dessert at the hands of the servers shifts the mood of the room, followed by a motley assortment of Native Indians shuffling in with musical instruments in hand. Dressed in a patchwork of European clothes and hats, their instruments are a ramshackle Mission-made assembly of violins, guitar, cello, drum, wooden flutes, percussion and tubular bells. Fernandez stands tall as he organizes them into the corner. With his hands held like a conductor, all is quiet. With an enthusiastic cue, the band plays a frontier version of a classical European piece in a foreign land. The only real emotion I've witnessed among the Mission Indians comes alive in a spark of joy as they come together in song. They play quite fluently with the crude arrangement, a good reflection of the conductor skills and musical talents.

The song winds down as Fernandez admires the band with a growing smile. "You see, gentleman, we aren't entirely uncivilized out here," he boasts, and then lets rip a belch.

"Bravo! They're quite good," Cabo confirms with enthusiastic clapping.

"A long way from the concert halls of Madrid, but they are quick learners in the ways of music," Fernandez says with pride.

"You have done wonders. They are just like real musicians."

"Naturally quite talented. It is merely a question of direction. Carry on in my absence."

"I look forward to carrying on your work with the Natives," he replies enthusiastically. "But I must know Father, how do you learn to communicate with these Native people?"

"You will figure it out, as I did. Their language takes much time and patience to learn. You will need much more patience to teach them Spanish," the experienced priest instructs.

I listen with great interest to the music being played, which sounds nothing like what I hear from the musicians of Noqoto. European hymns played by Natives feel oddly out of place, but then, there are many odd things here at the Mission.

Fernandez digs into his stewed dessert fruit bowl like a pig at the trough. Finished, he pushes back from the table, leans back in his chair with his empty wine glass held high. The young server sprints to his side, carefully pouring without spilling a drop as the recipient of her efforts sternly eyes her every move. "I prefer fermented fruit!" he quips.

"One thing we agree on!" Zalvidia raises his glass, followed by the others.

The servers finish the wine rounds, mine requiring very little with just enough of a pour to keep the others from noticing.

Fernandez chuckles on at his joke while setting down his glass, it catches the edge of the dessert plate and the wine spills across the table.

"Damn! I hate wasting wine!" he says as he wobbles to his feet to face the musicians. "Pick up the tempo! I want to dance!"

Waving his arms high in the air, he spins around in circles, performing stumbling dance steps fueled by the wine as the band struggles to keep up.

"Thank God! Almost delivered from here!" he shouts with joy, hands extended to rafters.

CHAPTER 28

The drunken dinner party guests take little notice as I say good night and slip away. Fading music accompanies me as I walk down the long hallway. Entering the soft glow of the candlelit guest room, an unintentional glance in the mirror helps me decide that my formal evening clothes will help me not draw the soldiers' attention.

Shuffling silently to the main entry, I pause when I sense eyes on me. I turn slowly, and find myself facing a portrait of angels haloed in silver in the ghostly light. Beyond stands the barricade of a thick door with industrial hinges and deadbolt to keep outsiders out, and insiders in. I open it and step into the cool night, the muted courtyard enveloping me in gray. I pause and let my eyes adjust; although the moon has not yet risen, its ghostly glow is visible.

I turn the corner of the main building, reaching the soldiers' quarters. Dark shapes slump on benches, others are splayed across the dusty ground. A barrel lies on its side, goblets strewn in the aftermath of what must have been a drinking rage, the soldiers' snores a guttural concert. The moon's reflective light gives the morbidly drunk an unearthly hangover glow, with portents of headaches.

I see no humans near the stables. Cautiously moving around the back of the paddocks, I follow the fence line to a corner post and open the gates to the unfenced hillsides. Working my way back to the stables, I gently open each rear door and coax the anxious animals through the open gates. With long grass to keep them browsing, I close the gates and make my way back to the tack room. Going from saddle to saddle, I slice each leather girth strap where it meets the saddle, rendering them useless. Working from bridle to bridle, I cut each strap through until the cruel bit dangles free.

A voice sends my heart skipping. "New look?" Yaqi whispers.

"A disguise."

"I see the real you in there."

"The soldiers are drunk."

"Talkitna?"

"In the prison, as you said."

"We go get her."

"Trust me, you need to stay away from the Mission. I can get closer, without alarm."

"I will be watching in the shadows," he assures and hands me my weapons.

Wishing I were invisible, I walk across the courtyard, the weapons partially hidden. The Mission buildings loom in the layered light of shadows. Slipping behind the bell towers, I duck into the cover of supporting walls and look toward the prison. The moon throws elongated silhouettes of the bells onto the courtyard. Slipping silently between the main building and the house of worship, I peer cautiously around the corner to see a soldier slumped against the wall near the prison door. I slide toward him and my heart races. He's armed, his pistol lying across his lap. His stout leather armor covers his torso, and his helmet lies in the dirt. My knife at ready in one hand, I slip the skeleton key from around his neck. Snoozing and reeking of booze, he doesn't stir.

"Talkitna," I whisper.

"Wave Dancer," she whispers back.

I sheath my unbloodied knife. The lock gives way to the key. Sliding the deadbolt free, I swing the door aside to see her standing in a shaft of moonlight. I rush the last steps to join her and hold her again. She buries her head in my chest. A jab on my shoulder spins me around. Talkitna leaps at her brother with a flying hug.

The three of us make for the door. Talkitna stops and stares at the slumped prison guard. Revenge descends over her as she motions for Yaqi to hand her his knife. Yaqi shakes his head and draws his Spanish knife. Like a hunter bleeding his prey, in one slash blood pours from the freshly cut neck of the jailer. Awakened to his own death sentence, the guard's final earthly vision is Talkitna spitting in his face.

Yaqi gathers the dead guard's pistol and dagger, adding to our arsenal. He hands me the newly acquired Spanish dagger, and I tuck it into my belt.

We stalk carefully around the main building until only the Mission courtyard stands between us and freedom. No sign of life from the soldiers. We run across the exposed land.

A shout freezes us. I turn to see a man standing at the Mission door—Zalvidia.

"Stop!" he yells again.

"Run, Yaqi!" I warn, as I glance back at Zalvidia.

Zalvidia moves briskly toward the soldiers, yelling for them to rise. Wasted words, only slight stirring and mumbles. We run like spooked deer across the open courtyard toward the ridgeline, aiming for the shelter of shadows, closing the gap to the cover of dense oak trees.

The report of a gunshot rips the air. Yaqi drops at my side. I kneel down and witness the fallen warrior from my Dream Walk come back to haunt me. My brother Yaqi is lying dead at my feet. A slow river of blood pours from his shattered skull. I didn't want him to come to this demise, but I had no choice. History had its way.

Talkitna screams out mournful cries, then muffles her agony in tears. She drops down to Yaqi's lifeless body and holds it in a final embrace.

Coming out of shock, I reach into the quiver to draw one of Paxa's arrows. Pulling back with deadly intent, I aim at the executioner as he coldly walks toward us, readying his musket for another shot. I pull back firmly on Paxa's bow, calmly aim true, and send an arrow whistling. The flint point strikes the target. I reach for the pistol still gripped in Yaqi's hand as Zalvidia struggles to finish reloading his musket. We both fire, his lead whizzing past my head, my shot grazing him. My only shot with the pistol, and I inflict a glancing flesh wound.

He drops to his knees. "You die!"

The sounds of exploding gunpowder begin to rouse the soldiers who struggle to stand.

Father Cabo appears at the open door of the Mission. "Don't shoot!"

Father Fernandez and Portillo stumble to the entry and freeze, trying to make sense of what they witness. Fernandez strikes off on his own, wobbling toward the Mission bells. He pulls on their ropes, frantically trying to raise an alarm.

As much as we want to bring Yaqi home, we must leave him behind. I pull at Talkitna's arm. She refuses to go. I don't give her a choice. Rising up to our feet, we run, only to tumble to the ground as our feet are taken out from under us. With a deafening rumble, the earthquake of August 1787 violently begins, hurling us down to Mother Earth.

I roll to my side and glance toward the Mission. No one is standing. Dust fills the moonlit atmosphere as bells clang with each roiling wave generated from deep within the earth's crust. Fernandez is down on his knees beneath the bells. Crumbling chunks of adobe peel off around him. Knocked flat to his face, he fails to see the bell breaking free of its mount. With a final toll, it tumbles until it is deathly quiet. Lying beneath the immense brass weight, Friar Fernandez's earthly body lies motionless in the dust. For him, Mother Earth has had her final say.

When the shaking temporarily settles, Talkitna and I leap to our feet. All around us Mission Indians stumble around the courtyard, the walls now tumbled adobe, the bricks they once assembled now lying in crumbled piles.

Zalvidia slowly rises and hustles back to the soldier's quarters, yelling for the men to saddle the horses and pursue us. His words are hollow as the still drunken soldiers can barely rise to their feet, let alone gather weapons and horses.

Looking across the field to Yaqi, the moonlight shadow of the courtyard cross falls across his lifeless body. Pulling Talkitna away, we stumble into a sprint for the cover of trees beneath the shaded ridge.

Cresting the ridge, we slow our pace to catch our breath. Below us the Mission is enveloped in a soft haze of dust-muted moonlight. Crumbled walls lie haphazardly in the courtyard, collapsed trusses and gaping holes mark the roofs, and the bell tower has split in two and is missing a bell.

A lone figure kneels beside the courtyard cross. Cabo the priest is on his knees, praying to the god of his Catholic faith.

CHAPTER 29

After what seems like endless running, we both slow to a halt. Looking at Talkitna in the gun silver landscape, I see that the murder of her only brother Yaqi hangs heavy, smothering her spirit. I hand her my spear for her defense, but she turns toward the Mission.

"Little Wave waits for you," I remind her, stopping her with a firm hand.

She spins around and starts running toward her village, spear ready.

Once we hit the valley floor, there's nowhere to hide. Our tracks become child's play to follow as very few trees throw shadows. We pick up the pace to the sounds of our feet striding onto El Camino Real, our labored breathing as we suck in air. My heart pounds in my chest to keep up with the blood pumping through my veins. On a flat stretch, I look over my shoulder to see Talkitna on my heels, her face grim with determination.

We reach the top of a rise. I glance back to see if I can catch a glimpse of anyone coming up from behind. No sign.

Coming to a small stream crossing the trail from a side canyon, Talkitna slows. My body wants a long drink and a chance to stop moving, but my muscles may seize. Picking our way upstream away from the main trail, we find cover in the shadows of oaks.

With hushed tones, we gasp between gulps of water. "Do you have food?" she asks.

Reaching into my pouch, I pull out the last of the dried venison, careful not to drop it as I hand it to her. "Take it, I had dinner at the Mission with them," I sheepishly confess.

"You had dinner at the Mission with them? Perhaps one was the soldier who raped me!" Talkitna hisses, trying to hold her fury.

"Raped!"

"The child is mine, even if it has the blood of the Spanish."

"If I hadn't sent you and Little Wave to the waterfall, this wouldn't have happened…"

Talkitna grasps both my arms and looks into my eyes. "I came out of hiding, we would have been safe if we had stayed at the waterfall."

Surrounded by oak branches reaching toward the moon, I reach out to Talkitna and embrace her, as tears stream from both of us.

Running across the valley floor, we watch the moon sink below the distant ridge. The first colors of the new day threaten to expose us to all who might see. A glimpse of sun peeks over the ridge, striking us with warming rays as I shed my Mission shirt and tuck it out of sight. I double-time it to catch up with Talkitna, now well ahead of me as she strides up the valley to the ridge. When I reach her, we slow the pace, running beside each other as the trail narrows.

Approaching the last cover of trees, I slow down and look back, seeing low clouds in the far distances. Is it morning mist? Talkitna's eyes show she knows the difference.

"Run," she decides for both of us, as she takes off sprinting up the trail.

Striding behind her, I match her increased pace, breath to breath, step for step. The terrain behind passes as we gain on the imposing mountainous ridgeline ahead. Talkitna's back beads with sweat until rivulets flow. Steadily we climb, but are still exposed, the growing heat of the glaring sun adding to our punishment. Looking back over my shoulder I see in the distance a cloud of moving dust—horses on the move. Our tracks will be easy to follow, and there will be no doubt of our passing. It's time to make it difficult for our pursuers.

"Time to leave this trail," I point out between gasps for air.

"Your plan?"

"Up the steep narrow canyon to the ridgeline," I say with fake confidence as I point to the imposing canyon ahead.

"I say we look for an ambush," she replies showing no fear.

"Not sure how many…"

The canyon continues to narrow and grow steeper as we climb. Shade from the tree-lined gully cools the hot air by few degrees as our pace grinds to a climb. In low gear, our legs muscles pump hard to get up the steep pitch, each step up sending us a half-step back thanks to the loose scree. Upslope, through the thinning trees, we see a band of limestone cliffs presenting few options of ascent.

"We hold the high ground. This is the spot to take them," Talkitna says with confidence.

I have seven arrows in my quiver, a knife at my side, and a very revengeful woman with a spear anxiously rotating in her hands.

Cresting a split in the rocks just wide enough for a man on a horse, I pause to peer over the edge the way we'd come. It's a good setup for a marksman with seven arrows against how many men?

Above us is even steeper terrain, impossible for a horse and mounted rider to cover. Even if we have to keep fleeing, our escape route is nearby. Hustling upslope, we set tracks in the loose alluvial fan and then carefully backtrack, trying to stay in our own tracks until we're back at the rocky bluff. Quickly and quietly, we gather rocks and pile them on each side of the gap, building a sizable rock ammo stash. Looking across the gap to each other, I motion Talkitna to stay low. I place an arrow in the bow and check that my Spanish knife is easy to reach. The more I think about armor and helmets, the more I like the idea of a well-placed rock barrage, if surprise stays on our side.

Dust stirs, branches snap, and loose rocks tumble as we remain crouched on our rocky perch. I signal to Talkitna. She's anxious. The labored breathing of the horse echoes towards us, the clacking of hooves against rock as the animal struggles to climb higher. Spurs click and whip slaps under shouts of abuse from the unseen rider. The animal grunts and strains with desperate sounds of being pushed to the brink.

I peer out from behind a sheltering branch and see the outline of a single rider driving the exhausted beast without mercy. The rider breaks into the clearing below, fully in my view. There is only one man—Zalvidia, arm blood-caked and a cloth bandage tied around his head wound. Looking to Talkitna, she fingers a fist-sized rock and glances my way for the nod. Patience will be in our favor, as long as the horse continues to climb.

Long seconds later, I give the signal. We both stand with rocks in our hands. Looking over into the gap in the cliff, the horse still struggles, with no rider. We both look at each other with panic, having lost our element of surprise against the veteran soldier.

We quickly scramble up the steep slope to put distance between us. The sweat-soaked horse stops and rests on the rocky bench, panting for breath. No sign of Zalvidia, who's likely staying tight to the cliff to avoid being an easy target. We flee, scrambling on all fours up the unstable slope, aiming for the cover of thick brush at the top of the rock fall. I dislodge a boulder and send it tumbling; it bounces, launches off the cliff and crashes down the gully.

Ducking into thick cover of brush well out of sight of anyone below, we face a lot of vertical to make it to the crest. We're forced to stay low and snake our way through dense thicket of manzanita and deer brush, trying to hustle as we clamber up the incline.

Wind whips at our backs as the heat of the day rises up from the valley floor, bringing with it the unmistakable smell of burning wood. The wind shifts and stirs, smoke enveloping the brush around us. Directly below, building flames leap up the slope, racing toward us with explosive sounds of popping pitch and crackling dry wood burning with intensity. Roaring towards us is a wall of flames fanned by gusty wind, the wild fire feeding ravenously on brush.

Racing for our lives in a frantic dash to safety, we aren't the only animals. Deer sprint by us like we aren't there with panicked eyes and tails raised in alarm. Rabbits scatter, a lizard scurries, a snake slithers, scattering squirrels chatter in distress. Above us, winged birds flee into the safety of the sky, leaving behind the unfortunate land dwellers. Almost to the ridge, the intense heat pulls what little moisture I have left to spare. Through the thick, gagging smoke, the rocky ridgeline looks enticingly close, and then it's gone in choking billows. A few more blind steps and we give a last push to get over the top of the crest to the relative shelter of the lee side.

Time seems to slow, the last few steps a smoke laden haze. Hand in hand, we pull each other over the ridge and dive downslope following intuition. Feeling our way, we tuck in next to a rocky outcrop. Intense heat builds as we seek relief in the rough rock, entering the shelter of a cool, damp cave. The roar of nature's fury beyond our sanctuary is deafening. Out the narrow window of the entry portal, flames lick threatening to engulf. Flickers of firelight shrouded in smoke envelop our shelter. Lit in front of me is a familiar scene filtered through swirling haze— my portrait of the dolphin spirit guide. Next to my totem, Yaqi's depiction of a killer whale. My eyes close. He's here. When I open them he's gone. At my side, Talkitna sheds tears down her sooty face.

Exhausted, we slump against the cool wall of rock. Pressing close to each other, Talkitna rests her weary head on my shoulder. And there, amongst the cave art surrounding us, we collapse.

When I awake, the roar of the flames has dissipated to a few random crackles and pops. Outside the cave, the sky is still smoky, or is it? It's foggy moist air rising up from the seaward side of the mountain. We have to find water.

"Wake up, Talkitna," I whisper.

"Wave Dancer," she replies as she opens her eyes.

"The spring," I choke from my parched mouth.

We exit the cave into a burnt world filled with swirling hot smoke mixing with the moist coastal fog. Black skeletal stumps and branches stand ghostly around us, the dividing line of the ridgeline stopping the spread of flames. The dense smoke and fog snuff out the sun, leaving me to wonder how much of the day passed since we saw Zalvidia. Dropping down into the thick fog gives me comfort, knowing the gray blanket will hide us. Where the Spaniard might be is another question that lingers. He may have returned to the Mission, satisfied that his ploy of lighting the fire engulfed us in a burning hell.

The green grotto of the spring soon calls to us with the sound of falling water. Well concealed in the dense, unburned brush surrounding it, I'm not worried about being seen. Still, I cautiously lead Talkitna toward the spring, stopping frequently to look around and listen for any signs. As we step into the clearing, the sight of cascading water into the clear pool below sends us both scurrying to quench our thirsts.

After drinking all we can hold, we step back and look at each other. "I'm smoked," I comment as I take a whiff.

"Are we safe here?"

"I think we are," I assure her as best I can.

We both step up to the cascade of clear water and take turns washing our faces. "I need a bath," I state the obvious.

She answers with action, wading in with a sigh.

I watch her dip below the surface. Coming up for air, she gives herself a vigorous scrubbing and flips back her head, water flying from it.

She watches me, watching her as water drips down her face, joining tears of sorrow for her dead brother.

CHAPTER 30

Not far from the village, we pause and rest at the overlook's rocky bench where we'd eaten our first picnic together. Below us, framed by the ocean beyond, is her home, the village of Noqoto.

"Almost there," Talkitna nearly shouts.

"No Zalvidia in sight," I say as I scan the surroundings, still nervous.

"Little Wave!" Talkitna tosses me her spear and scampers down from our perch. Below me now, she breaks into a steady run as she hits the main trail to the cluster of village huts. I can feel her renewed spirit and the rush of emotion on returning home.

I clamber down from the rocks and hustle to try and catch her, but as I come to the clearing, she's nowhere to be seen. I have an unobstructed view toward the village, and panic sets in as I look around frantically for her. My fear is confirmed. I see dust.

Coming over the shoulder of a ridge, I see the horse and rider with Talkitna fighting against the tension of a rope lassoed tightly around her.

It's a long shot. I grab an arrow from Paxa's sheath and place it in the bowstring. With a prayer, I pull back to the breaking point and let it fly. The arrow arcs high into the sky and finds a live mark. The horse lurches and rears up, throwing Zalvidia into a backflip and hitting the ground hard.

As he wobbles to his feet, Talkitna runs to get away. I sprint to her and see Zalvidia readying his pistol. I prepare another arrow, this shot more than a prayer. It cuts the air in a blur toward the man intent on our deaths. The arrow glances off him as he goes for the trigger. The bullet explodes the ground at my feet.

With adrenalin-filled furry, I grab the spear and run toward the soldier, hoping to get him before he steadies his aim. Closing the gap, I let the spear fly with every bit of strength I have. It finds the target. Zalvidia reels and falls forward.

No sign of movement. I cautiously approach the downed fighter with my bow drawn. Talkitna stands well away, in shock from her ordeal. I kick him over with my foot. The spear falls limp out of his lifesaving armor. In his hand he clutches his pistol in a death grip, aimed directly at me.

His eyes widen with delight at seeing me about to receive gunpowder-driven lead. My bow is drawn tight, the deadly obsidian-tipped arrow aimed between his eyes. Neither of us wanting to die, neither wanting a draw.

"Go back to Spain and leave these Indians to live in peace."

The professional killer slowly gets to his feet, his gun aimed directly at my face. "You think I would walk away so easily from the bastard of a whore who wanted my life?"

We stand so close I can see into the eyes of a man crazed with revenge. Strangely, I feel no fear, only calm. "Want to live to see your whore house in Mexico City?"

"You want to live? Who do you side with, half-breed, the Indians or the Spanish? We can both walk away from here alive."

"Are you a man of your word?"

"I'm a professional soldier, bound by the ethics of my officer's oath."

I laugh out loud, while keeping my aim. "You fire that gun and my tribe comes running, surely an agonizing death for you."

"My soldiers will return and seek their revenge, no one here will be spared."

"So much for your code of ethics."

"Those are regular foot soldiers, not officers."

"Since you claim to be so noble, put down your gun."

To my shock, he drops his gun to the ground. "What kind of man are you?"

I lower my bow and set it on the ground. "Remember who spared your life."

"Go back to your precious tribe and take this bitch who now carries my seed," he replies, nodding toward Talkitna.

I look over toward Talkitna waiting in the distance, a sudden look of panic on her face. A thud into my shoulder and searing pain almost takes me off my feet.

I spin to face Zalvidia. "I lied," he admits freely.

I reach with my healthy arm and draw the captured Spanish knife out of its sheath. Warm blood courses down my body as I grip the dagger. Zalvidia runs toward the sea, his closest escape. I fling my dagger, watching it twirl and then stick into his thigh. He hardly breaks stride.

I fight back nausea and pull his dagger out of my shoulder, an intense rush of pain sending me to my knees. Fighting to stay conscious, I get up and stagger after him, his knife now in my hand, and my knife now in his. He beats me to the cliff's edge, pauses to look down. He jumps and disappears from view. I shuffle cautiously to the crumbling cliff, my wound throbbing as I struggle to focus and remain alert. On the edge of coherence, my eyesight blurring, I creep closer to the edge.

"Wave Dancer!" Turning toward the voice, my fading vision shows Talkitna running my direction with the spear in her hand. Without breaking stride, she launches and sends the spear flying past me. I reel around with wobbly legs to see Zalvidia, her spear pierced through his throat, his hands clutching each side of the shaft. Death in his eyes, he tumbles backward and disappears over the edge.

Losing my fight with consciousness, I strain, through mind-haze, for my last glimpse of Talkitna.

Her distant screams of despair cry out to me as I fall into a black void.

CHAPTER 31

The sound of the sea drifts in. Seabirds call eerily from beyond. Splinters of light creep into my vision as a sunny day spills into my shattered mind.

I lie still as death, not sure of my current status.

Beneath my back, I feel the firmness of damp sand of the high water mark. I can hardly move. I turn my head to the side and look down the beach. Rocky Point shakes unsteadily on the horizon as I try to focus.

In the distance, a wavy dream forms of a woman running down the beach in slow motion. My head aches and eyesight fades as I try to calm the inner-ear carnival ride. She's only a pleasant looking silhouette picking up her pace as she gets closer. I try to rise up, but flop back in a full-loop head spinner. As she comes into sharper focus, she lowers to her knees and leans over, seemingly in prayer. Her eyes show kindness and concern, familiar eyes I have seen before…

"You're hurt."

"I fell," I offer, my mind clouded with confusion.

I attempt to sit up, and the earth seems to wobble on its axis. I try to hold in the nausea.

"There's blood, let me help you get your shirt off."

Gently she rolls me to the side, takes my pack off, and carefully lifts my shirt free of my body. "Nasty cut, bleeding's stopped. If you fell, you may have a concussion. I saw your truck and your camp on my way here, let's get you back there and get a dressing on the wound. Come on, I'll help you."

With strong arms she helps pull me up. I shakily wrap my good arm around her as the dizziness returns. The more steps I take, the more my head clears. I look over at the woman helping me, now able to fully focus. Her hair is sun-bleached dirty brown, tied in a thick braid that brushes my face. She has the look of time outdoors in the sun, muscles well defined. I lean against her as a crutch. I look down and see strong legs dragging me along like a drunken guy. She leaves prints of beat-up hiking shoes as she maneuvers us toward camp Rocky Point.

"You look familiar…"

"I'm Linda Diaz, from the Museum. Remember? The Native American village display? We had a brief conversation, and then I had to run. I did text you. Remember?"

My throbbing head gives pause long enough for me to remember. "Linda! Of course! How come you're here?"

"I'm a wildlife biologist. I scored the job from the Natural History Museum's Biology Department to do a native plant and animal survey of Rocky Point. Hopefully before ENRG has a chance of trashing this sanctuary. It's a good thing I came when I did, looks like you had a nasty fall."

"I was rappelling off the cliff when the rope broke. I blacked out when I hit the water. I woke up, and the dolphin helped pull me out of the impact zone and into a dream…"

I struggle to remember, trying to tie in missing pieces. The images of the burial cave float into my head as reminders I'm not crazy. To confirm my self-diagnosis of mental health, I quit walking and reach into my pocket to look for the rainbow dolphin amulet as evidence. Nothing. I reach around my neck to feel for my grandfather's green stone canoe. Gone.

"I lost them," I say with sorrow.

"Lost what?"

"A gift from my grandfather, a green stone canoe. And I lost the dolphin amulet I found in the cave. I shouldn't have taken it…"

Linda stops and slowly leaves me to stand on my own. She drops our packs to the sand and reaches into the front pocket of hers, pulling out the greenstone canoe by the familiar cord.

"Is this what you're looking for?" she asks with a smile growing as she dangles it in front of my wide-open eyes.

Astounded, I look at the Dream Helper. "Where did you find it?"

"Washed up in the sand, before I spotted you."

"You're an angel," I say, reaching for it.

She holds tight, looking at me seriously. "Let me give this to you properly."

Face to face, close enough to touch, Linda drapes the greenstone tomol over my head. Stepping back, she gives a smile and admires its charm.

"I'm no angel, just sharp eyes."

"My Dream Helper returns. Thank you, Talkit— Ah, Linda."

Holding the precious pendant in my hands, fleeting images appear in my mind, the faded recollections of a dream only partially recalled.

I look directly into her eyes and see something there much greater than this moment. Call it coincidence, call it a dream, but this woman standing in front of me had come to me for reasons I can't ignore. "Thank you again."

"Glad I can help. It looks like we'll be spending time together here at Rocky Point," she says as she takes my hand and wraps it around her shoulder. "You'd better hold onto me, I don't want you falling again."

My camp is as I'd left it, everything still in place. It seems like home.

"You stay in that chair. That cut on your back looks serious. I've got a first aid kit in my car. I'll put some butterflies on to hold it closed. I can stitch that up nice and neat too. First, we need to clean it and get all the sand out."

"Sounds like you know what you're doing."

"I've put my wilderness medicine to use a few times."

"Appreciate your skills. I'd rather not leave Rocky Point. Time's wasting, what day is it anyway?"

"August 11th."

"There was a big earthquake..."

"It sure rocked me. I was organizing my field gear when it hit. Six-point-four, epicenter offshore, not far from here, actually. The experts are saying it wasn't the San Andreas, but a newly discovered fault. There's plenty of scientific seismic evidence to support the direction, depth and strength."

Remembering the photos of the burial cave on my waterproof camera, I dig into my pack. On first glance, it looks to be intact with no sign of lens fog. I point the camera at Linda and fire a quick photo. "Just a test. I want to get this downloaded and see if it's functioning."

"Let's get you patched up first. I saw my old friend barbadensis miller growing on the hillside near where I parked. I'll go back and get a cutting."

She runs up the road like she's on the first mile of a marathon. In no time she returns, bumping my way in a stiff-shocked Land Cruiser with wide all-terrain tires and a cable winch mounted to a cattle bar. Her legs dangle from the door as she climbs out and hops to the ground.

"Nice wheels."

"I end up in remote locations. We can talk auto shop later. Let's get to that wound," Linda says, dragging out a first aid kit from the back seat.

She gives me a strong dose of painful pleasure as she cleans my cut.

"Cool tattoo on your other shoulder."

"What?"

"The dolphin in mid-leap."

"I faintly remember getting it, guess it's here to stay."

"Heard that one before. Your wound's clean, I don't think you'll need stitches. This aloe should help it heal quickly. How's your head?"

"Better, not so dizzy."

"You've got to be careful with concussions. I want you to look me straight in the eyes."

She kneels down in front of me and I stare into her eyes. "Okay, I want to track your eyes while I move my finger. Follow it wherever it goes."

Linda gives me a tour of her features as she tracks back and forth with her index finger. I return to her eyes, briefly peering into her soul.

"I want to feel your pulse, let me see your hand."

She gathers my wrist into her hand and finds my pulse while checking her watch. "Pulse is a little high. I'd like to keep an eye on you. You need to stay upright for a while, then rest and take it easy tonight. What are you planning on doing for dinner?"

"I was hoping to have dinner with my new neighbor. I've got plenty of food, if the expiration dates haven't expired…"

"I've got a salad in the chiller along with tortillas, cheese, fresh salsa and avocados. I was going to spend some nights camping here to keep from driving back and forth and burning up time and fuel. It looks like you beat me to the best place to put up a tent."

"Lady, you have a good eye for property—quiet, end of the road, short stroll to a white sand beach, freshwater lagoon in the backyard, established shade trees, and only one neighbor."

"Perfect. I'm your new neighbor, if you don't mind."

"No wild parties."

"Only wild animals and plants invited to my party."

"Welcome to the neighborhood," I say with a smile and a hand extended toward hers. She smiles back and meets my hand. Our handshake lasts beyond a mere pause, my pulse racing.

"I'll get my tent set up before dark," she says with a confident tone.

"I'd give you a hand, but I'm under orders to relax."

"Done it many times before."

Linda is my campsite entertainment as I kick back in my chair and watch. She competently picks out a tent site, lays out the tent, stakes it down, puts together the poles, strings them through the sleeves, cranks on the poles until the dome pops up, lays out the hold down ropes, drives stakes to secure them against the wind and adjusts the tension of the hold downs to perfection. I gain respect for her with every move she makes. With a final unfolding of the camp chair, the happy camper flops down into it and looks across at me with a satisfied grin.

"You could be a professional camper."

"I am being paid. You're not doing too badly yourself. Probably a better gig than that Wooden Indian routine."

"I need hazard pay on this job, when I do get paid," I reply as I touch my sore shoulder.

"What were you doing rappelling off a cliff?"

"Thought I saw something worth checking out when I was surfing."

"Thought you were supposed to be working."

"I took an extended lunch break. Noticed the rack on your rig, are you a surfer?"

"My minor was Campus Point. Now, I'm surf mom for my son."

"How old?"

"Nine, but thinks he's a pro surfer already. His dad got him into it early."

"His dad must be proud."

"He was very proud. Took his boat across to Santa Rosa in search of empty waves, gale-force winds caught him mid-channel on the way back. His engine failed. Got a mayday call off before the boat was swamped. Tried to paddle for it on his board. We never found him. His board washed up on Santa Rosa, with a shark bite sized chunk missing."

"That's heavy, must be tough on you."

"Mourning takes time. Though it wasn't a surprise. He was Mister Adventure. I've mostly moved on. I have our gift of a beautiful son."

"Where's your son? What's his name?"

"Jake. He's with my parents. All these questions about me, it's your turn. I only know you briefly from our Museum encounter."

"You're talking to a former Native American Heritage figure with a concussion. Now I'm even more confused about my current standing. My brain is so scrambled right now, I'm not sure what's past and what's present."

"Hopefully it will come into focus after you've had a chance to rest. I've got to plan out my day tomorrow, then I'll get to dinner. You take it easy."

"I could get a fire started, if I can find the matches."

"I got it, we don't want you face planting in flames."

"Cool by me, former wooden Indians have an aversion to flames. I'll get these photos into my computer."

What was a hazy recollection of the burial cave comes to sharp focus as I get the images on the screen. With each photo coming through, a rush of déjà vu helps to piece together the last moments before I took the fateful fall. Pausing to linger on the close-up photo of the rainbow dolphin amulet, I close my eyes.

Through the portal of my mind's eye, Talkitna walks to me through misty fog. She floats my way and gifts me the dolphin guardian. She fades away through Dream Walk clouds.

Next fade is the photo of the small skeleton resting on decayed wood. I stare beyond the computer screen and see a boy in my mind's eye. It's Little Wave with the plank of a wooden belly-board beneath him, riding the curl with joy on his face.

Next on the screen, lying side by side, the remains of the couple resting together. The man with white quartz hawk amulet around his neck next to the woman adorned with strings of shells placed lovingly. Sharing their journey together to the Other Side as they had shared their journey through much of life. The love of Paxa and Alapay lives on in my soul.

The next image brings me to the present. On the screen, the photo I shot of Linda. I stare at her face as another face comes gently into my mind. Talkitna's face ghosts over Linda's portrait. The two women who found me washed up on the beach in different eras of time, look like lost sisters. The sudden rush of realization vibrates through me and leaves me gasping for air.

"You okay?" Linda calls out.

"I want you to look at these, can't tell anyone. Promise?"

"I can keep a secret, depending on what it is..."

I pause to compose myself. "It's what I found on the cliff face, just before I fell."

Linda grabs her glasses and peers over my shoulder as I show her each image. She stands in silence taking in the photos of the burial chamber as they unfold. No words needed to convey the sacredness of the resting place and the respect for the dead.

"Peter! That's an archeologist's trophy room! What you found is amazing. You must be so excited to share your discovery with the world."

"Not really excited. It's complicated. Expose this cave, then what? Ship my ancestors and their burial items to a museum? Put their burial effigies on public display? Or stuff them in the back halls of an archive room in a cold steel drawer? Or, don't tell anyone, besides you. Then what might happen when they're discovered someday? And who am I anyway? Grave robber or archaeologist? These days it's so rare to find anything on this scale that hasn't been plundered and looted. This is a heritage discovery that could be worth a small fortune on the antiquities black market. Then there's ENRG with their huge money on the line pushing to get Rocky Point developed. The same corporation that wouldn't want you finding endangered flora or fauna around here. And then there's the job offer at Santos and all the cash being dangled in front of my nose. I need time to think this through. Will you keep this confidential?"

"I promise," she says with unquestionable sincerity.

"Shake on it?" Our hands grasp together.

Coming back to the cave photos, I remark, "Those people in the burial cave have shown me past lives of my tribe I could only imagine before my Dream Walk into their world."

Linda stares at me, not quite sure where I'm coming from. "Shown you? Dream Walk? Their world? Symbolically, right?"

"Sometimes I see vivid dreams into the past, like when I had my concussion, like a few minutes ago when I looked at the photos. I saw those people alive, I lived with them in their village."

"You'd better lie down."

"I saw one of these people from hundreds of years ago just a few days before I fell from the cliff. I was at Mission Santos and a warrior from my tribal past appeared in a dust devil, then I met up with him again in 1787. His name was Yaqi. We became tribal brothers."

"A knock on the head can do crazy things. I'll keep the straight-jacket handy."

"It all seemed very real, and it still does. In fact, there was a woman very much like you in the village of Noqoto."

"Like me? Now you're creeping me out."

"You could be sisters, from another era. Got me thinking Talkitna and I could be… And Zalvidia and I could be…"

"What tales you tell. You might want to write this all down before you forget."

Kicking back in my camp chair, recalls of past ancestral connections enter my mind. Staring at the dancing flames of ancient fire triggers dreams playing back. My tribe of Noqoto dance together in ceremonial costume around the raging bonfire. From the darkness, the voice of Talkitna singing brings a rush of emotion. I look at Linda, humming a song while placing plates on the table.

"I'll get your chair," I offer, getting up too quickly and sending me into a spin. Linda's comforting arm wraps around me as I find my legs.

"Peter, I can get my own chair. I don't want to have to pull out the first aid kit again."

"You're putting a damper on my manners."

"Your gestures are appreciated, but not necessary. Let me help you. That's what neighbors are for," she reminds me as she places her chair next to mine.

I savor every bite of the meal. Linda keeps my water glass full, insisting I stay hydrated.

"That was the finest meal I've had in ages."

"That's a nice compliment, coming from someone as well traveled as you imagine yourself to be."

"Imagine this; when I fell from the cliff and hit the water, what happened soon after I blacked out was an awakening."

Linda ignores her food. "Awakening after you blacked out, like a near death experience?"

"When I saw you on the beach today, our meeting was the end of my Dream Walk back in time. There was a whole journey between blacking out and seeing you."

"Here you go again... Are you feeling dizzy right now?"

"I'm not dizzy. The awakening was what I experienced in the Dream Walk. A journey back to California of the distant past. My ancestors once lived here, right where our tents are. In the morning I'll show you some antiquities I found. This place was teeming with village life from my tribe of the 1700s."

"And you say that someone like me was there?" she asks, wondering about my sanity.

"It could have been you in another time."

"I'm scientifically schooled, I don't believe in reincarnation. But, I do like to think I have an open mind... until proven otherwise. Tell me, Peter, do you Dream Walk to the future?"

"Often, when I visualize the future, many times what I envision comes true."

"What do you see in the future now?"

"I see us becoming friends."

"We share the same vision."

"Then you Dream Walk too."

We both stare off into the flames, returning at the same time to look at each other. Smoke swirls softly in the flickering light, the quiet of remoteness settles like a comforting blanket.

"It's interesting how we both ended up here after meeting at the Museum. What are the odds?" Linda comments.

"I'm no odds maker, call it fate."

Rising up from her seat, Linda extends her hands to help. I hang on to her hand to brace myself, feigning the need of support.

"You may need to feel my pulse again, my heart's skipping," I say with a fake wobble.

"I think you'll live. You've had a big day, plus or minus some centuries. I have a big day tomorrow. I'll put out that fire," she says as she releases my hand and douses the flames.

"See you to your tent door, in case of Grizzly bears?"

"Poor arctos californicus, never had a fair fight against guns."

"Or wooden stakes."

"The tales you tell. Good night, Peter."

"I'll tell that tale another time. Good night, Linda."

Watching her closing the tent flap, her questionable look at me disappears with a rapid zip.

CHAPTER 32

Outside the glowing fabric walls, nature's voices of dawn call as birds sing their morning glory stories. Behind the chirping choir, the rhythmic crest of breaking waves sends my surf-obsessed mind questioning the wisdom of surfing. I lie on my cot in my sleeping bag comfy and warm, quite willing to wait for the sun to directly strike the tent before I make any big moves.

The clouds and morning light moves leisurely across the mesh skylight of my fabric home. My neighbor enters my thoughts. From what I've seen so far, there's no way she's sleeping in. With a long pull, I unzip the bag and shuffle over to zip down the door. In the dewy grass, fresh tracks of a female biologist head toward Rocky Point.

Flapping in the breeze, a note attached to her tent: "Peter, I'm off to survey around Rocky Point. Suggest we meet for lunch here at midday. Surf's not good, so take it easy."

Slowly I organize myself. There are some less strenuous tasks I can get done. With an easy push of the red ignition button, I fire the stove to get water boiling. Steaming mug of coffee in hand, I stroll to the beach to check the surf. Not so good, as Linda said.

Facing the ocean with toes dug in the sand, everything around me is basically the same, but some changes are glaringly apparent.

The sky is littered with jet trails. Miles offshore, a container ship stacked ridiculously high cruises south, looking like it's about to collide with an oil platform. On the distant ridgeline, the chain-link fence with barbed wire looks like a wildlife internment camp. The Rocky Point access road slices down the ridgeline, ending where I stand, I'm reminded of Old Red parked and waiting.

Approaching Old Red is like seeing a friend after years apart. A mechanical companion exuding good memories of time shared. Moving to the back bumper, there's no visible reason for the rope to come loose. I clearly recall checking my knots and double-checking to make sure it wasn't going anywhere. And there where it should be, the trailer hitch, intact and with no rope to be seen anywhere.

Stepping around the back of the truck to get in the driver's side, I spot the unmistakable indentation of a boot print in the patchy dirt between crushed sagebrush. It's recent. A man's boots with pronounced heels. I don't wear boots or heels.

Sorting through my pack, I take out my camera to capture images of the tracks. Careful not to disturb the impression, I climb into the truck. I fire up the motor with the new battery and give a friendly pat to the time-faded dashboard as I begin easing the old girl toward camp. Bumping along the rough terrain, my wounded back makes me grimace.

I put Old Red into first gear and set the loose handbrake. I glance in the rear view mirror at camp. Rounding the good mirror of the truck, I catch a glimpse of myself reflecting back. I peel off my shirt and bend around to check my neatly dressed wound. Turning the other shoulder, I look at the dolphin tattoo. Rushing memories of my spirit journey rise up from my soul. Yaqi's art lives through me as an avatar guided by his dolphin guardian tattoo.

At the camp table's desk, I download the images from my camera onto my laptop. Staring at the indentations of the boot, I have an educated guess who may have circled my truck.

Walking toward the last survey marker with shovel in hand, I pull out the wooden stake with a shake and start to dig shovel-depth into geometric grid patterns of layers of earth. I scrape around the excavated zone and assemble fresh dirt to the side. With a detailed effort using a garden spade and dry brush, the pit starts to reveal a ring of darkened rocks. I flash on vivid reflections of my tribe gathering around a flaming communal fire.

With a screened sifter, I sort through the first of the loosened material like an artifact miner panning for clues. After many shaky efforts, the fine dirt falls through the mesh to reveal ancestral stories. It's an animal bone hollowed out with holes drilled, a lonely flute gone silent. I gently clean it with water and flush out the dirt. I give it a blow and it still whistles. I play random notes imagining who played a song long ago.

Sifting through more material, I reflect on historical layers of man built upon each other over centuries of centuries. I daydream that perhaps someday in the future, others will find the layered remains of what was once present-day Los Angeles. In a brief wink of geologic time, LA sinks beneath the globally rising sea to become another lost Angel of Atlantis.

Returning to camp wearing a thick layer of dust, my morning's dirty work has produced a handful of artifacts spreading across my table. A few fragments of arrow points, part of a pestle, a whale bone scraper. My quiet contemplation of the past is broken by an approaching vehicle, the security SUV with dust flying in a spreading cape behind it. In one sweep I gather up the collection on the table and place it inside my tent pocket. As the SUV gets closer, I see Linda in the passenger's seat. Pulling to a stop, she steps out while swinging a pack.

"Cheers, Steve!" she calls to the security guy.

Over her shoulder I can see the same security dude giving me a smile and a wink through the window. "Hey, Steve, turn that thing off!" I shout with a kindly wave of my hand.

Looking shocked at the unexpected hospitality, he surprisingly turns off the engine and follows Linda to our temporary tent homes.

"Cool of him to give me a ride," Linda says while slinging the daypack.

With shifty eyes, the uniformed ENRG militia man cases out our camp like he's watched too many cop shows. As he steps up to me with his familiar alpha stance, I take the opportunity to glance at his feet. His black boots leave clean tracks.

"Want a glass of water," I offer him.

"No thanks."

"There's something I thought you might be interested in seeing."

Curiosity gets the better of him as he follows me to my tent awning. I grab my camera with one hand and open the laptop with the other. I pull up the photos of the boot prints by my truck and lower my laptop next to his most recent boot prints in the dirt. I squeeze off a couple of photos showing the undoubtable boot match, then pan up and get a full body shot of him standing with mouth open.

"This is really interesting. These are photos of boot prints by my truck. I was doing a bit of exploring off the cliff when the rope I was hanging from let loose. Almost killed me. I couldn't help notice that the boots you're wearing look exactly like those I found next to my truck just before the rope came off."

Linda shuffles over and lines up all the angles, nodding her head. "They look the same."

Security Steve isn't too happy, looks like he's about to make himself scarce, but squeezes in words of defense. "Those photos don't prove anything, Sherlock Surfer," he says smugly.

"Someone was trying to shorten my lifespan. I won't have to look far to find him."

"Anytime you need a ride, little lady, you just let me know," he says as he winks at Linda.

"I'll walk," she replies, turning her back.

The corporate thug lumbers back to his truck. Firing up his engine, he gives me his familiar middle-finger salute. Testing the throttle, he throws up dust that drifts our way, guided by the rising wind.

I glance over at my camp mate. "I hate to lecture, young lady, but you need to be careful who you climb into cars with."

"He seemed like a nice man, the uniform and all. But that guy is twisted. He adjusted your rope for a fall. Now what? The cops?"

"No, I have to keep working this place."

"What about security cameras? Likely they've got them. Maybe there's a visual of him messing with your rope?"

"This isn't a reality show."

"Maybe it is, the cameras could be wireless."

"So, what if they are?"

Linda scans the ridge above our campsite. "That looks like a relay tower and dish, line of sight to Rocky Point, might have a lens pointed at our camp too."

"Then what?"

"If it isn't a closed system, you should be able to hack the signal. You just need the wireless frequency."

"Beyond me."

"Let me see your laptop."

Watching Linda's fingers fly through a mind-boggling maze of information is impressive. I don't comprehend any of the software programing technical backdoors she weaves through until I see the image pop up on the screen.

"Looks like a live feed," she says with pride. "Computer Science pays!"

I glance toward Rocky Point and confirm it's live when I see the flock of gulls gliding through my screen.

"Very clever of you, but I need footage of him untying my rope."

"I'll see if I can get into the hard dive on the main system. I need to hustle before the creep gets back to the guard house."

In almost no time she's able to reverse the time of the footage and scroll back through it until Old Red is parked in the frame. She goes back further until there's clear footage of Security Steve entering the picture. Slowing it down to freeze frames and zooming in on the detail, Linda and I can see him as he cautiously walks to my truck and makes his way around to the rope. Following it to the edge of the cliff, he looks over to the water below. Then, he makes his way back around to the rear of my truck and bends down.

"Can you zoom in more?" I ask.

Clearly I can see him loosen the rope from the hitch, leaving it barely wrapped. He walks by the driver's side and looks in the window. Linda downloads the footage and hits SAVE. "He's a sick dude," she comments on his character.

"You missed your calling at the NSA."

"I'm good at problem-solving issues I care about." She looks down at the image again with renewed concern, "Looks like he was playing the role of your executioner. Whether ENRG has anything to do with his actions poses another question," Linda says, with a bit of doubt.

"Huge money at stake. I'd bet the security footage now safely on my hard drive mysteriously disappears from the system in the guard house," I say as I file the images under "Free Fall" and shut my laptop, choosing to ignore the date on the image.

Remembering the bone whistle I'd found, I duck into the tent, pull out the artifacts and lay them out on the table. Linda steps over to look at them in closer detail.

"Nice, Peter, where did you come up with these?"

"They were around what looks to have been a fire pit I excavated." I pick up the whistle and play a quick few notes. "I may have played drums with this guy."

Walking back to her tent, she calls excitedly over her shoulder, "I've got some wonderful plants I found too! Let me download these photos and I'll show you!"

Across her screen come photos of an assortment of select plants. "These are two endangered plants on both the State and the Federal Endangered Species list. This gem is called California Jewel Flower, and this shrub is Franciscan Manzanita. I also found some plant species that aren't as scarce. These days, Leather Oaks are found only in a few small pockets. And, I believe this is Vandenburg Monkey Flower, but I've never seen one before. Rocky Point being so undisturbed is rare in coastal California."

"Would any of these endangered species stop the project?"

"First, they'll have to be peer tested for accuracy. If they are what I think they are, it may be enough to put the brakes on destroying their natural habitat. But don't hold your breath. Recent history shows how often developers find ways to get around environmental restrictions by making deals to set aside other land they have acquired elsewhere."

"Looks like an uphill battle. No fun being a California Jewel Flower confined to cracks in the concrete".

"Think positive. I haven't even gotten to the formal animal survey yet. Have you seen any foxes or owls?"

"I've heard owls calling, just before the earthquake."

"What about frogs, fish, newts or salamanders in the wetlands? This lagoon is a real rarity; most coastal estuaries in California have been filled in for development."

"I hear the frogs are happy."

"I can't wait to keep looking, but now I'm famished."

"I made some sandwiches."

"Thanks, Peter, I really appreciate it."

"Nice to give back to you after all you've been doing for me."

Sitting in the shade of the willow tree eating our lunch, time together seems timeless. "Hope that was dolphin free tuna," she says while finishing the last of her crust.

"You're talking to a man with a dolphin tattoo. Are you working late?"

"I'll be back about dark."

"You're putting in the hours."

"For a worthy cause."

"I've got dinner tonight, I'm staying close to camp."

"Thanks, appreciate that. How's your head?"

"Back to my normal..."

"Still having illusions of the past?"

"Call me Wave Dancer."

"Nicer sounding than Wooden Indian. Glad to be out of the casino and on this job?"

"No comparison. My track record doing fieldwork got me this gig. The past seems to find me. I'm a Dream Walker, says my grandfather."

"You're a time-traveler of your mind, but I'll need to peer test the physical theory."

"I scored a dolphin tattoo souvenir on my last big Dream Walk."

"I need undisputable evidence of the tattoo actually being created on you."

"You'll have to take my word for it. But right now, I'm just an Indian archaeological scout around here at Rocky Point. Evans will bring in the cavalry for the expanded site work excavation."

"Is that why you were at the Museum when we met?"

"I was showing Evans my most recent find at Mission Santos, then he broke the news to me about ENRG's attempts to rape the land of my sacred surf break and ancestral home. Next thing I know, he hires me to do the initial survey. Says it's because of the time I've already put in at Rocky Point chasing waves and my bloodline linkage of over 7,000 years. When I met you in the Native culture display, he was prepping a letter. I go from recently fired Indian Heritage Figure being replaced by a robot, to museum archaeologist. Now, if I can stop the oil depot, it will be a valid occupation."

"Just curious, is there a lady waiting for you back on the reservation?"

"I asked you to have coffee."

"Any kids in your past?"

"No, although I envy them."

"I hear you there."

"You say I should write down my tales. Does your boy read books, like real books?"

"Loves to read paper books. I'm keeping him away from electronic clutter crap as long as I can."

"My grandfather would approve."

"He'll have plenty of time later in life to decide if staring like a zombie at an electronic screen is a worthy of his time. One thing I can see already, like his father once did, when the ocean is nearby he'll drop everything to dive in."

"Sounds like you're happy to take him to the beach."

"The ocean calls us both."

"Too bad you didn't bring your surfboard."

"I thought I'd be working. Speaking of work, I've got to roll. Take it easy and don't reopen that cut on your back."

"I'll be playing in the dirt like a good boy."

As the excavating hours pass, I clear all around the top of the fire ring and expose the large blackened rocks to former ground level. From where the pit is located, I pace off in other directions where I recall from my Dream Walk other tribal gathering stations— the basket making area, seed grinding zone, boat builders location, shell pile of waste, and the tool and weapon manufacturing area where there could be a trove of lasting artifacts.

By late afternoon I have another nice assortment of ancestral odds and ends spread across the table, castoffs that weren't fit for use, broken pieces of fish hook, shaped stone pestles, broken arrow points, half-finished scraping rocks. Just this site alone would require a huge amount of time to sort through the many generations that once called this home.

The setting sun toys with my elongated shadow-self as I arm-puppet my expanded reach. Time to call it a fitting end to a long day. Settling back into camp life, I fire the gas lantern to help Linda find her way back and get to the food prep duties. Camp chef of the night gets cooking Italian red sauce with spicy sausage, onions, pepper and splashed with some California cabernet. Set the table waiter-like with my finest cheapo camp utensils, organize remains of a melted candle, light a fire, and cue music on my laptop. Time for a solar shower before getting back to task at the Rocky Point Bistro.

Headlamp beam marking her presence, Linda comes walking out of near darkness into our neighborhood of two.

"Hard day at the office?"

"Critter traffic was literally crawling."

"Saved you a solar shower. Dinner will be ready soon."

"Cool. Smells great, what are we having?"

"Italian tonight, spaghetti with red sauce, bread and wine. Table for two?" I ask as I drape a dishcloth neatly over my arm.

"Wonderful, if the entire staff of one will join me. Table outdoors?"

"Excellent choice on such a fine evening."

Linda disappears into her tent and zips up her door. I glance over to the solar shower hanging nearby. When I first rigged up the camp shower to the willow tree, I was here alone, didn't even think about privacy. It's the best location to hang the heavy black water bag in the sun, a branch high enough to hoist it with good drainage to keep the runoff from the lagoon. Before Linda's return, I quickly hung my only beach towel as a privacy screen after my shower. Untested, a gust of wind mid-shower would be visually challenging.

Appearing from her tent looking like a rare Rocky Point biological specimen of the beautiful human female species, Linda walks to the shower zone with towel wrapped around her, carrying implements of cleanliness. Being the gentleman I strive to be, I glance down at my cooking stove to the task at hand. Being the male of the species, I can't help but shift slightly. A gust of wind sends the tent rippling. My eyes turn to see the beach towel flying like a flag twisting in the breeze. Softly lit in the warm glow of the lantern light, my very pleasurable glance is kept secret as she washes her hair with eyes closed.

When she reappears through her tent door dressed for the night, she gives a contented sigh, sweeping a comb through her hair and smiles at me with enough radiance to freeze me. "Doesn't a warm shower feel great after a day tramping in the hills?"

Flustered by the newly scrubbed lovely lady standing in front of me, I'm left with only a few words and dribble, "Would Madame camper care for wine?"

"Big yes!"

I walk over and hand her a wine glass of red plastic. Looking directly into her eyes, I teeter as toastmaster. "To crossing paths once again here at Rocky Point."

"To new friends. And may Rocky Point remain untouched by the petrochemical industry," she adds.

Plastic touching plastic, both of us smile as California red flows.

I walk Linda to the table, and quickly return with two steaming plates of penne pasta smothered in red sauce. The candles on the table flicker and dance with last colors of day as the first stars of night appear in twilight sky. Dinner music serenades as crickets and frogs sing chorus of random scales.

"My complements to the chef," she says with a satisfied smile.

"When you're camping, almost anything tastes great."

"I really appreciate your efforts. How was your day? How are you feeling?"

"My health is improving, thanks. I made some progress on the excavations, found another site with some stone and bone fragments. I'm starting to get a good picture of what the village once looked like. How'd you do?"

"I did well. I'm getting a good feel for what animals are here. I found some interesting tracks, lots of signs and even some impressive mountain lion tracks high on the ridgeline. I set a few bait boxes for the little critters. I'd love to find a Pacific pocket mouse, they're so scarce."

"Most women wouldn't want to find mice in their pockets... How long do you plan on being here for your wildlife survey?"

"My parents are watching Jake through the weekend. Like you, I'm just the point person establishing the groundwork, setting the stage for more in-depth studies with a bigger crew."

"You must be very good at what you do, being first on the scene."

"I've been doing this kind of work since I was a volunteer in high school. I feel like I'm helping to save these plants and animals, giving them a voice in government short-term special interest-led legislation. I'm fighting for wildlife against globalized corporate irresponsibility for the environment, which is leading the way to our teetering at the edge of the environmental cliff. Most of our current threatened species are on the brink of survival due to human activities. Over seven billion people crowd the Earth, and the population's growing. It's all building up to more extreme weather patterns sweeping across the world. We are staring at the Anthropocene, the sixth mass extinction. We are losing species at a frightening rate. It's all interconnected in the ecological web. We're snuffing out plant and animal species like there's no tomorrow, including ourselves."

"Did you hear who won the finals of the playoffs? Was it Golden State Warriors?"

"I'm not amused."

"I can only take limited doses of impending doom. I really can see you're passionate about your work."

"I am."

"Not everyone can say that."

"I can tell you're passionate too."

"I feel like I'm helping to give a voice to those who got screwed by Manifest Destiny. Trying to fit together pieces of the archaeological puzzles of pre-European cultures before they got decimated by what others labeled, 'Progress'."

"Progress isn't all bad. Finding a balance with Nature is the key. Otherwise, we're all toast on this planet."

"Mother Nature will survive without us." I lift my glass, "Food is getting cold."

"I'll catch the dishes," she says with no argument.

Settled into kick-back mode in our comfy camp chairs, quiet contentment as the sounds of the nature-filled night surround us underneath a ceiling of stars. I stir the embers with a green stick and toss in a few more hunks of driftwood to feed the flames as dying embers swirl with the rising smoke twisting in infinite space.

"Peter, what you call Dream Walks, do you really believe they exist, or do you think they're vivid dreams not easy to forget? I have dreams sometimes and they seem so real I could swear they were, until I wake up and find myself disappointed I was only dreaming."

"I can't really tell you. Sometimes I'm not sure what to think. Like right now, I could be dreaming a very pleasant dream with you here."

"I can assure you, as a trained scientist, I'm not a dream."

"Linda, I have to confess something. When you were showering tonight a gust of wind blew the beach towel away like a flag. I couldn't help but see what I saw... I don't want you to think I'm a pervert. We'll rig up a better private shower in the morning."

Linda breaks into a giggle, then calms. "Since we're confessing, I came into camp from the hills earlier this evening. I walked around the willows, and there you were showering with nothing to hide. I was so embarrassed, so I slipped away and waited awhile. By the way, love your cool tattoo."

"Yours is cool too, what I accidentally glimpsed of it..."

"See you for coffee in the morning?" she asks with a hint of a smile.

"Looking forward to it. I'll be barista."

CHAPTER 33

After a very pleasant morning cup of coffee while chatting with Linda, we part ways, walking our commutes to work, me chasing long lost ancestors and she seeking out the remaining local residents of the plant and animal kingdom.

Today I decide to focus on the edge of the lagoon where the boat building would have been. If there were to be any surviving tomols, they would have been buried deep in the mud by a flood, the wood preserved. To find a Native boat intact would be a dream come true.

It didn't take long to figure out where the boat builder location was in relation to the sand bar enclosing the lagoon. It's a matter of functional convenience. With almost no rocks to get in the way, digging down through the sandy mud isn't too difficult. When I do finally hit something hard, I carefully clear the dirt away from the palm-sized object. Rinsing it thoroughly in the lagoon, I see it's a black obsidian stone shaped into a sharpened hand plane, a familiar tool for shaping wood projects such as boats and early surfboards.

The unmistakable sound of helicopter blades slicing the air draws my attention from my work. Flying in from the south, the dragonfly machine grows bigger until it swoops in, blocking the sun. I toss the woodworking stone in my pack and stash it.

The ENRG helicopter returns with a smiling Richard Thorne waving out the window. Dust is kicked up around me in a dry blizzard as the wind-maker pulls leaves from branches, spinning the air in a blender.

The mechanical storm calms. Thorne steps out the door as the blades wind down. "Looks like you have a new neighbor," he comments, nodding at the additional tent.

"Linda Diaz, biologist working for the Santa Barbara Natural History Museum. She's away in the field looking for endangered species for ENRG to eradicate."

"Harsh words, Peter the environmentalist. I'll have you know, as responsible corporate citizens, ENRG works within environmental protection laws of each jurisdiction we occupy. To show you I'm a man of my word…" He uses both hands to lug a metal strong box from behind the passenger door. Setting it down on the ground with a thud, he opens it. Stacks of golden Canadian coins glimmer in the sunlight.

"Took you awhile, you may have explored other options," I comment, the memory of the rope fresh in my mind.

"This is the deal we agreed on."

"We did not agree, only a consideration of your offer. I see now you were serious." I pick up one of the gold coins and toss it in the air, catching it blindly in my other hand.

"Three hundred thousand in 99.9 % pure gold coins, it's all yours, if you keep your end of the deal," he says as he shoves the strong box over with his foot, spilling gold coins across the earth. "Nobody will know. Think of all the good things you can do with this gold."

"I've given it a lot of thought, and you're right, wealth is not necessarily a bad thing. Money can do a lot of good for humanity."

"A deal?" he asks as he extends his hand to shake mine.

"All about how I earn the wealth, I need to be able to live with my conscience. What goes around comes around. The Golden Rule."

"Gold rules, like right now, here between you and I, here in The Golden State. My conscience is clear. I sleep well. This is the way business deals are made. I'm a businessman. I serve the interests of the shareholders and the corporation. I help make people money, including moms and pops that depend on ENRG dividend checks to put food on their table and keep their lights burning."

"They could keep the lights burning with renewable energy and help save the planet."

"You admitted yourself that you can't be a hypocrite when it comes to gas and oil. Can't have it both ways, you're an oil junkie too."

"I can't argue with you on my oil consumption," I sheepishly admit as I glance over at my gas guzzler on last legs of rubber. I spin the coin in my fingers in front of me, the glint of shiny gold reflecting the sun. Grandfather comes to mind. I toss the coin back.

"No deal."

"You're shitting me! All this gold! You sure? We can still make this happen, let me sweeten the deal more. How about you can have all these coins, and we buy you a brand new truck of your choice too? Pick the brand, model and color you want. Make it a hybrid to satisfy your green streak. That wreck you're driving looks like the rust has finally won."

"I told you before, it's got sentimental value," I answer firmly.

"Final answer?"

"Final answer."

The nice guy smile fades from his face. "Watch your back out here. Don't want any more accidents," he warns.

"Good to hear your corporate communications works so well. I've got some back up very interested in me staying healthy."

Thorne reaches down and shoves the coins in the box, clamping the top securely shut. Stepping back into the helicopter, he turns to me and gives that well-rehearsed smile before closing the door. "You've got my number. I'll be hanging onto the gold for now if you change your mind. Stop by the dealerships when you head back to see what new truck appeals to you. Amazing technology they're coming up with these days in efficiency and battery storage, check it out."

Watching the helicopter shrink into the blue sky, I briefly think about the gold coins lying at my feet a few moments before. It might be the largest amount of money, easy or otherwise, ever to come my way. A new environmentally friendly hybrid truck would be nice, since Old Red, the petrol sucking relic is almost dead.

On the table by my tent, I check the open laptop. Satisfied, I hit PAUSE.

When Linda and I meet for lunch at camp, I show her the recording of Thorne offering me the bribe. Adjusting the volume to maximum, the conversation is clear, all recorded on my laptop with images. She zooms in on his bribe offer.

"That could be very damaging to him, and ENRG," she states with a serious look.

"He makes it sound like it's all in a day's work, bribing people to get what he wants. He might have been in on the rope trick too, might have offered to pay off the guard's mortgage if he did the dirty work on me successfully."

"I feel safer with mountain lions."

"How'd you do with your traps?"

"Just common species, but I did a glimpse of Western Snowy Plovers, they're rare. I'd like to focus on setting traps and nets around the lagoon to see what wetland creatures are there. If I could find a California Tiger Salamander, I'd be elated!"

"Use my kayak, tiger hunter," I say.

"Thanks, I'll take you up on your offer."

"I'm going to head out of here on Monday. I need to meet up with Evans to show him what I have, regroup and get a plan in place to gear up for a more involved effort."

"I'll head out with you too. I want to spend time with Jake. I miss him."

We sit eating our midday meal together in the shade of the willow, an ultimate picnic setting. Looking across the lagoon, dragonflies dance in courtship, butterfly couples flutter around in harmonious flow until alighting on a cluster of purple lupines near the edge of water.

"Peter, I had a lovely evening with you last night."

"I want to see those photos of your son."

"Jake's not shy around a camera, as you'll see."

The first few images on her laptop are Jake at the beach, boogie boarding the white water with a huge smile planted firmly on his face. I look at another young boy in my mind, an image of joy on a wooden board as he too rides the whitewater. "Little Wave," I murmur.

"He's not up to the big ones yet," Linda replies not knowing whom I'm speaking about.

"I can see he loves the water."

"Saltwater in his blood."

A few photos later, one of Linda standing on a surfboard riding with style. "You do surf."

"I don't get out as much as I'd like to."

"Bring your board back, I'll see what I can do about increasing your water time."

"You're a bad influence on work habits."

"When the swells up, work can be overrated."

"Speaking of work, I need to get back at it. You did say I could use your kayak?"

"I'll help you get the kayak in the lagoon," I offer.

"Nice day to be on the water," she says.

Linda and I lift the kayak down from the racks of my truck and walk it to the edge of the lagoon. Following her from the stern, I can't help but watch her strong lean body leading my way to the water.

Sweat pours down our brows from the boat-carrying effort on this hot day. "If I go for a swim, will that mess with your netting?"

"As long as you're not wearing sunblock. That stuff's lethal for water creatures. Let me check that wound on your back first."

Dutifully I take off my shirt and turn my back to her as she lightly feels over the scar. "No sunblock for me. What do you think, doctor?"

She answers with a firm push, sending me into the water. I sink down beneath the surface, staying perfectly still and holding my breath as long as I can. I let out a few puffs of air and sink to the bottom. Slowly I rise to the surface and see her frantically diving in to save me before I disappear again. Stopping in front of me, her look of relief turns to anger. "That was mean, I thought you blacked out."

"I'm sorry, it's the little boy in me."

Casting her off in the kayak, she turns and gives a smile as she digs in the paddle and pulls away. The wake she leaves fans out in a smooth V, her little waves making their way to my feet as I stand at the edge of the water. Staring out at the lagoon, imagining the stream feeding into it and the waterfall up the canyon, memories of Talkitna arise.

Back to work for me, digging into the past history of the tribe of Noqoto at Rocky Point. Every bit and piece of fragments of the ancients I pull from the grasp of the earth confirm a guiding force leading me to discover artifacts at almost every turn of my spade. It's a powerful feeling that drives me on until the fading light at day's end.

With a bird-like whistle, I turn my attention toward the mirrored surface of the lagoon. Linda slices the paddle into the glass, pulling her along as she cruises toward me. I watch the perfect mirror reflection of her in the sunset laced clouds painted across the surface. She coasts up to shore in front of me, the colorful mirror fading into surrealism in her wake. I grab the handle on the front of the boat, pull her up on shore and give her a hand to help her out.

"Thanks, Peter."

"How'd you do, Captain Collector?"

She reaches down into the kayak and pulls out sample jars, some with small fish doing tight little laps.

"Too small for dinner," I muse.

"I need to get photos of these and release them pronto," she informs while holding up the jars to the colorful sky.

"What are those little fish?"

"Tidewater Goby! And it gets better, I found Rorippa Sambelii!"

"Lost opera singer?"

"Commonly known as Gambels Watercress. It's so wonderful to see a whole wetland ecosystem intact!"

Back at camp, our fresh food options are shrinking. "Hope you're okay with Mexican again, I'm down to some homemade tamales from my auntie I'm happy to share," she offers.

"Muy bueno!"

Post-dinner warmth glows from within, fired by the spicy tamales that were some of the best I've had. Dish duty done, I turn down the lantern to a dim glow. Grabbing my chair, I make my way to the fire to join Linda. We both cast a smile, settling into the comfort of each other.

"Peter, tell me more about your Dream Walk. You said there was a woman, Tal-kit-na?"

"When you found me on the beach I thought you were her, momentarily. She named me Wave Dancer because she saw me surfing waves."

"I like the name on you."

"Talkitna was a lovely woman, inside and out. You're both similar in many ways. And, she had a son, about your boy's age…"

"Speaking of dreaming, I'm calling it a night."

"Good night, Linda, sweet dreams."

"Good night, Peter, sweet dream walks."

The smell of morning coffee wakes me as I crawl out of the tent to find Linda already organizing her gear.

"Wish we could stay a few more days, but I'm really anxious to see Jake."

"I'm looking forward to meeting him too."

"Looks like we go our separate ways from here?" she questions.

"Temporarily, but I don't abandon good friends like you."

"I hope not, I'd miss you."

"It won't be long until we cross paths again. Promise?"

"I promise, Wave Dancer."

CHAPTER 34

I hold the scissors hesitantly above my head while looking in my bathroom mirror. With nervous hands, I've come to the compromised conclusion it's time to cut my hair. Squeezing the scissors together, I watch a hair curtain fall into the sink. Another squeeze and the bulk of my hair drops away in an instant despite the time it took to grow it to that length.

Upon opening my closet, I realize I haven't worn my only suit and tie since graduation from high school over a decade ago. It's pinched in the corner like a skinny, flattened mummy, the dry, shrunken flower my Mom pinned to the lapel still in place. Trying it on is a struggle as I wiggle in to see if it fits. Musty smells grab my nose as I pull the jacket around my shoulders; it fits like a well-tailored straitjacket. Time to go shopping; a secondhand suit will suffice.

The thrift store industry appears to be doing very well. I'm amazed walking into the well-stocked second-hand store and sort through racks and racks of men's suits, many of which look as if they were hardly ever worn. The place smells like a bunch of somebodies have died in these suits. I wonder how many of these men passed away into a world of no responsibilities, leaving behind wives and families to sort through the remains of their stuff, hoping to make a few bucks and free up storage space.

Help is on the way as the lady behind the counter puts down her romance novel and makes her way to the bewildered. "Can I help you there, honey? You look like a fish out of water."

"Got that right. I need to look professional in front of a big meeting I have coming up."

"Glad it's not a funeral, too much of that around here lately." She takes me by the arm and leads me to another aisle. "Some nice stuff just came in, haven't even hung it up yet."

Shuffling through a stack of clothes on the counter, she pulls out a dark brown suit. "This looks like you. The lady who brought these in said she didn't want to have to sell them, but hard times make hard decisions. I feel real sorry for a lot of folks that come in here."

"Guess you're doing them a favor and are helping them raise money. You're helping me out since I don't want to pay full gouge for something I'll wear maybe once."

"What size suit do you wear? How about your collar size? What about your inseam?"

"Seriously? I have no idea, I'm into comfort wear," I say with open arms displaying my shorts, T-shirt and flip-flops.

She holds the suit and pants up to me. "These are in the ball-park. There's the dressing room. You let me see you when you've got it all on."

The musty mortuary aroma follows me into the dressing room. I close the curtain and don the suit. Looking in the full-length mirror, I feel like I'm ready for a corpse costume party. I pull the curtain aside and step out in front of my one-woman audience.

"Well, honey, I've burned through a lot of novels sitting over there in that chair, and I've got to say, that's the nicest suit I've seen on anyone. Even the shoes look like they fit you!"

"I won't be wearing it for long. And the shoes are torturous. Maybe you can help me please? I couldn't get the tie tied."

"Come stand in front of the mirror, dear, I'll help you."

And soon, with limited funds, I have the entire getup, including shoes and tie.

The mini mall I step into has one of those no appointment quickie haircut places with posters of too perfect people with too perfect hair splashed liberally across the walls. Mirror, mirror everywhere as all eyes in the lineup of occupied chairs shift to me. The haircut lady with the well-manicured appearance looks a bit confused as I sit in the adjustable chair.

"I've seen haircuts like yours before and usually they need booster seats," she comments, as she looks me over, trying to decide on a course of action.

"Pretty much sums it up."

"So, what'll it be?"

"Trying to stay low profile, give me a regular," I request.

"Regular what?"

"I'll take a regular guy in a suit look."

"Got it, generic suit guy. I'm Charlene, what's your name?"

"Hi Charlene, I've been called a few names, but just Peter will do."

"Well, Just Peter, what do you do for a living?"

"That's an open question. Still trying to sort it out."

"When I'm all done, you'll look presentable for your next job interview."

"I need all the help I can get. Big meeting with big players."

"Big players, are you trying out for some kind of team? Couldn't help but notice how fit you look," she comments as she shifts around me, brushing against my shoulder.

"I'm into individual pursuits."

"What about you?" And that's all I have to ask, she rambles on like she's topped up with a dose of truth serum.

CHAPTER 35

I'm missing the nice lady at the thrift store and her tie-tying skills. Mimicking her motions trying to tie my own, I struggle with the reverse-mirror challenges of the gag-inducing accessory. Alone in my apartment, no one to consult, I finally search the Web. I feel better knowing I'm not the only global citizen inept at the necktie question. I even find directions on how to tie a hangman's noose, as I struggle to breathe.

Cruising in Old Red with both windows open for ventilation, I'm the best-dressed man in the worst looking vehicle driving south on Highway 101. A passing semi-truck kicks the wind into my window, making my tie dance around randomly in my field of view.

When the ocean vista opens up, there's clean swell visible with offshore winds feathering the waves. The latest test of my resolve, I fight the wheel gravitating to the sea and put on my sunglasses, hoping they'll help me stare straight ahead.

Approaching Santa Barbara, I'm low on fuel again in thirsty Old Red. Time to fill up again. An electric hybrid sure would be nice. Pulling the handle from the pump, I'm extra careful not to spill any of the refined crude oil on my ironic suit made from 100% petroleum derived rayon fabric.

With a full tank allowing me to once again spew out the exhaust of burnt fossil fuel behind me, I drive up State Street to the city municipal building, which takes ages as the traffic backs up to a creeping pace. At this point, I could run faster than sitting in the truck, but in the hot sun I'd probably get heat stroke and collapse on the sidewalk in my cheap suit and air-lock shoes.

Still a few blocks away, I find a place to park costing a small fortune a day. Stepping out from the shade of Old Red, I'm hit with a hot wave of atmospheric rise in global temperatures that can't be ignored.

On the steps of the municipal building, a pulsing crowd gathers. My spirit lifts seeing concerned people holding signs in protest against the ENRG oil and gas depot application. Camera wielding news crews poise to capture sound-bite commentary as they stalk the crowd pressing toward the main entry.

A blip on my radar. A person wielding brochures on a collision course with me. A dread-headed dude with an earthy attitude steps up to me, announcing he's a member of the Green Party. Earth-guy hands me a pamphlet featuring my animal totem that explains why I should join the Greens. He flips aside the dense weight of his dreadlocks and shows me his credentials—a Green Party badge hanging below his beard. Taking him in, I'm jealous of his loose and comfortable cotton clothes, down to his open-toed sandals. Decked out in my business suit with encased feet, we look so different on the outside, but on the inside, we're in agreement on the health of planet Earth.

Reading me, he starts to look doubtful. "Excuse me, sir, the Green Party is here to protest the petrochemical plant proposal at Rocky Point. As you can imagine, defending our planet against the well-funded globalized corporate machine isn't cheap. Being in the red makes it hard to be green, we can sure use donations to keep us going," he says as he holds out a change can adorned with photos of whales and dolphins, along with a wireless transaction pad in his other hand.

"We also take credit cards."

"Sorry, left my wallet in the limo," I say with a straight face.

"Sure, right, man," he judges, while looking me up and down. "You look like you're a member of the Green Money Party. You work for ENRG?"

I look down at the costume I wear. "I'm in disguise," I inform him before walking away from green guy across green grass.

I stay back from the crowd by stepping into the shade of a tree, trying to keep cool in my dark solar-gain outfit despite the midday sun. As my neck swells with sweat, I carefully loosen my tie, not wanting to fumble through another frustrating experience.

Appearing like a mirage, coming my way across the far reaches of State Street is a high-heeled jaywalking vision of Linda amongst the rippling asphalt waves of rising heat. Her long hair flying free against blue dress hugging her trim body, she crosses the path in front of me, focused only on the doors to the city council building. With laptop in her hand, she's tunnel visioning and not noticing it's me.

She stops suddenly, turns and looks at me with shock. Slowly stepping closer, she speaks her surprise. "Is that you in there, Peter?"

"I'm trying to look respectable for my presentation. It was Evans's idea."

"Wow, you look like you could be a formal-wear model."

"We could be a couple on a wedding cake."

She gives me a kiss on the cheek. "Good to see you again, handsome."

I take a step back to take in all of her from high heels to neatly parted hair. "What a change from hiking shoes. All ready for your speech?"

"Got my presentation nailed down. How about you?"

"Power point presentations aren't my strength."

"Passion is your strength, that's what matters most."

"How about we go out for dinner after the hearing?"

"A date, or a celebration dinner?"

"We can call it what we want."

"It's a date. I'd love to have dinner with you, Peter."

"Awesome, it's a date."

Walking across the lawn with the help of his cane is Evans. He gimps right by me until I call out his name. "Doctor Evans, its Peter!"

Adjusting his glasses, he looks my way until his face opens into a smile. "You clean up nice, boy. Glad to see you took my advice. And hello, Linda, I'm anxious to see your presentation."

"Hello, Doctor Evans. I'm anxious to do what I can to save Rocky Point."

"No one as passionate about what you've both found at Rocky Point."

Linda and I look at each other and confirm feelings.

"Peter, I want you to know your presentation today completes your final thesis on Native Americans in California. With the work you've done toward the critical preservation of Rocky Point, I consider this your final passing grade, no matter the outcome of today. It's been an honor to have you as a Native American student, and it's my pleasure to tell you that you're now a formal member of our chosen profession."

I'm temporarily at a loss for words as a warm glow of accomplishment rises from within. "I get my degree?"

"You get your degree. Well done."

"Peter, that's wonderful!" Linda gushes as she gives me a hug.

"I'll leave you two to your thoughts. Good luck to you both and I'll see you inside," Dr. Evans says as he heads to the door.

"So now you'll have a piece of paper with your formal name and a fancy seal to tell others you're an expert on what you already know," Linda comments while she does up my tie. "There. Now you look like you're ready to take on those big bad ENRG corporate cronies." She stands back and admires my disguise.

"Give it your best shot, Wave Dancer."

CHAPTER 36

The doors open to the conference room and a human tide rushes in. Two lowly looking security guards attempt to slow the onslaught in vain. It's going to be standing room only.

The room is packed as Linda and I jockey our way from the back to our reserved seats in the front row. Each of us goes to our own designated tables and sets up our laptops to prepare for the presentations. Once again, my tech savvy lady friend comes to my rescue and sorts out my nervous last minute attempts with my laptop and the large overhead screen.

My opening image is the photo taken from the Apollo mission as blue-green Earth rises above colorless moon. The audience goes quiet with the visual reminder of our fragile planet with no political borders floating in the blackness of the universe.

Returning to our seats, we can see table place cards and water glasses awaiting the arrival of the Commission members, who will take their seats in luxurious leather thrones facing the audience. The American flag hangs limply at one side of the expansive podium, the California flag on the other. An oversize wooden gavel rests on its side on the podium, waiting for some action.

I turn around and scan the room to see anyone I know, and almost instantly lock eyes with Richard Thorne. His expensive looking smile is missing, and he's looking at me like I'm the enemy. I give him a smile and a wink, followed with an enthusiastic thumb's up. On either side of him sits a small tribe of overpaid lawyer types in tailored suits and ties, thick files full of documents stacked before them. They all look over at me like a pack of hyenas sizing up prey, already posturing to move in for the kill.

Dr. Evans sits at my side and notes the gang of legalese slingers across from us. "Maybe you can have a beer with your buddies over there later," he comments dryly.

"I could swear one of them was salivating when he looked at me."

"A lot of money at stake here, my friend, and you're about to present a major hurdle."

Behind the podium the door swings open and the commissioners enter the room, each taking a seat behind their names. All wear proper business suits and ties, even the lone woman minus the tie. As they settle into their seats, their air of authority reverberates in the room. A few reveal slight smiles with nothing behind them, only superficial gestures beneath the mask of authority over others.

These people in front of me are some of the most powerful people in California. With a single vote they can determine the fate of any project proposed under their realm. Some of the most valuable real estate on the planet falls under their jurisdiction, not just in monetary terms, but also in terms of ecology and history. The fate of sensitive lands such as Rocky Point rests in their hands.

Glancing over at Richard Thorne, flashing his perfect white-toothed smile, I wonder if he had offered better paying consulting jobs to any of the commissioners who might be looking to move to a nicer neighborhood.

I look over at Linda sitting next to me. She takes a deep breath, straightens her back and poises herself, calm on her face.

I follow her example and seek inner calm, preparing for what I hope will be a game changer for ENRG's plans for Rocky Point.

Loud cracks of wood on wood snap me to attention as the Chairman pounds the gavel. The crowd goes quiet as the meeting is called to order.

I turn to look back at the faces behind me and notice my mom sitting with a whole group of my fellow tribe members. All of them gesture encouragement, and not entirely silently.

The gavel slaps down on hard wood again, bringing my head swinging back around to face the commissioners. The Chairman clears his voice to reprimand my Noqoto tribe cheering section. "This hearing will take place in a civil manner. I will not tolerate this kind of disruption. If you persist, security officers will escort you from the room. I hope I make myself clear on this point," he snorts.

The Native crowd quiets down and the Chairman resumes order. "We now have Ms. Linda Diaz representing the State of California Department of Natural Resources. I remind you, Ms. Diaz, that you have a time limit of thirty minutes. Any accompanying documents can be left with the secretary."

Standing confidently to her feet, Linda approaches the screen with the overhead photo of planet Earth. Turning directly to face the Commissioners, she commands their attention. "As you well know, there should be serious consideration for something as important as deciding the fate of this rare natural ecosystem known as Rocky Point." She changes the image on the screen to a zoomed capture from space overlooking all of Rocky Point. "This photo shows Rocky Point where the proposed petrochemical facility will forever alter what is now there. It's a good lead-in to a series of images I photographed at Rocky Point and its immediate surroundings. First, if you please, I'd like to see a show of hands as to how many of you Commissioners have visited Rocky Point in person?"

Only one raises his hand, hesitantly explaining, "I did a flyover in a helicopter. Can't say we landed."

"Don't you think a decision as important as this should require each of you to spend time actually walking in this amazingly beautiful environment, which is unlike any I've worked on in coastal California before," she asks, a mix of disappointment and passion in her voice.

The Chairman chimes in. "Ms. Diaz, I remind you that we are not required to visit proposed projects and would appreciate if you would just present your facts. Beauty is in the eye of the beholder."

"How disappointing. I thought seeing and being in such a rare, undisturbed stretch of coastal California would be a requirement for making an important, informed decision. My presentation will provide you with the facts, and I'll leave the beauty interpretation to each individual."

"You requested facts, so here's what I found and documented on or in the near vicinity of Rocky Point. I've collected samples of each either physically or photographically. These samples have been independently tested by the UCSB Biological Studies Department for authenticity. Follow-up field studies were performed by independent researchers to verify my findings. As you are aware, the letter of the law protects these species at both the Federal and State level. It is unlikely another location in coastal central California could be found offering such diversity of flora and fauna in such a compact area."

Switching from the graphics to a photo of Rocky Point from the ridge above, Linda carries on. "What follows is a series of photos I took in my biological survey at Rocky Point. None of these images have been digitally altered or manipulated in any way."

She has the crowd in her hands as she presents each image and gives a quick explanation on what they're seeing. Switching to night-time, she shows remotely triggered strobe shots capturing a small fox, bats in flight, owls swooping down with claws wide open, bobcats, mountain lion, porcupine and even a skunk with its tail raised. Back to daytime, images of snakes, lizards, horned toads, newts, rabbits and mice flash on the screen. Red-tailed hawks, ospreys with their nests near water, brown pelicans gliding over waves, California quail, hummingbirds and Western Snowy Plovers fly across the screen.

"These next photos show an increasingly scarce freshwater lagoon and the species that call it home, one of the few remaining intertidal lagoons in California that has not been drained and filled in for development. I remind the Commission members that this lagoon is slated to be drained, filled, and turned into a storage zone for petroleum tanks. This lagoon is a nursery for a host of fish and amphibians, and without the lagoon, they will be gone. This photo captures a California Tiger Salamander, an endangered species on the Federal and State list. This is a Freshwater Goby, also listed as Federal and State endangered."

"These next images illustrate the wide variety of plant life at Rocky Point, some of which is very rarely found anymore. Several of the plants are on the Federal and State endangered species list."

There are murmurs from the audience at the images of large fields of bright orange California poppies carpeting the hillsides, valley oaks clinging to rocky crags, wild plums, waving grasses caught in the wind, spiky cactus clinging to dry hillsides, dune grass, miniature plants captured with a macro lens, their small flowers brought to life on the large screen.

A bright graphic replaces Linda's photos. "This shows the decline of these endangered and critically endangered species found on Rocky Point. As you can see by the shading showing their historic range and what we now know exists, there are only very small pockets of these plants and animals struggling to survive the ongoing pressures of increasing human encroachment on their habitats. The question is: When does the natural habitat shrink so much that the species can no longer survive? Unfortunately, history shows the answer usually comes when it's already too late. It's critical that we preserve what's left of the habitats of these rare species if they are to survive."

She moves on to coastline photos showing tide pools at low tide with colorful anemones, stretched-out starfish, clinging abalone, tightly-gripped muscles clustered together, clam shells, thick kelp, sea birds cruising the beach, seals napping in the sun, sea otters floating on their backs in lush kelp, whales breaching offshore, and dolphins riding the waves.

"As you can see, this coastline is alive with sea life. The upwelling from the deep channel offshore brings nutrient rich cold water to the surface, constantly mixing with the current. It's a supermarket of food for marine mammals such as dolphins and gray whales that migrate just off shore where the point juts into their path. As we have unfortunately witnessed in many parts of the world, including Santa Barbara, contamination by oil spills in such a concentrated area would be devastating for marine life both in the ocean and the tidal zone. Sea birds and marine mammals such as seals and otters are particularly hard hit by oil spills. Think about the images from the Deepwater Horizon disaster for wildlife and humans."

"From what I've found in the short amount of time I was at Rocky Point, it's obvious that this oil depot project would be an environmental mistake of epic scale. The coastal environment at Rocky Point is irreplaceable. I urge each one of you California Coastal Commission members to weigh this proposed project against the environmental costs. And I hope that someday soon you can put your own feet on the ground at Rocky Point and see for yourself why it must be saved as a wildlife reserve. Think of your children, their children, and the generations of your family into the future that deserve to see Nature in the wild. They thank you, and I thank you for your wisdom to keep Rocky Point a sanctuary."

What starts as sporadic clapping grows into an ovation including whistles and yells as Linda turns to face the audience and makes her way back to my side.

The Chairman frantically pounds his gavel as the audience winds down to a murmur.

"Thank you, Ms. Diaz. Next up will be Richard Thorne from ENRG Incorporated. You have the same time limit of thirty minutes, Mr. Thorne"

Thorne stands to face the Commissioners, turning on the charm so heavy I can feel it, even with his back to me. The guy radiates confidence and knows how to use it.

"Thank you, Coastal Commissioners, for letting me speak before you today," he says, as he works his laptop power point show.

On the screen appears an image of a dad, mom, two kids and a dog in the driveway of their freshly painted suburban home as they pack up the family car for a holiday. It's one of those over-produced, digitally-altered images, everyone and everything looking perfect, including the driveway without oil stains, the brilliant green grass without brown spots, every hair on every head in perfect order, not a wrinkle to be found on any clothes or faces, no dirty tennis shoes from the boy who dribbles his basketball, the teenage daughter abnormally happy to be going on vacation with her parents and brother, model-slim mom carrying the picnic basket, and designer dad easily hefting the empty luggage into the trunk. The car sports a "Support Our Troops" bumper sticker complete with American flag." It's Pleasantville USA.

"Without oil and the refined products that come from it, this car wouldn't be going anywhere, and neither would this American family. You can say whatever you want about oil, but today's reality is that this country and most of the developed world depends on oil to keep the rubber on the road. I'd ask to see a show of hands as to which of you drives a car that depends on oil, but I think we already know the answer."

The next photo is a shot of US Army troops dressed in full desert combat gear on patrol, following an armored Humvee with a manned machine gun mount. In the background, oil well rigs burn as black smoke pours into the sky in a scene that looks like blackened Armageddon.

"This is what dependence on foreign oil looks like when Black Swan events unfold. This is why we must continue to develop our oil infrastructure here in America, to keep from being held hostage by terrorists in countries where democracy has no meaning. Without oil to keep our troops supplied, our brave soldiers would be stranded in their valiant efforts to protect the freedom of Americans in the homeland."

I groan under my breath at what might come next. Thorne is laying it on like the marketing pro he is, and pulling at patriotic heartstrings.

"What I'm about to show you next are images in which most every item you see has come to the consumer in some way by oil. If not used in the actual manufacture of the item, then used in the transportation to get the item into the consumer's hands."

The quickly unfolding series of images shows almost anything and everything imaginable as a by-product of oil. I shudder when he shows a pair of shoes looking much like the ones on my feet. The last shot in the series is the classic bowling alley with the bowling team buddies cheering a teammate's strike.

"As you can see, there's almost nothing the modern American consumer uses that in some way doesn't come from oil. I don't think most people would prefer to go back to the horse and buggy days when the average American life span was less than fifty years. Oil makes this modern world we live in such a better place, and we take much of it for granted … until there is no more oil."

Turning to the audience, Thorne preaches his message.

"Now I know every one of you here today cares about the health of this planet, cares about the beauty of California, cares about the plants, animals and sea life that surrounds us in places like Rocky Point. I do too, whether you want to believe it or not. But I'm a realist and I see oil as a necessary part of doing business and living in America. If you don't use oil in some way in your life, than you must be living in a cave. That's the reality of it. We need the infrastructure to get oil to the consumer as safely as we can, that's reality too. We at ENRG believe that Rocky Point's location is the best choice to achieve that goal. Our systems have been refined to minimize risk to the environment. We will strive to ensure that happens."

The crowd is mostly silent; even the greenie hypocrites have nothing to say. Thorne turns back to the Commissioners and brings the sales pitch to a close as he changes the final image to the Global logo.

"I know each one of you here in front of me has a major decision to make today that will impact all of us for years to come. I ask you to look at your own lives and see what you use every day that comes from oil. I think it's a fair question to ask and I'm counting on you for a fair conclusion. I thank you for your time and thoughtful consideration."

The Green Party recruiter suddenly stands up and shouts toward Thorne, "Bullshit! All you care about is money!"

By the time the sacrificial Green Party guy gets to the word "money," the beefy security crew is on to him and hustles him out of the room.

"Thank you, Mr. Thorne. Next up will be our last speaker, Mr. Peter Martinez, from the Santa Barbara Museum of Natural History. Mr. Martinez, you have a thirty-minute limit, please."

My support crew of tribal friends and family including my mom burst into applause to an embarrassing degree. This prompts the Chairman to once again bang his gavel and cry, "Order! Order!"

I click on the spacecraft image of Rocky Point and turn to face the Commissioners.

"I'm Peter Martinez, I've been asked by Dr. John Evans from the Santa Barbara Museum of Natural History to present my findings from my research at Rocky Point. I was appointed by Dr. Evans to conduct the initial field study for Native American historical culture around Rocky Point in part because of my 7,000-year ancestral ties to the area, and my passion to discover links to the past. I've been well trained by Dr. Evans in the formalities of archaeological fieldwork and the procedures required. I have an advanced degree in archaeology from UCSB. As you can see in this photo behind me of Rocky Point, there are almost no signs of modern man except for an access road and fence lines at each border. The layers of archaeological time here haven't been touched by any major modern coastal development, a very rare occurrence in present day coastal California. As I did my work at Rocky Point and peeled back its layers of time like an historical onion, I discovered the remains of a well-established Native American village site at the edge of the lagoon. The same area that ENRG plans for its massive oil storage tanks. According to my findings, which have been substantiated by Dr. Evans and his team at the Santa Barbara Museum of Natural History, this village had been in existence at least 7,000 years ago, long before the first European ever set foot on the shores of the west coast of the North American continent.

"The first of the artifacts I discovered was actually the last of the artifacts left behind when the village was abandoned soon after the establishment of the nearby Spanish Missions in California in the 1790s. What you are about to see on the screen are photographs of my findings, and clear evidence of a once thriving culture of Native Americans in the exact location where the most major impact of the development proposal by ENRG would occur. What you see in these photos are not just inert objects absent of connection to the living. They are, in every way, very alive in their connection with a past people who lived at Rocky Point for hundreds of generations. "

I click on the slide show button and let the images roll through, dissolving like ghosts from one image to the next. The first series is a set of still life photographs of artifacts I'd found and grouped together against a neutral white background. Set to Native American flute music with dissolves between photos, the images fill the screen and the mood in the crowd grows noticeably somber at the discoveries in front of them. All eyes remain fixed on the screen and none wander, including the Commissioners'.

"The next photos you will see show the relation of the locations where the artifacts were found in relation to where ENRG plans its development."

I show an overview with graphics on where the cluster of archaeological finds was discovered, allowing time for people to take in the overhead image of the village site. The next visual is an artist's rendering of the village of Noqoto as I had remembered it in my Dream Walk—the huts, canoes, work areas and tribal gathering places. Next, a dissolve of an artist's conception of the lagoon filled and leveled, the massive oil tanks sitting right where the village once was. A few noticeable gasps come from the crowd. I pause on this image for effect.

"And now, I'd like to show you a human element of the people who once lived at Rocky Point. In my wanderings I discovered a burial site. I'd like you to imagine that these people were very much alive, like you and I in this room today. Families with children, loving each other, loving life, living in this wonderful place they once called home."

I fade into my images of the burial site in the cave, each image slowly dissolving into the next as the crowd remains rapt and quiet. As I watch each image, my eyes water with emotion at the memories I hold of the people of Rocky Point. People I'd come to know and love through my Dream Walk into their world. The next image is a close up of the rainbow dolphin pendant hanging around a skeleton neck.

I turn to the Commissioners as they turn their eyes from the screen to me. "This is the final burial resting place for village leaders and their family. These images you have just witnessed have been seen by very few since they these Native people were laid to rest hundreds of years ago. Rocky Point is a sacred spot, and to be buried so close to what the Native Americans considered the portal to the Other Side is indicative of their status in the tribe. This is where hundreds of generations gathered to say goodbye to life as we know it. Rocky Point was sacred, and still is to local members of my Noqoto tribe today."

I next flash on the moving element of my show. "But some people who pursue profits don't want such discoveries to be made by people like me. No respect for the dead, the living, no respect for history, only chasing a short term dollar, no matter who gets in the way."

I click on play and the security footage rolls showing me fixing my rope to my bumper and rappelling off the cliff. The next shot shows the ENRG security guard slipping the rope toward the end of the hitch, the rope getting tight, the knot slipping from the bumper, and the rope sliding quickly into the sea.

"I was almost killed when this rope was tampered with and fell into the sea. I still have a large scar on my back from a fall that left me unconscious. You will clearly note the ENRG logo on the uniform of the man who tampered with my lifeline."

Thorne offering me the bribe rolls next. The helicopter with ENRG logo standing idle in the background, him removing the strong box from the helicopter, the gold coins spilling to the ground, Thorne scooping up the gold coins and putting them back in the helicopter, and then flying away. The dialogue and the images of our conversation show the obvious attempt to bribe me, and my turning the bribe down. I look over at Thorne and his cronies and note their concern.

"As you can see from the evidence, a high ranking executive of ENRG Incorporated named Richard Thorne, who is sitting here in this room, considers very large bribes an effective way to get what he wants when other methods fail. What does this tell you about the integrity of a company that will attempt almost anything to move this project ahead, including attempted murder? How does this make you feel about the future plans ENRG has for Rocky Point? How would you feel if you were at the end of your rope, as I was?

"May I remind the Commissioners that these discoveries of past human habitation and burial sites at Rocky Point are protected under the California State Historic Places Act. This is a very rare find of a historical Native American village not destroyed by development or grave robbers. The skeletal remains I found are only part of the very human story that once played out daily at Rocky Point. This sacred site deserves to remain undisturbed, and is protected by law. The proposed ENRG oil depot site would destroy this peaceful resting place for the dead. It would also destroy the sanctuary and refuge for the living creatures that call it home. I ask you not to be intimidated by the well-funded tactics of a soulless corporation pursuing its bottomless thirst for profits. Don't let the bullies of the bottom line tell you what you can or can't do. I urge you to vote no and leave this stretch of coastline called Rocky Point as Mother Earth and the Great Spirit intended. Please give my ancestors who once called this place home the respect and dignity they, and this spiritually powerful place, deserve. Thank you." I click back to the image of Rocky Point from above and leave it on the screen.

Applause erupts behind me as I turn and notice almost everyone standing up and clapping, except the ENRG team. Their look of resignation is impossible not to see; even Richard Thorne's car salesman smile is absent. He looks like his mind is elsewhere, maybe wondering what kind of settlement money I might be looking at to keep him out of jail.

Walking back to my seat, Linda, who is beaming and clapping, bows her head at my performance. Evans brings his hands together and nods a sage smile.

As I settle into my seat between them, he turns my way and whispers in my ear, "Well done, Peter, that was your final paper and I'm giving you a perfect score. Let's hope you and Linda opened up the Commissioners' hearts and minds with what you've presented."

Linda leans over and whispers in my other ear, "That was awesome, Peter! I loved the security footage. You should have seen the ENRG suits as their smug looks faded!"

The pounding of the gavel brings the crowd noise down to a low murmur as the Chairman rises to his feet to address the audience.

"There will now be a recess of the California Coastal Commission. We are presently scheduled to return to this room at three o'clock with our final decision on the proposed development of Rocky Point. You are invited to remain here in this room if you wish, or you may return here before three."

Most of the room begins to clear out. As I exit the door into the bright sunshine with Linda and Dr. Evans at my side, I'm barraged with reporters sticking microphones into my face and asking questions. Dr. Evans comes to my rescue. "There will be other opportunities for the story to be told, but now is not the right time. If you would please excuse us, ladies and gentlemen, we have to consult."

CHAPTER 37

As fast as Dr. Evans can limp, we hustle away from the crowd and slip off into State Street looking for a quiet place to eat. We are unanimous on the choice of a Mexican restaurant and take seats by the window. A look around shows the trendy version of my last restaurant meal, prices adjusted upward to cover the prime location. I scan the menu, looking for my usual order, when I sense a presence. I look up from the menu and there, in front of the window, is my Mom, stopped in her tracks looking in at me.

"May I join you?" she calls to me in sign language.

Opening the door for her, I give a well-received hug. "Thanks for coming, Mom. Seeing you in the audience means a lot."

"I'm so proud of what you've achieved, son. You did a wonderful job with your presentation," she says with pride.

"Had my heart and soul in it. I want to introduce you to Dr. Evans from the Museum of Natural History in Santa Barbara. He's my course instructor, the man who gave me the job at Rocky Point." I escort my mom inside to our table. "Dr. Evans, this is my mom, Theresa Martinez."

Standing to shake her hand, Evans looks her square in the eyes and says with sincerity, "It's very nice meeting you, Mrs. Martinez."

"Call me Theresa."

"Please, call me John. Theresa, I want you to know what a wonderful young man you've raised."

"The tribe raised."

"The more time I spend with him, the more I've grown to respect him. He's done an amazing job with the Rocky Point project and you should be very proud to have him as a son."

My mom is backpedaling after our last meeting at the casino. Looking over at me, a smile grows as she looks into my eyes with new clarity and understanding.

"He is a good son, John. The tribe is so proud of him too," she says with a wink at me.

I reach over and take Linda's hand, bringing her to her feet.

"Mom, I want you to meet someone special. This is Linda Diaz. She and I have been working together at Rocky Point."

Linda steps up to my mom, bypasses a handshake and gives her a hug. "It's very nice to meet you, Mrs. Martinez. I have to agree with Dr. Evans, you have a wonderful son."

"Very nice meeting you, Linda, and please call me Theresa."

"Sit down, Mom, and let me buy you lunch for a change."

"I've got lunch covered for all of you. This one's on me. No arguments," gruffs Evans.

"Thank you, John," my mom acknowledges as she looks appreciatively at the man who knows more about the history of our tribe than most of its living members.

I slide into the booth close to Linda until our legs touch.

"Mom, you and Dr. Evans have a lot in common. He knows so much about the history of our people and you've always been like a sponge when it comes to learning about our tribe."

"You should come by the Museum sometime, Theresa, I'd love to show you around, take you into the archives to show you what we have that relates to your tribe."

"I'd like that very much," she answers, with a hint of a schoolgirl crush. Turning to Linda, she adds, "I very much enjoyed your presentation at the meeting. Seeing all those plants and animals, I have so much respect for what you do. You painted a very clear picture of the need to keep Rocky Point as a sanctuary for such rare wildlife."

"Thanks for your kind words, Theresa."

"Mom, all of us sitting here feel strongly that there's a decent chance ENRG won't get the green light to go ahead on the development at Rocky Point, but still, it's up to the Commission. If ENRG can't utilize the land for their business needs, it becomes a liability instead of an asset. If the Coastal Commission turns them down, they'll be looking at options for selling the land they own at Rocky Point."

"Not a good return on investment you mean. So, what's your point?" she asks in her casino manager's voice.

"The tribe should make ENRG an offer to buy the land. We're the adjoining landholders with an historical stake. It makes sense."

"What do you propose our tribe do with the land?"

"Give the wildlife room to live. Do nothing but preserve the land. Leave it as it is. Provide a sanctuary for the living and the departed."

This leaves her quiet. I can tell the thought of purchasing such a property without any sort of guaranteed financial return for the casino is digging deep into her profit-driven conscience. "I'd need to take this to the Tribal Council, of course. The elders would get their say, including your grandfather."

"You know Grandfather would be all for it."

"And of course, it will come down to price. If it's worthless to ENRG, our tribe might be the only logical choice to purchase it."

"It's not as if our tribe isn't cashed up. We're raking it in at the casino. Let's give something back to Mother Earth and give our ancestors a place to rest in peace."

"We'll see how the future unfolds, but I like your idea, Peter. There's more to life than money, and this would be a wonderful thing to do."

"How is Grandfather? I've been so busy with the dig and preparing for this presentation I haven't seen him."

"He wanted so much to come here. His knee is really acting up, arthritic and swollen and he's in a lot of pain. Of course he wouldn't go to the hospital to get any help. At least he charged his phone."

"I'll go see him as soon as the dust settles from Rocky Point."

"I propose a toast!" Dr. Evans says as he lifts his water glass. "Here's to Rocky Point."

CHAPTER 38

Nervously I settle back into my seat in the meeting room as we once again await the return of the California Coastal Commission. By this point in time, my feet are numb from the pressure of the shoes, my neck itches agonizingly from the collar and tie, and musky odor clings to the inside of my suit with its limited ventilation escape routes.

Looking over at Thorne, the group of yes-men huddling around him, whispers of plotting occasionally spilling out for the ears of others. Surely their focus is on damage control options as the security footage I presented threw a wrench into their plans. Combined with all the evidence Linda and I presented, stock option bonuses are looking questionable.

At last the door swings open and the Commissioners enter the room, settling into their seats behind the podium. Poker faces on all of them, no hint of a decision. The audience volume fades as the Chairman picks up his gavel and threatens those in the room with some loud whacks.

"We will now bring this hearing to a close. With a show of hands from the Commissioners, a final tally of votes will be presented to the residents of the State of California, and to the residents of the Noqoto Indian Reservation. A simple majority will determine the final outcome of the proposed oil and gas depot site at Rocky Point by ENRG Incorporated."

Everything is quiet. Linda and I look over at each other, anxious to hear the verdict.

The Chairman stays standing while clearing his throat. "All in favor of ENRG's proposed plan for Rocky Point raise your hand."

Hesitantly two, and then a third Commissioner, raise their hands.

"I note that three of the Commissioners are in favor of the development."

The crowd boos so loudly that the gavel banging on the table has little effect. Finally raising his voice and yelling into the microphone, the Chairman brings the noise level down with the threat of canceling the meeting.

Order restored, he continues. "All opposed to ENRG's proposed plan for Rocky Point, raise your hand."

Three commissioners raise their hands almost in unison. Given the deadlock, the Chairman's vote will decide the fate of Rocky Point. All goes quiet and all eyes turn to the man with so much riding on his shoulders.

"I note that three of the Commissioners are opposed to the development. I will now cast the final vote to determine the outcome of Rocky Point." Pausing, his eyes closed, he stands like he's the only one in the room.

Slowly they open. "I cast my vote in opposition of the proposal by ENRG Corporation at Rocky Point."

Leaping to our feet, Linda, Evans, and I group hug together as a wild, deafening uproar from the audience fills the room. I can hear my name yelled into the mix from the cheering section of my tribe.

Linda and I hug each other as Evans steps toward the Commissioners to shake each of their hands. We follow his lead, shaking even the hands of the three who voted for the project.

Evans steps up to me as we return to gather up our gear at our table. "Congratulations, Peter, your ancestors are smiling down on you."

"Thanks for giving me the chance to find them."

"We have a new job opening up at the Museum."

"Job? Like a regular job, time clocks, suit and tie?" I shudder.

"No time clocks. No suit and tie. It's a Native American educational program designed to give public school children a more balanced view of California history, especially during the Spanish Mission period. I'd like you to help put the program together. We already have a grant from the state. You'd be doubling the salary you get now."

I don't need much time to consider the offer. "I'd like that, Dr. Evans. Thanks so much for offering it to me, only, there's one thing."

"What?"

"The bones of my ancestors at the Museum need to return to a proper resting place. I'd like to be the one to help make that happen."

"I give you my word that I'll work with you and the tribes to see that it happens," he promises as he seals the deal with a shake of hands.

"Oh, and one other thing, when the surf's really good, I need to go surfing."

"As long as you get your work done, I don't have any problem with a flexible schedule."

Gathering up our laptops and paperwork, I glance over and watch the Commissioners disappear behind the door. Most of the crowd has made their way to the exit doors. All I can think of is getting the cruel shoes off my feet, the noose of a tie off my neck, and the stiff suit off my body. The comfortable shorts and sandals waiting in my truck call to me.

We make our way outside and are met by cheers from the lingering crowd. My mom wedges her way through the bodies and gives me a huge hug, tears in her eyes.

"Congratulations, Peter, I'm so proud of you! You make me proud to be your mom, and proud to be a Noqoto! I wish your Grandfather was here..."

At that moment, a lone cloud floats over the sun, casting a shadow.

I turn and see Thorne and his crew emerging from the building. "Hang on a second, Mom, there's the man you need to talk to," I say, stepping toward him, not wanting him to slither away. I purposely herd him away from his yes-men to the side of the building.

"Well, Richard, you win some, you lose some big time."

"We may appeal the decision."

"That would be costly and I think you know there's a good chance you'd be shot down again."

"What are you thinking, Martinez? You coming after me personally?"

"I might, but first, I want you to talk to my mom."

"What? Aren't you a big boy?"

"She sits on our Tribal Council and is General Manager of our casino. She wants to talk to you about the option of purchasing Rocky Point from ENRG now that it's such a liability for you. Our tribe would be willing to discuss purchasing it and leaving it as a preserve forever. I think you agree that no one would buy Rocky Point if they can't develop it."

"Forever is a long time. Your tribe could change its mind in the future and opt for a casino and golf course."

"Our connection to Rocky Point is not profit driven. We can write it into the purchase contract and title—no further subdivision or development of the land."

"I can't speak for my company on selling Rocky Point, but I'll see what I can do," he says with a promising look.

"If you helped see to it that ENRG sold the land to our tribe for a reasonable price, I won't file a criminal complaint against you or your company. Think of the costly trial you'd avoid, the long jail term waiting, the bad publicity put on the corporate name, the lost revenue, your wife divorcing you and taking half your wealth."

Thorne attention becomes much more focused. "Sounds like a deal in the making," he says, slightly relieved at his newfound freedom.

"Of course there would be a finder's fee. Global would pay me for putting the land deal together," I inform.

"What kind of finder's fee?"

"Our original deal, with the new truck. I believe you hold Canadian gold coins?"

"Deal. I've still got the coins. Where's your Mom?"

"Follow me."

Mom steps up to Thorne with newfound enlightenment. "I believe I can help arrange a purchase of Rocky Point, Mr. Thorne, if you would be interested in discussing terms."

"I'm all ears, Mrs. Martinez. I'd like to talk about this in more detail over dinner. What are you doing tonight?"

"We can dine at our casino. I'll see you in the California Cantina at seven?" she proposes, wisely establishing the negotiating place.

"I'll see you there."

"Leave your lawyers in their cages."

"Just you and me," he assures her with that salesman smile.

I give Mom a thumb's up and a big smile. She smiles back, a new woman.

I turn to find Linda and spot her patiently waiting for me in the shake of an oak.

I make a beeline for her. Leaning against the tree with laptop under her arm, she looks like a gorgeous gunslinger who just shot down the corporate bad guys.

"Hey there, handsome, what do you say we get out of here and go for a walk on the beach," she propositions me with a wink.

"Sorry beautiful, I don't want to get sand on my new shoes."

"I have a feeling you won't be wearing those ever again."

"I'd like to toss them in the recycling bin."

"Might want to recycle the cheap suit too."

"With pleasure, although it was money well spent."

"You still have a nice haircut."

"I need a swim in the ocean," I say while removing my tie. "Waves are up, I brought my board."

"Where are you parked?" Linda asks.

"Not far. Hope I don't have a ticket. I lost track of time. Let's go out to dinner and celebrate, it's on me tonight, I got a new job." I peel off the jacket and open my collar.

Making our way across State Street, Richard Thorne pulls up to the red light. I'm shocked seeing he's behind the wheel of a Tesla. I knock on his window and give him a thumb's up. He rolls down the window as the light goes green.

"Zero to a hundred in three seconds, on clean electricity!"

In a flash, he's silently gone to the next red light.

Linda and I pull up to the town beach in Old Red, and I'm amazed at the number of people attempting to surf the inside break.

Over a hundred people all clustered in one zone battling for the few meager waves rolling through. Stand-up paddle boarders dominate the outside line up. On the other end of the scale, short boarders on thin foam chips sink in up to their chests far on the inside, hoping to pick up meager wave leftovers. A two-wave set rolls in and I count seventeen people riding the same knee-high wave as rails collide and tensions arise.

"Wow, I think I'll pass," I decide with an easy change of mind.

"Look at all those people," Linda comments. "Water doesn't look very clean does it?"

"Not like Rocky Point."

CHAPTER 39

Steve in the guardhouse waves to us like we're old friends.

I bring quiet New Red to a stop without pushing in a clutch, put it in park, notice the lack of miles on the odometer of the hybrid truck fully equipped with lightweight camper resting solidly on the bed. I feel a bit like I'm cheating on Old Red, now put out to pasture in my driveway.

Steve steps up to my window and I roll it down with the tip of one finger.

"You steal that rig?"

"Finder's fee. It's an electric hybrid."

"You deserve it. ENRG would have trashed this place, like a lot of other beautiful places they've fucked up."

Shifting his attitude to gratitude, he continues. "I really appreciate you cutting me slack. I'm truly sorry for my actions. I'm a changed man. I've given my notice to ENRG. Thank you," he confesses with sincerity.

"In a way, I owe you more than you owe me. A lot of good came my way after I hit the water," I tell him while glancing to Linda.

He opens the gate as if to royalty. "And thanks for what you both did to keep Rocky Point the way it is. Not sure what I'll do for a job when this all shuts down, but it doesn't matter. In the big Earth picture, that's not important."

"I've got an in at the casino if you need to keep paying the bills."

With Linda at my side, I crank up the tunes on the surround sound and roll away from the unguarded gate.

Approaching the high lookout, I pull over and shut off the engine. Looking down at the land meeting the sea, emotion ripples through me, shaking tears from my eyes. When I look over at Linda, tears roll down her cheeks as she gazes toward Rocky Point.

I pull to a stop at our former camp. It feels like we've returned home, although all signs of our old camp are now gone, and the wind has erased our footprints. We open the doors of New Red and take in our surroundings, letting them soak into our being.

"It sure feels good to be back here." Linda confirms what I'm thinking.

"A good place to be with you."

Our hands warm together as the wind creases the grasses near the edges of the lagoon. "Offshore!" I say, noting the gust, as I go for the ladder to unstrap our boards on the solar paneled roof.

With wetsuits in hand, we run toward the beach and crest the sand dunes. Before us, small, shoulder-high peelers break right and left in perfect peaks. We have it to ourselves, no one in sight. We leap into our wet suits. Paddling out together into the lineup is a dream coming true.

Linda spins around and catches the first wave. I watch from inside as she cross-steps to the nose and hangs five with a graceful arch of her back. The wave picks up speed and she responds by stepping back and crouching down into the pocket, picking the fastest line. The wave barrels along with her in the tube, a smile of joy on her face.

I shout a hoot and watch her glide past, her path clearly visible in the back of the wave. On the inside she kicks out and paddles back out without wasting a move.

My turn comes when the biggest of the set waves lures me in. I only have time for a quick bottom turn and then grab the rail to set up for the barrel. The lip folds over me as I drag my hand along the face to meet it. Linda is now the audience, and she pauses to sit up on her board. With a loud hoot, she now cheers me on as I release my hand and break into the clear, followed by a cut back banking off the white water. She waits patiently for me to return to the lineup and I can't paddle fast enough to share our mutual stoke.

I slow my strokes as two dolphins drop in on the next wave, free gliding just beneath the surface. My Guardian Spirit has returned with her mate. She's happy, and so am I.

With pleasurable exhaustion, Linda and I lie down in the hot sand to relax and warm up, the blood pulsing through our hearts. Looking out to the horizon, it seems so long ago that I first surfed Rocky Point to today. I think of Grandfather and his early lessons with me at the water's edge, how his passion to show me the pleasures of the ocean have led me to who I am, to myself. His interest in the past lives of our People instilled in me the same curiosity. I'm truly fortunate to have such a man in my life and I look forward to helping other young people share in the same interests he had shown me. My new job with the Museum will allow me to do just that. Gently I hold the Dream Helper he gifted me, along with his words of wisdom.

"I'll make lunch. I can tell you need some time to yourself," Linda wisely observes.

Looking down the beach at her footprints left behind in the sand, a wave pushes up onto shore leaving behind a soft outline. I follow her foot impressions now half-filled with water gleaming in the sunlight until something attracts my eye. An iridescent rainbow shimmers back. I kneel and pick up the polished abalone shell in the shape of a dolphin.

Returning to the truck, Linda waves out the window as she organizes lunch in the camper. I set down my surf gear and gently place the dolphin in the center console. After a quick shower, I open the awning with a few cranks of the handle. Stepping to the rear storage locker, I grab the chairs and table and set up under the shade.

Linda comes through the screen door and walks down the steps. "That's a nice little kitchen to work in, running water!"

She settles into her chair as I make my way back to the camper on a mission.

"This is such an awesome rig!" she excitedly points out the obvious.

"I feel a bit guilty."

"You should be proud, you deserve it for helping save Rocky Point. Now you have a hybrid, solar powered mobile base camp wherever you go. Besides, Old Red was almost dead."

"Linda, when I was down on the beach just now, I really came to appreciate all that I've been through to bring me here with you."

"We're both lucky."

"What we have together is something more than luck. Like what I found on the beach just now, it isn't by chance." I dangle the rainbow dolphin in front of her, its reflection lighting her eyes with bursts of color.

She gasps at the sight of it. "Peter, it's beautiful. Is that the dolphin that went missing when you fell from the cliff?"

"How many grains of sand on this beach? In my Dream Walk I had given the greenstone canoe to Talkitna. I know now, she would want you to have it."

"You're giving me chills."

I get to my feet and help Linda to hers. Facing her, I place the rainbow dolphin over her head, letting it settle against her tan skin.

"This rainbow dolphin belongs on you." I step back to admire it resting perfectly around her smooth neck like it was always meant to be there.

Tears come to Linda's eyes as she looks back at me. "It's so beautiful, Peter. I love you."

"I love you, Linda." I hold her hands, pulling her close and wrapping her in my arms.

CHAPTER 40

When I get back within cell range, I pick up a message from Mom. Grandfather has not returned the calls she's left on his cell phone and she's panicking. Not that unusual in both cases, but she said she couldn't help but be very concerned for his health, and could I get up there to check on him and make sure he charges his phone. I text her back, assuring her I will, but by the time I say goodbye to Linda, it's too late to wander up in the dark.

The morning brings with it the first rain in many months. Lightning flashes and thunder booms overhead as I work my way up past the newly swollen creek to my grandfather's. Rain comes down in wind-driven sheets as I fight my way up the ridge. Staying dry is impossible as horizontal rain finds its way into every break in my parka. I'm soaked to the bone as I top the ridge and descend down to his house. Visibility is almost nil in the dark clouds clinging to the crest, only my memory and internal compass guide me to where I know he will be.

When the house comes into view in the dense clouds, there's not more than a few steps to get to the porch. Peering through the rain spattered living room window, all seems very quiet with no sign of him. I knock on the door while letting myself in.

"Grandpa!"

Concern comes through me, there's no answer. I make my way to the door of his bedroom and open it slowly. Not wanting to look, but knowing I will, I peer through the door and see him lying peacefully in bed, covers pulled up to his chest, eyes peacefully closed.

"Grandpa?"

There's no sign of movement beneath the sheets. I step to the side of his bed and reach to feel his forehead. Cold. I pick up his wrist and feel for a pulse. None. Placing his arm gently down, I stand back and take in the scene before me. He has died in peace, no sign of struggle, face calm and serene. I know he will not want me to cry for his passing, wanting me to instead happily remember the good times we've shared.

I cry so long I'm dehydrated.

I make myself a cup of tea and sit down at the kitchen table to see a note written in his hand. Final words addressed to me: "Peter, I'm with you always in spirit. Enjoy this home we've built together, my gift to you. As a last gift, which can't be returned, is the name of your real father. Arguello the priest violated your mother when she was a teenager. Looking back, the gift is you. When you look up to the cosmos, I'll be looking down at you. Keep on Dream Walking, Love, Grandpa."

Arguello is my father. I realize now that his "my son" comments were beyond religious symbolism. I really am his son. And I can now understand why my mom and the tribe raised me. All those unknown Father's Day cards unsent by me no longer apply.

I sit with Grandfather, drinking my tea and not wanting to leave. I want to tell him all about Rocky Point, our victory in defending it, the tribe purchasing it as a sacred place to preserve, the new love in my life, my new job. But the person I most want to share these successes with is no longer alive. I touch his still heart with my hand, and then touch mine. He's physically gone from this earth, but spiritually he's still with me, as he promised.

It's the toughest phone call I've ever made. Telling my mom about the death of her father rips into me emotionally so much I can barely talk. I tell her there's no need to come to his home now, to wait until the storm clears and we'll bring him down then. With sobs of sorrow, she agrees with my thoughts of staying with him until the weather clears, freeing her to deal with his passing in her own way.

In the morning there will be a new day, and life will go on without him, like the planets, stars and galaxies of the cosmos.

CHAPTER 41

Drawing in a deep breath, I'm honored my grandfather entrusted me to scatter his ashes. After his memorial service had come to a close, it's just he and I heading to the beach together, one last time in the seat of Old Red, his stardust seat-belted next to me in a clay urn.

Pulling up to the abandoned guardhouse, I swing the gate free.

Sunset is rapidly approaching as I pick up the pace down the dirt road to the lagoon. The stiff shocks of the truck resist a large pothole, sending the top of the urn floating in the cab of Old Red. I pluck it from midair and return it to its place.

"Sorry, Grandpa, I'll slow down."

Pulling to a stop at the overlook to Rocky Point, I stare at the beautiful landscape, feeling very blessed that Mom's negotiations with Richard Thorne and the Tribal Council have secured the future of this sacred land. The Noqoto tribe now controls the fate of Rocky Point. Our ancestors' legacy on the land returns to the rightful guardians. Grandfather would be proud. The sun moves on toward another day, peering through scattered clouds and throwing rays that pierce the sky. One beam of cosmic light spotlights Rocky Point like a star performer on Earth's stage.

Old Red and I roll down toward the gateway to the Other Side. I pull into the site of the village from long ago and shut off the engine.

With Grandfather's ashes in my pack, waves of gratitude flood through me for being able to fulfill his final wish. Clambering up to the top of the point, I cautiously creep out to the end of land. Looking over the edge, waves from a distant storm crash against rocks, shaking the land beneath me. Looking out to sea, I see the sun glowing deep orange as the flaming ball of life-giving creation touches the horizon.

I open my pack, remove the urn and hold his ashes before me. "May you be in peace in Similgasa, Grandpa," I pray for his next journey.

With a wave of my arms, his ashes spill from the urn and float on the offshore wind in a dusty cloud. A gentle breeze stirs his ashes as they drift down to the holy water of the sea. The ocean's waves burst into spray on the rocks below, droplets of salt water like orange diamonds at sunset reaching up. His ashes settle into the mist, the cosmic dust of creation meeting Mother Ocean. The outgoing wave takes my grandfather to the Other Side.

The sun disappears below the horizon as I stand alone on the crest of Rocky Point, surrounded by the Pacific Ocean. I turn to look back at my surroundings—the cliff face, the coastal range of mountains reaching to the sky, the long beach stretching out toward the lagoon.

Far in the distance, I spot a lone figure on the sand.

In the fading light of day, he walks away.

I close my eyes.

He's there with me in my soul.

I open my eyes.

My grandfather is gone.

A tear runs down my face and trickles toward Mother Earth to land in the ancient dust of Rocky Point.